"LOWER YOUR BLADES AND BACK OFF, OR I'LL AXE YOU BOTH DOWN!"

Such was the ear-splitting quality of that voice that both warriors stopped their fighting and stared. There, towering over and out-bulking everyone in the room, stood their chosen war leader, Bili the Axe. His eyes were slitted and cold rage blazed out from the narrowed openings. Instinctively, everyone backed off from that glare, knowing that it could only presage violence or death.

"Neither of you sought or received my permission for a duel," Bili grated out. "I should axe you both down where you stand, but since you are new to my command, I will grant you another chance. You both are full-armed and so, too, am I. If you want to shed some blood here, I'll help you shed more than you can afford to lose. Make your decision, do it now!"

Great Science Fiction by Robert Adams from SIGNET

The
Witch
Goddess

A Horseclans Novel

by

Robert Adams

A SIGNET BOOK
NEW AMERICAN LIBRARY

COPYRIGHT © 1982 BY ROBERT ADAMS

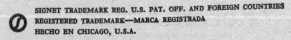

SIGNET, SIGNET CLASSIC, MENTOR, PLUME, MERIDIAN AND NAL
BOOKS are published by New American Library,
1633 Broadway, New York, New York 10019

FIRST PRINTING, SEPTEMBER, 1982

4   5   6   7   8   9

PRINTED IN THE UNITED STATES OF AMERICA

To Drs. Roger Schlobin and Jeffrey Eliot,
gentlemen and scholars, both;
To Dr. Jean Lorrah and Catherine Crook
De Camp, two most talented and charming
literary ladies;
To Pat and Miriam Kelly;
To all my friends of the NYUSFS;
To Maryann Palumbo, publicist extraordinary;
To Elinor Mavor, Editor-in-grief;
To George and Jennie MacCaulay;
And to André Norton, my treasured and
most supportive friend.

PROLOGUE

Sir Bili of Morguhn lay dying in his palace. Fifty years before, after lengthy and strenuous persuasion, he had assumed the title and duties of Prince of Karaleenos, and he had served that office well and faithfully, it and the farflung Confederation of which the principality was a sizable part. Early in his long life he had become a legend, but now he was an old man, a very old man, dying as all old men must, soon or late.

But the legend would not die with his ancient, suppurating flesh; he knew this as well as did all those powerful notables who had hurriedly gathered to attend his passing. The deeds that the younger Sir Bili had wreaked with his huge and famous axe, with his prowess and courage, with his matchless mental attributes, would continue to be recounted as long as there were Eastern Kindred, mountain Ahrmehnee, Ehleenee, or a Confederation.

"Aye," the dying old man thought, chuckling to himself despite the slowly increasing agony of his infected wounds, "and those damned Witchmen will have cause to remember Bili the Axe, too! Between us, Lord Milo and I scotched more than one of their hellish schemes, over the years.

"They never seem to give up, those unnatural monsters. At least once in every generation of normal men, they're out to foment trouble somewhere in or around our Confederation. Twelve . . . no, fourteen or fifteen years back, it was that vicious bastard Gardmann. Before him, it was that phony Freefighter. What did he call himself, anyway? I forget, now, after so long . . . Close onto forty years; but I remember the name—his real name—that he gave under our tortures, Morton Flachs. It's too bad he managed to chew through his wrist veins, that night after he finally broke; we might've gotten more out of the bastard the next session.

1

"Then there was that man who tried to kill Lord Milo and Aldora and me that time in Kehnooryos Atheenahs. We never knew for sure if he was really a Witchman, but Lord Milo assumed that he was because of his weapon—that booming, fire-spitting thing Lord Milo called a *pisztuhl*. He struck all three of us and killed two guards, outright, but the missiles did no permanent harm to the two Undying, of course. The one that sped toward me failed to strike me solidly, thank Sun and Wind, it just tore through my shirt and furrowed my arm before killing the guard behind me. Before Lord Milo could make himself heard, the living guardsmen had made a blood pudding out of the man . . . but they couldn't be blamed for it, they knew their duty and they did it despite the terror they all must have felt of that witchy weapon.

"Of course, I'd seen and heard one like it before that—a bigger, much longer one. She called that one a *ryfuhl*, that damned Witchwoman who'd set herself up as 'goddess' of those outlaw Ganiks, the ones we fought for Prince Byruhn.

"Hmmm, what was her name, now? In nigh eighty years, a man can forget so much."

As old Bili's mind, cloudy now with drugs and age and suffering, sought recall of the name of that Witchwoman who had so many years before, led the savage, cannibal Ganiks in the then-unknown mountains to the west and south of the Ahrmehnee lands, he began once again to relive those exciting times. It had been those times which had given birth to the legend of Bili the Axe.

Born to one of the two wives—sisters, they had been, and daughters of a Middle Kingdoms duke—of Hwahruhn, the hereditary chief of Clan Morguhn, Bili and all of his younger brothers had been sent in childhood to foster at various royal or archducal courts of Middle Kingdoms maternal relatives. Then, in Bili's eighteenth year, the chief, his father, lay ill unto death and he had been summoned back from the north by his mothers.

Although barely eighteen, the Bili who had ridden back south had been a full man and a proven warrior, already knighted into the Order of the Blue Bear of Harzburk by the king who had fostered him. Nor had that knighthood been a meaningless gesture; Bili, the king's distant kinsman, had earned the honor with his strength, arms skills, and stark ferocity, axing down a full-grown nobleman in a single combat, and then the two men-at-arms who treacherously attacked him in defense of their foresworn lord.

And young Bili's prowess, coupled with his qualities of natural leadership, quick and accurate judgment of men and situations, and some highly unusual mental attributes, had served him, the duchy and the Confederation well in the very hard and fearsome times that immediately followed his return, his father's death and his accession to the chieftaincy and title. For rebellion had long been brewing among certain elements of the Ehleenee—whose distant ancestors had ruled over most of the lands of the Confederation prior to the coming of the Kindred Horseclans. Incited, aided and abetted by a murderous gaggle of priests of the Old Ehleenee Church and by two spurious bishops of that church, both of whom proved to be actually agents of the Witch Kingdom—that realm located among the swamps of the far south—the situation had exploded bare days after he had come back to the lands of his birth.

The young warrior's initial encounter with the rebels had very narrowly missed being his last. While riding back to Morguhn Hall after a visit to the hall of a kinsman-vassal, *Komees* Hari Daiviz of Morguhn, he and his small party had been viciously attacked on a forest road by more than a score of sketchily armed but coldly murderous rabble.

"What a night that was," ruminated the dying Bili. "And what a glorious fight!"

Then, suddenly, in his mind he was there again.

The young Bili would have taken the lead into the place of lurking danger had not his companions—*Vahrohneeskos* Ahndee, Bard Klairuhnz and the two Freefighters on loan from *Komees* Djeen Morguhn—argued him down. So when the mounted column trotted in a single file toward the bridge, Bili was third in the line, with Ahndee ahead of him and one of the Freefighters, Dzhool, at point. Behind Bili rode the bard, Klairuhnz, with Ahndee's servingman, Geros, between him and the other Freefighter, Shahrl.

The closer the little party came to the forest, looming darkly just beyond the bridge, the stronger grew Bili's apprehension. Now he knew for certain that they were riding into a battle, and he so mindspoke Ahndee and Klairuhnz.

Awed, Ahndee silently asked, "You can *far-gather*, then,

Bili? That's a rare and a precious ability. We were told of it
at the Confederation Mindspeak Academy, of course; but not
one of the instructors had ever met a man or woman or cat
that actually possessed it. Can you sense how many foes? Or
how far ahead they be?"

"No," Bili readily admitted, "never have I been able to
judge numbers, but we are near to danger and drawing ever
nearer."

The thick, old planks of the bridge boomed hollowly under
the impact of the ironshod hooves, then they were into the
forest. Bili found the forest proper far less dark a place than
it had appeared from without. Except for the oak-grown
fringes, the growth appeared to be principally tall old pines,
unbranching for many feet above road level, and the wan
moonlight filtered through the needled branches high above,
making for dim visibility.

The road ran straight for a few dozen yards, then began a
gradual ascent and a slight curvature to the right, following
the lower reaches of a brush-grown hillock. They splashed
through a tiny rill which fed down into a small swamp before
joining the larger stream. Beyond the rill, the road commenced another slow curve, this one downward and to the
left. As they descended this reverse slope, the moon dove for
cover and Bili's hackles rose. The still-unseen danger was now
looming terribly near!

"Soon!" he urgently mindspoke Ahndee and Klairuhnz,
while bringing his axe up so that its fearsome double-bitted
head rested against the steel plates covering his right shoulder. He dropped his reins over the pommel-knob, for, in
battle, he guided Mahvros solely by mindspeak and knee
pressure, not that the battlewise and faithful stallion required
a great deal of guidance. Then he lowered and carefully
locked into place the slitted half-visor which served to protect
eyes and nose. By that time, the peril lay so very near,
pressed so heavily upon his senses, that he could hardly bear
it.

"Now!" he beamed with mind-blasting intensity. *"It is all
around us!"*

Ahndee and the bard drew their blades, and the sibilant
zweeep of steel leaving scabbards alerted the two troopers,
who bared their own weapons. The servant, Geros, awk-

wardly gripped and regripped the haft of his boar spear in a sweaty hand.

Up the slope, to their left, the trees abruptly thinned out . . . and the fickle moon chose that moment to again start a slow emergence from the clouds.

There was a scuffling noise at the head of the column, a strangled grunt, followed almost immediately by a horse's shrill scream of agony and terror, then came the unmistakable clash-clanking of an armored body falling to the ground . . . and the moon came fully out.

Bili could see the trooper, Dzhool, twitching on the roadway. A stocky, black-bearded man had a foot on the dying Freefighter's chest and was frantically striving to jerk the point of his spear from the body.

The rebel bushwhacker never got the weapon free, however, for Bard Klairuhnz kneed his mount past Bili and Ahndee, and his heavy, cursive saber swept up and then blurred down. The bearded head, still wearing its old-fashioned helmet and a look of utter surprise, clattered across the road and into the weeds. The headless body stood erect for a brief moment more, geysering great, ropy spouts of dark-red blood, then collapsed atop the still body of its victim.

From around the far side of the screaming, hamstrung lead horse charged another of the rebel ambushers, lacking either helm or body armor, but swinging up a short, broad-bladed infantry sword. This man was as short and stocky as the first, but beardless, with thinning gray hair. His lips were pulled back in a grimace, revealing his rotten and discolored teeth. There was fresh blood showing blackly on his swordblade, and he ran directly at Bili, shouting something in Old Ehleeneekos.

Ahndee watched Bili—seemingly effortlessly handling his long, massive weapon with but one hand—catch the swordslash on the steel shaft of his axe and allow the blade's own momentum to propel it into the deep notch between shaft and head. Then a single twist of Bili's thick wrist tore the hilt from the old rebel's grip and sent his sole weapon spinning off to clatter into the roadside weeds near his companion's severed head. But the spike surmounting the twin axebits was jammed deeply into the oldster's chest well before the sword came to ground.

Dead Dzhool's crippled mount was still screaming. Then

the servant, Geros, began to scream, too; no warrior, he, he was frightened beyond words and could only scream and point his spear up the brushy slope. There, a line of riders—at least a dozen of them, the moonlight reflecting from their arms and armor—was issuing out from amongst the trees which had concealed them.

"*Back!*" roared Klairuhnz. "There're too many of them to fight here; back to the bridge!" Suiting action to words, he reined his mount about and set off in the wake of Geros, Sharl and Ahndee.

Bili lingered long enough to split the skull of the suffering horse, then he set off toward the narrow bridge just as the line of mounted ambushers came tilting down the rise. This granted Bili a closer look, and his battlewise eyes informed him that though numerous—nearer a score than a dozen—the charging horsemen were not nearly so well armed as they had at first seemed to be.

All of them had swords of one kind or another and a few even bore the weapons as if they understood them and their proper use, but the uniformity ended there. The big man in the lead had a full panoply of longsword, shield and suit of three-quarter armor that looked to be decent-quality plate.

But all of the men he led might have been outfitted from a hundred years' worth of battlefield pickings. Their helms were of every description, from true antique to almost new. One man's body armor was naught save a dented breastplate, another had squeezed into a shirt of rusty scalemail, two or three went in ancient jazerans, one in a cuirass of boiled and lacquered leather and another in an old, threadbare brigandine. Bili thought that the ruffianly crew certainly looked the part of the brigands they probably were.

Mahvros' powerful body responded to Bili's urgings, and the big, steel-shod hooves struck firelight from the pebbly roadbed. The black stallion splashed through the little rill, and then they were descending back along the road's first curve.

Suddenly, twenty yards ahead, riders emerged from among the treetrunks to block the way back to the bridge. A shaft of moonlight silvered their bared blades.

Bili mindspoke Mahvros, "Faster, brother mine; be ready to fight."

The huge ebon horse increased his speed and beamed his

approval and impatient anticipation of the coming conflict, one of his principal joys in life being the stamping unto death of anything or anyone he was set against. Raising his head, he pealed a shrill, equine challenge, then bore down upon his promised victims.

"Good old Mahvros," thought the ancient Bili. "I've forked many a strong, faithful, pugnacious horse in the years since he went to Wind, but never has there been another that was his equal in any way. Sacred Sun shine ever upon his brave spirit."

One horse and rider went down in a squealing, screaming, hoof-flailing tangle, while Bili took a ringing swordswipe against the side of his helmet in passing. Still shrilling his challenge, Mahvros came to a rearing halt, pivoted and returned to savage the downed horse and man, while Bili axed the second rider out of the saddle with a single businesslike stroke. The stallion knew the brief elation of feeling man-ribs splinter under his hooves before Bili urged him back along the road to the bridge.

Scores of hooves were pounding close behind them as Mahvros cleared the last of the trees to see Ahndee and Klairuhnz, their blades gleaming, sitting their mounts knee to knee a few paces out onto the span. Three yards behind them, the trooper had uncased and strung his short hornbow and nocked an arrow and was calmly awaiting the appearance of a target for that arrow.

"Bili!" Ahndee shouted exuberantly. "Sun and Wind be thanked. We'd thought you slain back there." He began to back his big gelding that Bili might have his place.

But Bili signed him to stay, positioning Mahvros a little ahead of the two warriors. "This will be better," he stated shortly, adding, "An axeman needs room." He did not see the smile that Ahndee and Klairuhnz exchanged at his automatic assumption of command over them.

The trooper proved himself an expert archer, putting his shaft cleanly into the eye of the first pursuer to gallop out of the dark forest. His second arrow pinned an unarmored thigh to the saddletree beneath it. He nocked a third, quickly drew . . . and the bowstring snapped. Cursing sulphurously and most feelingly in four languages, he cast away the now use-

less bow, drew his saber and ranged up close behind
Klairuhnz and Ahndee.

The next four attackers took a brief moment to form
themselves up, then launched a charge, apparently expecting
their prey to remain in place and await their pleasure. They
none of them lived long enough to repent their error or to
recover from the counter-charge.

The leading man held up his shield to fend off Bili's axe,
while he aimed a hacking cut at Mahvros' thick neck. But the
stout target crumpled like wet paper and the axeblade bit
completely through, deep into the arm which had held it, the
force of the buffet hurling the man down to a singularly
messy death beneath the stamping hooves.

Mahvros roughly shouldered the riderless horse aside, while
Bili glanced around, seeking another opponent. At that very
moment, Ahndee was thrusting the watered-steel blade of his
longsword deep into the vitals of his adversary and Bard
Klairuhnz looked to be more than a match for his shaggy
foe. But the hapless Freefighter trooper had troubles aplenty.
First his bowstring had broken, and now his saber blade,
leaving him but a bare foot of pointless steel jutting up from
the hilt. With this stub, he was fighting a desperate defensive
action.

In a single, mighty leap, Mahvros was alongside the mount
of the ruffian. Shortening his grip on his axehaft, Bili jammed
the terminal spike deeply into a side made vulnerable by a
wide gap between the back and breast plates of an ill-fitting
cuirass. Shrieking curses in both Old and Modern
Ehleeneekos, the wounded man turned in his saddle to rain a
swift succession of swordblows on Bili's head and shoulders.
Although the stout Pitzburk plate turned every blow, Bili was
unable to retaliate, for at such close quarters, his long-hafted
axe was all but useless.

Unexpectedly, the swordsman hunched his body and began
to gag and then retch, spewing up quantities of frothy blood.
At this juncture, the Freefighter reined in closer, used his
piece of saber to sever the man's swordknot, then virtually
decapitated his late opponent with the man's own antique
blade.

They had almost regained the bridge when the main body
of attackers caught up to them. First to fall was the rearmed

Freefighter, his scaleshirt unable to protect his spine from the crushing blow of a nail-studded club.

Bili's better armor turned a determined spearthrust before he axed the arm from the spearman. Then he turned Mahvros full about and, straightening his arms, swung his bloody axe in several wide arcs before him; he struck nothing and no one, but did achieve his desired effect of momentarily halting the van of the oncoming force and granting Ahndee and Klairuhnz a few precious moments to regain the bridge.

Bili's vision, somewhat restricted by the bars of his visor, failed to record the man who galloped in from his left . . . but Mahvros saw him. With the speed of a striking serpent, the mighty horse spun about and sank big yellow teeth into the flesh of the smaller equine.

The mare thus assaulted was not a warhorse, not even a hunter, and she harbored no slightest intention of remaining in proximity to this huge, maddened stallion. Taking the bit firmly between her own teeth, she raced back into the forest, bearing her shouting, cursing, rein-sawing rider only as far as the low-hanging branch which swept him from her back and stretched him senseless among the dead leaves and mosses.

Mahvros' forehooves were already booming the bridge timbers when a hard-flung throwing axe caromed off Bili's helm, nearly deafening him and filling his head with a tight-spiraling red-blackness, shot with dazzling-white stars. Only instinct kept him in the saddle while Mahvros, well-trained, battlewise and intelligent animal that he was, continued on to the proper place, then wheeled about just ahead of Ahndee and Klairuhnz.

Reaching forward, Ahndee grabbed Bili's arm—limp under its sheathing of steel and leather—and shook him. "Are you all right, Bili? Are you injured?" he shouted anxiously.

Then he let go the arm and turned to Bard Klairuhnz, saying, "Your help, please, my lord. He's barely conscious, if that. We must get him behind us ere those bastards cut him down."

Bili could hear all and could sense movements on either side of him, but neither his lips nor his limbs would obey his dictates. Fuzzily, he pondered why *Vahrohneeskos* Ahndee, a nobleman of this duchy, would have addressed a mere roving bard as his "lord."

In his great bed in the dimly lit room already smelling of death, old Bili smiled to himself. "That was the first fight I fought beside the Undying High Lord, though I knew not that that same Bard Klairuhnz was my sovran until much later in the rebellion."

Against so many attackers, holding at the bridge, where a flank attack was impossible, had been a good idea. The blades of Ahndee and Klairuhnz wove a deadly pattern, effectively barring their foemen access to the dazed and helpless Bili, now drooping in the saddle. Because of the narrowness of the span—it being but just wide enough to easily accommodate passage of a single hay wagon or ox-wain—only two men at a time could attack the defenders, thus doing much to nullify their numerical superiority. And on a man-to-man basis, the ill-armed, ill-trained crew were just no match for well-equipped and seasoned warriors. The length of the Forest Bridge, from the far side to the center, was very soon gore-slimed, littered with dropped weapons and hacked, hoof-marked corpses.

But the repeated assaults had taken toll of the two stout defenders, as well, for flesh and blood can bear only so much. Ahndee sat his horse in dire agony, his left arm dangling uselessly at his side. He had used its armored surface to ward off a direct blow from a huge and weighty club, while he slashed the clubman's unprotected throat, and he now sat in certainty that the concussion of that buffet had broken the arm beneath the plates.

Klairuhnz's horse now lay dead and the bard stood astride the body. Hopefully, he had mindspoken Mahvros, but the black stallion's refusal had been unequivocal. Moreover, he had promised dire and fatal consequences should any two legs attempt either to unseat Mahvros' hurt brother or to take said brother's place in the warkak.

Bili regained his senses just in time to see Klairuhnz sustain a vicious cut on the side of his neck and be hurled down, blood spurting over his shoulderplates. Roaring, *"Up Harzburk!"* through force of habit, Bili kneed Mahvros forward and plugged the gap, admonishing the horse by mindspeak not to step on the man.

A swing of his axe crushed both the helmet and the skull of Klairuhnz's killer. As the man pitched from the saddle,

Bili belatedly recognized the twisted features—it was the face of Hofos, *Komees* Hari's majordomo.

Then there were two more enemy horsemen on the bridge before him. But this time it was Ahndee who was reeling in his kak, kept in it only by the high, flaring cantle and pommel, and unable to do more than offer a rapidly weakening defense.

Bili disliked attacking a horse, but the circumstances afforded him no option. He rammed his axe spike into the rolling eye of his opponent's mount, and in the brief respite allotted him while the death-agonized beast proceeded to buck its rider over the low railing and into the cold creek, he swung his axeblade into the unarmored chest of Ahndee's adversary. Deep went that heavy, knife-sharp blade, biting through hide jerkin, shirt, flesh and bone and into the quivering heart, itself.

Someone in the decimated group between the bridge and the forest cast a javelin, and Mahvros took it in the thick muscles of his off shoulder; he screamed his shock and pain and made to rear, being restrained only by Bili's mindspeak. Grimly, the young man dismounted and gently withdrew the steel head—blessedly, unbarbed.

Then he backed the big warhorse and turned him, beaming, "Go back to the hall of *Komees* Hari, Mahvros."

"This horse still can fight, brother!" the black balked, stubbornly.

"I know that my brother still can fight," Bili mindspoke with as much patience as he could muster up. "But that wound is deep. If I stay upon your back, you might be permanently crippled . . . and that would mean no more war for you, ever again, brother." Thinking quickly, he added, "Besides, the other man can fight no longer and must be borne back to the hall. A horse of your intelligence is needed to keep this stupid gelding moving, yet see that it does not move so fast that the man falls off."

Bili was not exaggerating. Ahndee had dropped his reins and his sword dangled by its knot from his wrist. Though his booted feet still filled the stirrups, his body was now slumped over the pommel and his two arms weakly encircled the neck of his mount.

The young *thoheeks* grasped the gray's bridle, faced him about, slapped his rump sharply and shouted. Even so, the gelding made to stop at the end of the bridge until a sharp nip of Mahvros's big teeth changed his mind.

Laying aside both axe and javelin, Bili took Klairuhnz under the arms and dragged him back from the windrow of dead men and horses, propping his armored body in a sitting posture against the bridge rail. Odd, he thought vaguely, I think he's still alive, and he should be well dead by now, considering where the sword caught him. . . .

Striding back, he picked up the short, heavy dart that had wounded Mahvros, drew back his brawny arm, chose a target and then made a running cast.

One of the ruffians with only a breastplate was adjusting his stirrup leathers when the hard-flung missile took him in the small of the back. The sharp steel head tore through rough clothing, then skin, kidney, guts and fat, standing far enough out from the man's belly to prick the horse when he stumbled against its flank. Scream of horse almost drowned out scream of man. And as the still-screaming man fell to kick and writhe his life away in the dust, most of his fellow rebels made to follow the riderless horse up the road and into the forest.

But a big, spike-bearded man—he who wore a full, matching panoply and sat a large, fully trained destrier— headed off the fleeing men and beat them back with the flat of his sword. Driving them back to their former places, he began to harangue them. Bili, leaning on his gory axe among the dead men whom he expected to soon join, could pick out words and phrases of the angrily shouted monologue, for all that he had not heard Old Ehleeneekos spoken in ten years.

". . . cowards . . . to fear but one, dismounted man . . . and he a God-cursed heathen . . . creatures of filth . . . gotten on diseased sows by spineless curdogs . . . gain your freedom? . . . lead all men to the True Faith? . . . treasure and land and women? . . . Salvation . . . killing heathens for the one, true God?"

Bili shook his head, vainly trying to clear it of the residue of dizziness. A true product of his race and upbringing, he had no fear of death, of "going to Wind." He was a bit sorry that he was to go so early in his life, but then every warrior faced his last battle soon or late. He would have liked to have seen his ill father and his sweet mothers just one time more, but he knew that they would rejoice when they learned that he had fallen in honor, the blood of his foes clotting his axe from spikepoint to haftbutt. And his brother Djef, six months his junior, would surely make a good chief and *Thoheeks* of Morguhn . . . maybe even a better one than he, Bili, would have made.

"*Dirtmen!*" he shouted derisively at the band of ruffians. "Rapists of ewes and she-goats! Your fellow bastards here are lonely. Are you coming to join them, or are you all going to run home like the curs you are to bugger your own infant sons? That's an old Ehleen custom, isn't it, you priest-ridden pigs? An old Ehleen custom, like the eating of dung?"

He carried on in the same vein, each succeeding insult more repugnant and offensive than its predecessor. The spike-bearded leader wisely held his own tongue, hoping that Bili's sneering contumely and racial insults would raise an aggressive spark in his battered, demoralized band, where his own oration had so clearly failed.

At length, one of the tatterdemalions was stung to the very quick. Shrieking maniacally, waving his aged saber, he spurred his horse straight at that lone figure in the center of the bridge.

Bili just stood his ground. To the watching rebels it appeared that he was certain to be ridden down, but Bili had positioned himself cunningly and he correctly judged the oncoming rider to be something less than an accomplished horseman.

The rebel's horse had to jump in order to clear the bodies of the two dead horses lying almost atop each other and thoroughly blocking his route to the axeman. Before the rider could recover enough of his balance to even think of using his sword, Bili had let go his axe to dangle by its thong, grabbed a sandaled foot and a thick, hairy leg and heaved the rebel over the other side of his mount.

Dropping his weapon and squalling his terror, the Ehleen clawed frantically for a grip on the smooth-worn bridge rail; but he missed, and commenced a despairing howl which was abruptly terminated when his hurtling body struck the swift-flowing water thirty feet below. He had been one of the "lucky" ones—attired in an almost-complete set of three-quarter plate—and, since he could not swim anyway, he sank like a stone.

But Bili had not watched the watery doom of his would-be

attacker. No sooner was the man out of the saddle then he who had unseated him was in it, trying to turn the unsettled and unfamiliar animal in time to meet the fresh wave of ruffians he could feel pounding up.

Feel, hear, but not see! For, once again, the sick, tight dizziness was claiming his senses. When, at last, he had gotten the skittish horse to face the forest, it was to dimly perceive the backs of the motley pack of murderous skulkers pounding toward that forest, a small shower of arrows falling amongst them, the shafts glinting as they crossed a vagrant beam of moonlight.

Bili's brain told his arm to lift the axe, his legs to urge the new horse on in pursuit of the fleeing Ehleen rebels . . . vainly. His legs might have ceased to exist, might have been severed from his trunk, while his axe now seemed to weigh an impossible ton or more. The weight became just too much to even hold, and he let it go, then pitched out of the low-cut hunting saddle to land precariously balanced on the narrow railing above the deep, icy stream.

"I was later told old Djeen and Hari grabbed me just in time to keep me from being just another armored corpse on the bed of that creek," ruminated old Bili. "For all of the troubles I had with Count Djeen shortly after that night, he was still a doughty old fighter, especially for his age—he was older than my sire—and lacking an eye and a hand. But, if memory properly serves me, it seems now that all men and some women were harder, tougher and more concerned with the really important aspects of life then than are most folk today; even my own kin—my grandsons and their get—seem addicted to frivolities and luxuries, sneering behind their soft hands at those few who still adhere to the old, good ways. The bulk of the Kindred are become as dissipated as Ehleenee."

"But the Ahrmehnee, now, *ha,* they're as stark and fierce and hardy as ever they were; they've become the backbone of the Confederation armies, and I hear tell that one of them— well, he's not pure-blood Ahrmehnee, since his grandsire was Kindred, Hahfos Djohnz, the first Warden of the Ahrmehnee Marches, but I recall that old Hahfos became outwardly more an Ahrmehnee than his wife or any of her kin. Anyhow, they say that his grandson, Moorahd Djohnz, will be the next senior *strahteegos.*"

He chuckled to himself, a bit evilly, thinking of the cold rage of his eldest son, Senior *Strahteegos Thoheeks* Djef Morguhn of Djahreht, now retired from active soldiering, when he told his father, Prince Bili, of the High Lord's plans to make a "wild Ahrmehnee" foremost military officer of the Confederation.

Bili had simply grinned in the face of his son's towering anger, saying, "Well, Djef, *you* were Senior Strahteegos, as I recall, and your dear mother was pure Ahrmehnee . . . or did you conveniently misremember that fact, Lord *Thoheeks*?"

Old Bili chuckled again, thinking of how his aging son had stamped out, livid in his rage, snorting and shouting and cursing in several dialects of Mehrikan, Ehleeneekos and—Ahrmehnee.

"I always was good," thought old Bili, "at roiling already troubled waters and at spreading oil on smoldering fires."

Then, he mentally sobered. "But the boy . . . I guess I'll always think of him as a boy, for all that he's pushing seventy-five winters, now . . . no, more than that, he's only a bit more than nineteen years my junior, after all.

"But he's wrong, nonetheless, and he should know better, he above many another, for not only is he half Ahrmehnee himself, but he commanded Ahrmehnee troops for years and they won many a victory for him and our Confederation. I know this and the other princes know this and the High Lords, too, so Djef's petulant objections to Moorahd's well-earned elevation will get all the consideration—or, rather, lack of consideration—that they and he deserve in this instance from the powers that be."

He silently pondered, then thought, "Djef must have gotten this strain of racial intolerance in the army, probably from some of those stiff-necked, overproud Ehleenee officers, the boy-buggering bastards. No, no, now I'm getting as bad as him or them. Not all the Ehleenee are overweening degenerates, there were quite a few with me in the mountains who were fine, stark warriors, men of normal tastes and preferences, who despised the Ehleen perverts as much as I did and do.

"Ah, those, too, were good days. Those days when we had scotched the Great Rebellion, then ridden into the western mountains to bring the Ahrmehnee to heel. That was true, old-fashioned warfare, and I was a young man, full of strength and juice and vigor, able to ride or hike from before dawn to dusk or after and then fight a battle before bedtime.

"In those days, I would hardly have noted these few bear-bites and scratches that will shortly be the death of me. But, of course, not even that brave bruin would've gotten a chance at my flesh, back then, before age had slowed my reflexes and stiffened my joints enough to let him charge in under my spear. True, it's not as good a death as my brothers, Djef and Tcharlee, died—full-armed, facing their foes in battle to the last breath—but it's a far better death for a warrior than the one our poor father died.

"Even my dear, ever dear, Rahksahnah—Wind keep her—for all the tragedy of her death, she had a cleaner, quicker death than this one I will presently die. Although I have ever thought that a part of me died long ago with her; had it not been for the children and my people's need for me, I'd have followed her to Wind before her husk had become cold."

As he lay with eyes closed, thinking of the long-dead, irreplaceable love of his youth, his mind again returned to those happy days of near eighty years before.

Subsequent to the surrender of the last stronghold of the Ehleen rebellion, Vawnpolis, the great army, reinforced by the addition of some hundreds of former rebels, had been split into uneven thirds for a three-prong invasion of the mountain lands of the Ahrmehnee tribes.

Thoheeks Bill of Morguhn, commanding some thousands of Freefighters and Confederation nobility, had been assigned the task of bringing fire and sword to the southerly reaches of the Ahrmehnee *stahn*, with the ultimate goal of so savaging the villages, croplands, kine and inhabitants that the warriors—all then gathered in the north and making ready to invade the westernmost *thoheekahtohn* of the Confederation—would feel impelled to break off their planned aggression and return to their own lands to defend their families.

Then, of a night, Bili received an urgent farspeak from the High Lord, Milo Morai, ordering him and his forces to immediately cease their depredations, break off contact with the Ahrmehnee and withdraw back into Confederation lands.

Bili was to proceed north and west with a picked force of

squadron strength. His basic mission was to intercept a large pack train, slaughtering the Witchfolk who led it and destroying all of the ancient machines or devices the animals bore. The Witchfolk, said Milo, had looted these antique devices and machines—along with a vast store of treasures—from the Hold of the Moon Maidens, after having slain or incapacitated all the inhabitants of that hold, then destroyed the tunnel leading into the fastness.

The High Lord also cautioned Bili to be on the lookout for a party of Moon Maidens, with whom he was to attempt to effect an alliance. The last warning was to be cautious, as it was said that bands of savage cannibals called Muhkohee were possibly raiding into the western Ahrmehnee lands in the absence of the native warriors.

So Bili had ridden west and north, with a nucleus from his reserve squadrons. He had given the High Lord's orders to each of the western squadrons as he met them, then fleshed out his own ranks with the very best of their various forces. Loud had been the outraged howls of Confederation noblemen when he had forced them to trade their fine, expensive armor and armament and big, well-trained destriers for the less fine equipage and lighter mounts of Bili's mercenary burkers. The only way that a country nobleman kept his suit of Pitzburk and his charger was by dint of convincing Bili that he himself would be a valuable addition to the squadron.

The result of these forced "loans" was that the force that the High Lord's young deputy finally led far, far to the west, off any existing maps, was compounded of the best available warriors on the best available horseflesh and with the best armor and weapons obtainable. And, considering all that was to befall him and them, it was well that he had so equipped them.

Chapter I

Erica Arenstein lay on her belly on the rocky earth, drops of sweat cutting rivulets through the dust that layered her face and dripping from her nosetip and chin. Just to her right lay Jay Corbett and, to either side of the pair, lay or crouched some dozen Broomtown men, all of them armed—as were she and Jay—with powerful, scoped, autoloading rifles.

But where all the men held their weapons ready to fire, butt at shoulder, hand on pistolgrip, forefinger caressing trigger, Erica's was laid aside within easy reach while she used both hands to hold a pair of large, heavy binoculars to her eyes. Without removing the glasses, she spoke to Corbett.

"Well, whatever godforsaken sty they crawled out of, they are certainly not Ahrmehnee. Compared to those ragged, shaggy wild men, the worst of the Ahrmehnee would look like twentieth-century executives. And if they keep to the direction they seem to be headed, they'll be no danger to us.

"Moreover, they're running like the devil himself is on their tail. Quite a few are afoot, and several appear to be wounded, too."

"How many, would you say, Erica? How many, so far?" asked Corbett, adding, "Don't take time to count, estimate."

"No way of knowing how many came off that plateau before we got here, of course," the woman replied, "but I've seen a good six hundred hotfoot it southwest."

Corbett pursed his lips, slipped the safety catch back on his rifle, then rolled onto his side to face her. "Then I think that it might be a good idea if we stay where we are long enough to see just what it is that has sent above six hundred wild mountaineers stampeding off that plateau."

"You're right, of course." She nodded once, the glasses still at her eyes. "Thank goodness for a military mind. My apologies for the row I raised when Dave Sternheimer assigned you to this mission."

She lowered the binoculars, turned to face him and laid a sweaty, grubby hand atop his own none-too-clean one. "And, Jay, double apologies for what I said back up the trail, when the big boom failed to materialize on schedule. More than likely, it's actually Harry's fault. All you did was prepare and lay the charges based on Harry's calculations."

Corbett shrugged his solid, muscle-packed shoulders. "No matter, Doctor, there's been no pursuit, anyway . . . knock on wood." He tapped his knuckles once on the polished butt of his rifle. "And the blame could lie anywhere—I could have goofed as easily as Dr. Braun, or the fuses could have been faulty, or the timing mechanism, for that matter. Yes, we took extra precautions in protecting them, but even so, some hundreds of miles on muleback could easily screw up delicate devices like that.

"But if blame must be laid, leave the onus on me; as long as I get you and this pack train safely back to Broomtown, I don't give a damn about those charges, Doctor."

The woman tightened her fingers on his hand and parted her dark-red lips to smile lazily. "Why can't it be 'Erica', Jay, as it was last night? Or do you forget so quickly?"

The massive black-haired man grimaced."No, I've not forgotten you . . . or last night, *Doctor*. But there's a time and a place for everything, and *that* is something I should have remembered last night; had I, Dr. Braun wouldn't be pouting on rearguard right now."

The olive-skinned young woman snorted derisively. "Harry Braun is a pompous, conceited, supercilious, oversensitive ass, Jay. And I know, believe me—we were married once, very briefly, five or six hundred years back. I took his possessiveness and his professional jealousy as long as I could, and when he reached the point of trying to beat up on me, I injured his then-body so seriously that he had to transfer, *that night*.

"Ever since then, David—Dr. Sternheimer—has been trying every sneaky, underhanded way that he knows of to get us back together. Why, I have no idea. That's the real reason, I'm sure, that he picked both of us to transfer to these Ahrmehnee bodies for the initial part of the mission, before I found out what those lesbians had in their valley.

"But this dark, sexy body would have died virginal—and

not one of the bodies I've spent any time in over the years has—before I'd have coupled with Harry Braun . . . and he knows it, too, Jay. It's not you he's pouting at, it's me."

Corbett opened his mouth, but before he could speak, the small, short-range transceiver lying on the slope between them crackled into life and a tinny voice demanded, "Well, what are we going to do, Erica? I hope we aren't going to camp here. According to the map, there's a sizable creek only a few kilometers farther on, and I need a bath . . . you most likely could use one too, after humping that damned Corbett all last night."

Both of them reached for the transceiver, but the woman's hand reached it first. "Dr. Braun, Major Corbett is the commander of this expedition, militarily speaking, and his is the decision regarding where we camp, how far we go each day or when and why and for how long we halt on any occasion. But you know the facts, I don't need to repeat them to you. And what I do in my tent at night is my affair, not yours. I nearly killed you once; I can improve upon that effort if you press me too far with your spite and your unjustified jealousy, Doctor.

"Now, Doctor, for good and sufficient reasons, Major Corbett has elected to stop where we presently are to wait until one group of armed men pass across our route and to see if any others will follow them. So halt the pack train, Doctor. Major Corbett or I will notify you when he feels it safe to march again. End of transmission, *Doctor!*"

With a sigh, Harry Braun turned off his own transceiver and rehung it on the pommel of his mule's saddle. Erica got bitchier toward him every year. Surely she was aware that he had never stopped loving her, not even when she had undercut him while they were still married—taken unjustified credit for the success of what had been a joint project—not even when she had flagrantly humiliated him by sleeping around with half the adult males in the Center, not even when she had very nearly ended his existence permanently by almost killing that fine young body he had had for only a few years.

He set his jaw, his lips forming a thin, hard line. Yes, she knew. Erica-the-Bitch knew that he still loved her and used the fact to torment him ceaselessly, giving whatever body she owned to anybody but Harry Braun. She—

"Mighty One . . . ?" The man forking the mountain pony at his side spoke diffidently.

Harry shoved his righteous rage far back in his mind and turned to the Broomtown man. "Pass up the word to halt in place, Vance, then take over the rearguard. Don't shoot unless you're attacked; otherwise, lie low and pass the word up to the van. That's where I'm headed now."

So saying, Braun nudged his well-trained mule into a smooth, distance-eating trot. He headed south, along the outer verge of the narrow track skirting the low cliffline of the plateau, occasionally deigning to acknowledge the deeply respectful greetings of the Broomtown packers and guards.

Broomtown was in that area once, long ago, known as Tennessee—or so stated David Sternheimer. But Harry privately disagreed with the senior director of the J&R Kennedy Research Center; he thought that it was actually located farther south, in the former state of Georgia. Not that the actual geographic location or their disagreement over it really mattered a rat's ass anyway, thought Braun.

Broomtown had been established some century and a half earlier, when the settling of the formerly chaotic Southern Kingdom of Ehleenee under the direction and aegis of Milo Morai and his Confederation had made the base in central Georgia untenable.

"Damn that meddling mutant, anyway!" Braun muttered to himself. "If not for him and his western nomads *we'd* control most of the East Coast by now. The damned Greeks had become so weak and decadent that anyone could've taken them over with fucking little effort."

As Braun trotted past a small group of guardsmen, their leader reined his pony about, drew his saber and saluted with a flourish. Half smiling, Harry raised a hand from his own reins and gifted the Broomtowner a curt nod in return.

Rough and hopeless as they had seemed at the start, each succeeding generation of the Broomtown folk was turning out better and better. To begin with, they had been only a small group of mountaineers—all related in one degree or another—living in miserable hovels behind a hilltop palisade and scratching out a meager existence from farming played-out land and raising a few skinny animals. In the leaner years, they raided smaller, weaker groups, and they lived constantly in dire fear of raids by larger, better-armed folk.

But the decision of the directors of the Center had radically changed all of that. Broomtown was now a village of some thousands of souls, living safely, securely, peacefully in rows of neat, well-built houses, some of which boasted as many as five rooms.

The technology of the Center had brought Broomtown the awe and respect of all its neighbors, and raids now were a dim fear of the past. That same technology had enriched the townspeople's lives in other ways, as well—advanced methods of farming and scientific stock-breeding had given them far more food for far less labor, carefully selective breeding of the Broomtowners themselves was, Braun and his colleagues felt certain, the principal reason for the quantum advances of intelligence and abilities in the last few generations.

The sergeant who had just saluted him and that noncom's elder brother, Sergeant Major Vance, were excellent examples of the sagacity of the Center's breeding program for their base-cum-colony. Not only could these two read and write—something which all Broomtowners had been able to do for the last three generations—they and many of the once simple and primitive natives were now quite competent in the understanding and use of Center technology.

Broomtown now included small shops and factories, even a small foundry. Practically all of the Center's firearms and ammunition were products of Broomtown, as were the large and the small transceivers and powerpacks. Moreover, the younger Broomtowners were becoming quite inventive and otherwise talented, constantly developing ways and means to render their products smaller, lighter in weight and yet still more effective than the Center-produced models they copied.

But there were many needful items of high technology that Broomtown could not produce at all and that the Center turned out only with immense difficulty and hideous expenditure of energy. That was precisely why the packloads of ancient machines and spare parts for them were of such unheralded potential value to the Center, why acquisition of them had been felt to be well worth the cold-blooded murder of hundreds of men, women and children, not to mention the expense of fitting out and dispatching this packtrain and the necessary armed guards to accompany it.

Nor were the refined metals to be sneezed at; gold, silver and copper, in both coins and bars; bars of tin, lead, zinc, nickel, chromium, tungsten and aluminum; spool on spool of wire of differing materials, gauges and degree of resistance. And too there were quantities of tools and technical equipment of varying sorts.

There had never been any sure way of ascertaining just how and where those strange, savage women had gotten the combined trove, how long they had had it or why they had transported it from place to place—if, indeed, they had, for some of the devices looked to Braun as if they had been in place for far longer than the Hold of the Maidens had been occupied.

Had matters been different and the decision been entirely his to make, Braun would have preferred to extirpate the population of the hold, use the big copters to fly up equipment and personnel both from Broomtown and the Center, then observe and study the functions of the devices in their places, before beginning to dismantle them. That, he knew, would have been the proper, scientific way to do it, but the discovery that the hold lay directly atop a volcano on the verge of erupting had precipitated the Board's decision to proceed as they had.

Some of the devices were unfamiliar to Braun and Erica Arenstein, not to mention Corbett, who was not and had never been a scientist, only a professional soldier; but from what little he had had time to skim from the ancient, crumbling books, charts, servicing manuals and blueprints, Braun could assume that most of the equipment was from a communications and/or tracking installation—a military or NASA facility, he surmised—although why a partially natural cave in the southern reaches of the Appalachian Mountains had been chosen and enlarged to contain it was beyond his imagination.

When he at last came within sight of the low, brushy ridge which twisted and turned across the track at a more or less right angle to the line of cliffs, Braun dismounted, removed his rifle from the scabbard and slung it diagonally on his back, clipped a pouch of spare magazines to his belt, then, after hesitating for a moment, added his binoculars to the load, before hitching his mule's reins to a small pine.

The Broomtown trooper on the other side of Erica yielded Braun his place with alacrity, when the scientist came bellying up the incline.

"Now, goddammit, Harry," Erica hissed venomously, "what the hell are you doing up here? You were supposed to be in charge of the train and the rearguard."

She might have said more, but Corbett quickly interposed, "Oh, don't make an issue of it, Dr. Arenstein. Since there's been no pursuit by now, I doubt very much there will be any. Besides, Sergeant Major Vance is a competent professional, I'd make him and several others commissioned officers if Dr. Sternheimer would agree."

"But Dr. Braun deserted his post," snapped Erica hotly. "He willfully left the place to which he'd been assigned. Under conditions like these, I thought that that was punishable by death, Jay."

Corbett sighed tiredly. "Doctors, you are both in charge of the scientific aspects of this mission, *I* am in charge of the military aspects, and, militarily speaking, you both are rankless supernumeraries. Neither of you has any assigned posting, as you both lack the ability and experience to satisfactorily fill a military command capacity. The commander of the rearguard is Vance; his brother, Sergeant Major Vance, and Sergeant First Class Cabell are each in charge of one segment of the train, and Master Sergeant Gumpner commands this vanguard, here.

"That you two doctors have been at murderous odds for centuries has been common knowledge at the Center and at our various bases. Who is or was or will be right or wrong in your feud is unimportant to me just now, nor would I particularly care if the two of you killed each other here and now. But Dr. Sternheimer impressed upon me the critical necessity of bringing the cargo of this train safely into Broomtown, and I gave him my word of honor that I would assuredly do so.

"So, Doctors, I hereby serve you both a warning: If any more of your ongoing hostility seems to me to be disrupting or even demoralizing my command, I shall have you both disarmed and bound to your mounts, or I shall personally shoot you, whichever seems the best course to me at the time. Do I make myself clear, Doctors?"

When neither answered immediately, Corbett went on in a lower but intense tone, "Please recall who and what you are. No matter how adult and sophisticated our Broomtowners may seem, from day-to-day contact, remember than in many respects they still are as primitive and childlike as were their ancestors of a century and a half ago. They all bear a degree of respect that borders upon veneration toward the Center and toward any of us from the Center, but especially for you scientists.

"Such spiteful, petty behavior as you two have evinced on this return trip has upset them more than you, or even they, realize. Dr. Sternheimer has great plans for Broomtown, you know, and intends to start to implement them soon after we get back, using some of the very men who are with us. So, for the sake of the Center, for the sake of all that we have worked for and suffered for over the centuries, for the sake of the United States of America—which we still are serving and which we can soon begin to rebuild—I beg of you both not to show these Broomtowners any more of your feet of clay. Save your mutual hatreds until you're back at the Center, among your own kind. Otherwise, Doctors, I'll find it a necessity to place my duty ahead of friendship."

When a full hour had passed with no more of the shaggy fugitives coming down from the plateau and no appearance by whoever or whatever had put them to such panic-stricken flight, Corbett dispatched his subordinate, Sergeant Gumpner, and a small mounted patrol to scout out the route of march. Within another half hour, the noncom radioed back that no living mountaineers were anywhere in sight, only a couple of dead ones and a few stray ponies, which he and his men had rounded up. At that, Corbett mounted the rest of the van and signaled the bulk of the train to resume the march.

As they proceeded on, he kept both of the scientists with him, placing Braun ahead of him on the narrow track and Erica behind. They had ridden on without incident or spoken word for the best part of an hour when suddenly the air seemed filled with birds. Birds of every description soared aloft from nests and perches, all screeching, crying and whistling insanely.

Then, just as suddenly, it was all that the men and woman could do to control their riding and pack animals, which not only gave the appearance of unnatural edginess—even the placid, dependable mules—but were being driven to near hysteria by the hordes of small leaping, crawling, slithering and scuttling wildlife with which the ground suddenly seemed alive.

Corbett halted atop a hill and reined about to ride back and see if he and his men could help with the screaming, rearing, kicking pack beasts. But before he could make another move or speak a single word, the rocky ground beneath his mule's hooves seemed to shift. Shrieking and thrashing, the mule staggered and fell, Corbett managing to clear leather barely in time to avoid going down with the animal.

Braun was not so quick or fortunate. His big, powerful mule fell with a thump on the heaving ground, pinning his left leg, movements of mule and ground serving to further mangle the crushed limb. He screamed once, then, mercifully, lost consciousness.

Erica's mule, though it kept its feet, proceeded to buck her off to land, winded, stunned and gasping, in a thick clump of thorny brush. Freed of its rider, the once-docile saddle mule went savagely berserk, attacking ponies and men indiscriminately, before Sergeant Gumpner drew his sidearm and shot the murderous beast.

The near pandemonium which had earlier engulfed the pack animals was now complete, total, affecting not just the ponies and mules but many of the men as well. And Major Jay Corbett could not bring himself to blame those men anymore than he could fault the frantic animals, for few were as stolid and stoic as Master Sergeant Gumpner and fewer still had the benefit of his own centuries of self-discipline.

Not only was the ground heaving and tossing like storm-roiled sea-waves, with trees crashing down or splitting asunder, but animals—wild beasts of all descriptions—still were terrifiedly crossing the track along the base of the cliffs, a brown-black airborne river of squeaking bats was issuing from at least two cave mouths somewhere on those cliff faces, and rocks and boulders were being torn loose to plunge down among the frightened agglomeration of men and animals.

The sight of the falling rocks awoke a horrifying presentiment in Corbett's mind. As icy chills raced up and down his spine, setting his nape hairs to rising, prickling, he staggered over to the still-downed mule, disregarding the danger of its thrashing long enough to secure his transceiver from its place.

"*Vance!* Sergeant Major Vance! This is Major Corbett, Sergeant Major, over!" Twice and part of a third time he had to repeat his transmission before the voice of the noncom acknowledged.

The subordinate sounded a little breathless, panting, but relatively calm. "Sergeant . . . Sergeant Major Vance here, sir. Over."

"Vance, don't interrupt, just hear what I say and do it, immediately! You and the rearguard get away from those cliffs. Ride if you can, run if you can't, but pass the word to get any men and especially pack animals that are still on that track off it, west of the line of small hills, as quickly as possible. *Do it Vance!* Out!"

Then Corbett turned back to those immediately surrounding him. Braun's mule just then regained its feet, trembling like a leaf, its eyes rolling whitely, and Corbett quickly stepped over, grasped the dangling reins and secured them to a nearby bush, lest the animal take it into its head to bolt. A brief glance at Dr. Braun told Corbett's experienced eye that he was probably hurt, possibly badly hurt, but still alive and breathing, though unconscious.

In the hollow ahead, Gumpner and a handful of his men were trying to either raise downed ponies or to quiet the few still on their feet and within reach.

As the movements of the earth began to slack off a bit, Corbett went back to his own mount, stroked it while speaking soothing, meaningless words and, when it had calmed down a bit, superficially examined it for broken bones or injuries, then slowly, carefully guided it back onto its feet.

With his arm through the reins, the officer continued to verbally soothe the big beast, while examining the saddle and the various items of equipment. The canteen was an utter loss, crushed by the mule's weight and holed by a sharp rock, but all the other pieces seemed to be intact and still usable, if somewhat scuffed. The rifle scabbard was scraped, with a buckle almost torn off, the stock was scored in places, but the action still operated smoothly and the sights showed no damage or misalignment.

Aware that mules and all herd animals tended to be calmer in proximity to others of their kind, Corbett led his mule over to where he had hitched Braun's mount. It was just then that Erica came slowly limping out of the brush, her face and hands thorn-scored and dripping blood, her black hair in wild disarray and filled with leaves and twigs.

"Where's that bastard of a mule I was riding, Jay? Have you seen the fucker?"

He handed her the reins of Braun's mount. "Take this one, Doctor—Braun won't be using one soon, I'm afraid. Yours is dead. After it threw you, it went bonkers and Gumpner had to shoot it."

"If he hadn't shot the misbegotten son of a bitch, *I* would've," Erica said grimly. "I couldn't've easily been killed, blinded by those goddamn thorns."

Corbett shook his head reprovingly. "Doctor, you can't fault dumb beasts for fearing earth tremors. Or men, either, for that matter."

"But, damn it, Jay, I . . ." And the earth heaved again, ferociously, tripping her still-wobbly legs from under her.

Both of the mules brayed their terror and reared, their big, steel-shod forehooves flailing. Corbett let drop the scabbarded rifle he had just removed from his own mount and, placing himself between the terror-stricken animals, took a tenacious grip on their headstalls and rode up and down with their rearings, using his weight to bring them down more quickly and his voice to calm them.

Because of his preoccupation with the mounts and the fact that he and they were facing south, he did not see the calamity that in the mere blinking of an eye befell the bulk of the precious pack train and the men accompanying it. But he heard it. He heard and felt it, and he *knew*. Even before he turned to see, *he knew*.

Sergeant Major Vance, obediently following Corbett's order, had himself ordered most of the rearguard off the track and well out from the cliffs. Then he and a few picked men, on half-maddened and barely controllable ponies, had galloped south along the track, trying desperately to see the other order carried out—getting the pack train off the track, away from the beetling line of cliffs and over the line of low hillocks to the west.

But, due principally to the hysterical state of most of the riding and pack beasts, it was a nearly impossible task, and precious few men and animals were beyond the point of danger when the second massive series of shudders shook the rocky earth and, with a grinding-crashing roar, the entire line of cliffs buckled and tumbled down, burying men, beasts and loads beneath uncountable tons of shattered rock.

Chapter II

"Oh, sweet Jesus," Corbett said softly, sadly, looking at the rocky mass grave the line of cliffs had so suddenly become. Where the two scientists—Arenstein and Braun—might and soon would bewail the loss of the devices, books and metals, the officer could think just now only of his men, his dead men.

He had known those men most of their lives, had trained and worked with them from their mid-teens, just as he had with their fathers, before them. He had ridden and marched and, occasionally, fought beside them; he had shared camp and fire and cookpot and hooch with them, heat and cold, danger and privation. He had long ago earned their warm love and their deep respect, both of which he had returned. And now they were dead, most of them, and he knew that he never again would even see their bodies.

And a part of him harbored a deep hunger to be there with his command, to lie dead beside them under those chunks of rock, to be finally, fully dead at last, as he should have been centuries ago. Major James Hiram Corbett, USA, had been a deeply religious man; indeed, only paternal pressure and his appointment to the USMA at West Point had kept him out of a seminary and the ministry.

He had retained his faith through the academy and through the service years, thereafter. He had remained religious up until the first time he had had to choose between a painful death and a transfer of his consciousness into a younger, vibrantly healthy body. And each succeeding transfer over the hundreds of years since that first one had chipped off a bit more of his original faith. But still there remained a flinty core of the edifice which once had been so grand and imposing, and that core still nagged him, troubled him on occasion.

It troubled him now. "Dave Sternheimer, that pompous ass, throws fits every time someone forgets and brings up what the mutants call us—vampires; yet, that's precisely what we all are—unnatural creatures, maintained in our deathlessness by a godless perversion of science.

"We all should rightly have died with the nation, the world that spawned us, and since we didn't, we have remorselessly levied a tribute of young men and women—living flesh and blood to sustain us—from every succeeding generation. Small wonder that normal folk and those mutants call us 'witches' and 'vampires,' for to this world we are the very monsters of antique legend. Minotaurs we are, and Kennedy Research Center the maze. How long, I wonder, before this world produces a Theseus to finally rid mankind of the murderous, unholy parasites we've become? Perhaps this Milo Morai, the mutant who has lived since before the War, will extirpate us, will one day cleanse the world of our sinful works and send our souls on to whatever hellish torments our misdeeds have earned us. Not even sweet, gentle Jesus could be expected to be merciful toward such a pack of selfish, merciless . . ."

His mind came abruptly back to the present situation and to the knowledge that something was wrong, very wrong. He had assumed that the high-mounting dust from the collapse of the cliffs had been dimming the sun, but though that dust was subsiding, the light still grew steadily paler, and he cast his gaze to all quarters seeking a reason.

Then that questing gaze was suddenly locked upon the northern horizon. There, looking close enough to reach out an arm and touch it, towered an immense, furiously roiling cloud of multihued smoke, steam and dust. Thick as any mountain, it stood, rising to a height of at least a full mile!

"The volcano!" he whispered to himself in awe. "My God, my God, what have we, what have *I* wrought?"

So rapt was Corbett that when Erica hobbled up again and touched his arm, he started. "That . . . that *thing* is a volcano, Jay; I've seen them before, in Cuba. Do . . . do you think it's possible that . . . that *our.* . . ?"

"Oh, yes, Doctor," he interrupted her, his voice savage. "It's our own, devil-spawned, twentieth-century witchery that's responsible for that . . . and, God forgive us, for that!" He waved his arm at the site of the deadly rockfall.

"Of course!" She nodded quickly. "With his knowledge of

geology, Braun should have expected this mess or something
like it. Sternheimer will have a fit when he hears of it, of the
loss of all those machines and devices, but we can still bring
a crew up here, after we get back to Broomtown, and salvage
the metals, most likely, even if nothing else. We— For the
love of . . . !" She took a hasty step back, her hands raised
defensively, instinctively, before her. "*Jay!* What's *wrong* with
you? You . . . you look as if you . . . you're ready to . . .
to *kill* someone!"

"You and Braun and Dave Sternheimer and your goddam
precious, priceless ancient relics! Doesn't it matter one damn
bit to you, you harpy, that they're likely half a hundred dead
men under those rocks—*my* men, good, loyal, decent men?
Can't you realize that it was *our* larcenous selfishness that
murdered not only those helpless folk up yonder where that
volcano is now, but our own Broomtowners, as well?"

As a soul-deep agony began to replace the killing light in
his eyes, Erica's fear too ebbed and she felt it safe to shrug,
saying, "Fortunes of war. You're a soldier, Jay, and so were
they. You all take the same risks in that trade, don't you?"

Before he could answer, Sergeant Gumpner mounted the
knoll to salute and render a brief report. "Sir, one pony dead
of a broken neck, three more had to be put down—with the
axe, to save ammo; I had to shoot one round to save Trooper
Jenkins's life from the doctor's mule, and that animal is dead,
too. A couple of ponies were bitten by the mule, but not so
badly they can't be ridden. Both Jenkins and Pruitt were
knocked down and bruised, but neither is hurt. Your orders,
sir?"

The order did not come, for at that moment, the boiling
column on the northern horizon was suddenly shot through
with flames and objects glowing so brightly that it blinded
one to look at them. And, within split seconds, came a sound
so loud that the barely quieted beasts were set once more to
rearing and screaming, while men clapped hands to their
abused ears and writhed on the ground in pain. But as
quickly as the unbearable noise came, it was gone.

Corbett had just jumped up and grabbed the bridles of the
two near-hysterical mules when he heard Erica shriek. A
quick glance over his shoulder showed the battered, bloody-
faced woman pointing mutely at the sky, through which a
veritable host of dark somethings were hurtling out of the

flame-riven column of gases from the volcano. In all directions they spread trailing plumes of smoke.

The first to ground anywhere near Corbett bounced down onto the rocky rubble covering the pack train and his men. It struck and bounced, once, twice, then shattered into many chunks and pieces . . . pieces of dully glowing rock. Almost immediately, a strong wind commenced to blow up from the south, its passage ruffling the sere grasses, brush and trees. In nearby places where other superheated rocks had grounded, fires sprang up rapidly and, fanned by the sudden wind, became instant conflagrations, sending animals and ponies that had fled into the forested areas racing back onto the relatively open areas flanking the track.

Erica limped again to Corbett's side. "Jay, I saw something very much like this happen in Cuba. It was about five hundred years ago, at the time of those worldwide seismic disturbances, the ones that ended by turning Florida and most of the Gulf Coast into swamps and sank so much of the East Coast. I know, therefore, what will happen now, and we've got to move fast if we mean to live through it."

By radio and by voice—for the fine, falling ash and the consequent lessening of sunlight had made a twilight world of their surroundings—Corbett and Gumpner and a corporal who happened to own a fine, far-ranging tenor began to rally such men as had survived the hideous disaster, then led them all, with their mounts and such pack animals as were easily caught, to an area chosen by Erica. There, hard by the rockfall beneath which lay the bodies of their comrades, the men moved out in a wide arc, firing the brush.

The slice of hell to the north was still sucking in cooler air from every direction and the swift-flowing wind currents had soon whipped the series of small blazes into a holocaust of truly monumental proportions. Northward and westward the fire raced, to join here and there those fires set by the first shower of hot rocks.

From within the depths of those merciless flames came the agonized death screams of countless beasts, and a violent explosion a few hundred yards to the west told of the demise of one of the panicked pack mules with a load of munitions. Another pack animal—this one a largish pony—stumbled out of the blazing brush, obviously blinded and screaming like a lost soul, until Sergeant Gumpner ran to its side and ended its suffering with his short-handled, heavy-bladed and already bloodstained battle axe.

Braun and the other wounded men and animals were very fortunate, for that one pony axed down by Gumpner near the rockfall was the beast on which had been packed the bulk of the expedition's medical supplies and drugs so that far more men lived through the terrible night than might otherwise have done so. It was likewise fortunate for them all that Erica included among her degrees an M.D.

After she had set, bandaged and splinted Braun's leg and administered those medications available, she went on to clean and cover wounds and burns and handle broken bones for first the men, then the riding and pack animals. But she refused to attempt surgery on the two unconscious troopers obviously in need of such treatment.

"Yes, Jay, I was and still am a very gifted surgeon, in my mind, that is; but good surgery is more than simple knowledge of procedures. The body must be trained as well, you see, and this one is not. I've not been in it long enough to even get to know it very well. And even were I in my original body—the one I was born in, I mean—under the existing conditions and with the available equipment, I very seriously doubt that I could help those two. Probably the kindest thing to be done is to have Gumpner put them down as he did that pony with its eyes burned out. But best to do it now, before they have a chance to come to and start to suffer again."

But Corbett did not delegate the soul-wrenching task to his subordinates. He borrowed Gumpner's axe and did the two mercy killings himself, driving the backspike of the axe accurately and deeply into each wounded man's skull at the confluence with the spinal column.

When Gumpner inquired as to burials, Corbett could only shake his head and sigh. "We lack even a single spade, and besides, the soil's too thin hereabouts for a real grave. No, Sergeant, strip them—clothing, too; we aren't out of this mess yet, not by a long shot, and we may have need of all their effects before we are—then get them farther up on top the landslide and try to cover them with rocks.

"Have a detail get the gear off that pony and then butcher the carcass. Have another detail scrounge any pots or pans, then send some men out there to drag some of those charred treetrunks back here to cook the meat.

"Corporal Cash," he said, turning to the junior noncom, he of the high-tenor voice, "take a head count—how many sound men, how many wounded, how many weapons and how much ammo for them, quantities and types of supplies or equipment left or salvageable, important items that are missing, that sort of thing. And find out how much water we have. It will have to be pooled and rationed tonight and maybe tomorrow."

The night came down quickly, was long and unremittingly hellish, with neither moon nor stars visible, but the whole area lit by the dim and flaring glow of near and distant fires. Ash fine as dust continued to drift thickly down, occasionally interspersed with showers of glowing coals blown by the shifting winds from the blazing forests on the hillsides.

The animals on the picket line had to be constantly tended. Every protectable inch of their hides had to be covered and their nostrils and eyes hooded with wet cloths. The humans too found it necessary to shield exposed skin surfaces from the corrosive, blistering ash, and to breathe through damp fabric. In the dearth of water, Corbett ordered that the animals' cloths, at least, be wetted down with their own and human urine.

No one got any sleep, three of the wounded died, and it seemed to all that that endless night of fire and horror would never come to an end. But, like all nights, end it did, in a wan and hesitant dawning.

"Were it feasible," Jay Corbett informed Erica, "I'd stay here at least another day, but we and the animals all must have water, and soon, and the map shows a sizable stream only a few klicks farther along this track. Except for Dr. Braun, for whom I'm having a horse litter made and rigged between my mule and that one that strayed in, last night, Gumpner has determined that all of the wounded left alive this morning are fully capable of sitting a pony. You've got Braun's mule and the rest of us will walk."

She nodded understanding and approval, but said, "Fine, Jay, but before we do anything, we must radio Broomtown or the Center or both, let them know what's happened and have them on standby, ready to copter up and get Harry and the few loads left as soon as we're within range."

He shook his head. "Impossible, Doctor. Even with booster units—which we no longer have—these saddle sets won't range much over twenty miles."

"But the big transceiver . . . ?" she began, then frowned, remembering. "Oh!"

"That's right, Doctor. It was near the end of the train, along with all of our supplies, ammo, tents and so on, so it's either under the rocks back there or somewhere out in those burned-over areas; useless to us, in either case, even if we took the time and were lucky enough to find it. No, Doctor, forget about help from the Center or Broomtown or anywhere else. We're on our own, and we will be for some hundreds of kilometers more."

Twice before they were formed up to begin the southward march, stray ponies—two of the four still bearing pack saddles—wandered in, three of them forming a small herd and the other in company with a full-sized horse.

The horse seemed a bit skittish, but Corbett, who had always had a way with equines, quickly won the big gelding over and, after petting him for a while, examined him and his equipage.

The big bay's neck and throat were armored with steel chainmail and plates of stiffened leather; a chamfron of thicker leather edged with metal protected the beast's face and a brisket plate of similar construction his chest. The saddle also edged and studded with metal, was a warkak, such as were made and used in the Middle Kingdoms, to the north and east. From the off side of the pommel hung a short-handled mace, its angular iron head clotted with old, dried blood and hair. From the near side hung a waxed-leather waterskin containing over a quart of brandy-water.

"Where in the world . . . ?" said Erica. "Jay, those primitives who crossed the track yesterday—none of them was riding anything like this horse."

He nodded. "More than likely this is from the force they were running from, Doctor. Remember, I told you that they looked like survivors fleeing a lost battle. Although he's armored like a destrier, this fellow is not war-trained to the extent that a destrier is, else I'd never have gotten near him without getting mauled. He's probably a troophorse, such as most of the northern mercenary cavalrymen ride. And there clearly was a battle. Not only is that mace thick with blood,

but the entire near side of the saddle and gear is crusted . . .
and it's not his, either; he doesn't appear to be injured, except
for a few small burns here and there."

The march down to the targeted creek was uneventful,
save for the ingathering of several more ponies and a couple
more mules. However, at the creek—or, more precisely, on
an island in the middle of the creek—Corbett and his party
were very pleasantly surprised to find Sergeant First Class
Leon Cabell and four other Broomtown men, all a trifle
singed and their mounts, as well, but otherwise uninjured.
With them were a few more pack beasts laden with metals
from the looted hold, another riderless warhorse of the
northeastern breed . . . and a bound prisoner mounted on a
shaggy, ill-kept pony.

Cabell's report was short and terse. He and the party he
now led had left the track before even the first earth tremors,
riding in pursuit of a knot of pack animals stampeded by the
flood of wild beasts fleeing the plateau. They had been two
ridgelines away from the track by the time of the initial
shocks and farther than that when the second series of tremors, the blast of noise and the rain of hot rocks had
occurred.

They had never really caught their quarry, rather the
pack beasts, moved by the herd instinct, had straggled to
join them during the long, fiery and danger-filled night, as
they rode first in one direction, then another, in order to
avoid the forest fires. Indeed, in the smoky darkness, it had
been some time before any of them noticed that the saddled
troop horse was not one of their mules, the big beasts being
about the same size.

When they had come upon the creek, Cabell had led them
upstream, recalling that the track crossed it somewhere to the
east of their position. The prisoner had been taken, he and
his pony together, upon the tiny island. The tall, rawboned,
extremely filthy man spoke English—of a sort, very slurred
and much debased—but so far had said nothing more than
what might have been prayers to a god or gods and what
were clearly curses.

"He seems to be under the impression, sir," concluded Sergeant Cabell, "that we are 'ghost-pale Ahrmehnee,' whatever
that group or race is. From what little he's said so far, and
precious little of that of a repeatable nature, I would imagine

that he was part of a large raiding party that was mauled, routed and chased off the plateau by a better-armed band of warriors. He had an arrow through his left forearm when we found him, but we removed it and bandaged him up."

"Where is the arrow?" demanded Corbett. It was produced, and after studying the black-shafted missile for a few moments, the officer turned back to Erica.

"It's not Ahrmehnee, Doctor, or Moon Maiden, either. And it's no hunting arrow. Offhand, I'd guess a Middle Kingdoms origin, and that would tend to fit in well with these two warhorses. But what the bloody hell are northern mercenaries doing over here in the western mountains? The Ahrmehnee have no need of them and never, so far as I've ever heard, hire them on. The Confederation employs them, of course, but no unit of Confederation troops could possibly have gotten so far west; the Ahrmehnee would've exterminated them well east of here."

She shrugged helplessly. "I have no ideas on the subject, Jay. But let me give that prisoner an injection. Maybe he can tell us more."

"Doctor, he's not one of ours, in any case. Whoever attacked and wounded him back up there before the quakes and eruption can be of no interest to us just now. What is of immediate importance is getting quickly to an area that wasn't so thoroughly burned out, where there will be graze for the animals. And that's why we'll halt for only an hour, here, then push on south, so if you want a bath, you had better go on downstream and get about it; we'll water the animals here and a detail will fill our containers a bit farther upstream."

"But, Jay, I think we should take the time to interrogate this prisoner. Right now, we have no slightest idea just what we may be riding into. And we're less than half our original numbers, too."

"Doctor," he replied firmly, in a tone that brooked no argument, "I'll say again what I said yesterday to you and Dr. Braun: *I* am military commander of this mission, *you* are of no rank, militarily. This is a command decision I have just made, based upon my training and experience.

"Insofar as our reduced numbers are concerned, there are still thirty-two troopers and noncoms, plus you, Dr. Braun and me. For all that our ammo supplies are critical, Doctor, for this time and place we are well armed, possessing as we do the only firearms on the entire continent, north of our Broomtown base; you've seen what superstitious awe our rifles aroused in the Ahrmehnee, so just imagine what the reaction of primitives like this prisoner would be.

"No, Doctor, although I hereby register your objection, we march on in . . ." He consulted his wristwatch. "Fifty-four minutes."

With the addition of the spare animals from Cabell's group, there were now sufficient to bear the remaining packs, and mount every trooper, as well. As the worst of the mountains now lay behind them, both Erica and Jay forsook their sure-footed but rough-gaited mules to mount the strayed-in warhorses, and they covered far more ground during the afternoon's march, for all that Corbett enforced a routine of alternating gaits and an hour on foot for every hour in the saddle.

By the light of a breathtakingly lovely sunset, the vanguard rode back to lead the main party into a small, bowl-shaped vale thickly grown with winter-sere grass and bisected by a tiny rivulet trickling down from a small, spring-fed pool high on one of the surrounding hills. Although fires had clearly raged all about this minuscule oasis, during the preceding day and night, it had for some reason remained untouched.

After Gumpner had seen to the posting of guards and the hobbling of the unsaddled and unloaded animals, the senior noncom approached Corbett. "Sir, we're going to need food for the men. We could send out hunters, but I think the prisoner's mount is dying."

The skinny, shaggy little pony had been wobbling and stumbling for most of the afternoon, causing Corbett to at last have the barbaric-looking man tied into the saddle of one of the two mules supporting Braun's makeshift horse litter. Now he went with Gumpner to examine the runty animal, which stood listlessly, swaying, head hung low and not even trying to graze; Corbett mentally agreed that the beast looked more dead than alive.

Nor were the two men long in finding the reason. A narrow stab wound on the near-side flank just a bit above the stifle was sullenly oozing serum; the wound had apparently closed soon after being inflicted and, hidden from easy view under the thick, woolly winter coat, had gone unnoticed by either the rider or his captors, with what little old blood visible being attributed to drippage from the arrowed arm of the man.

Corbett nodded curtly. "A gut thrust. From the poor creature's looks, he'll be dead before sunup. Go ahead and put him down, Gumpner, then have the men butcher him for us. As soon as the detail has the prisoner securely staked out, Dr. Arenstein will inject him with the truth drug, then she and I will question him; I'd like you and Cabell to be there when we do."

"Sir!" The grizzled noncom drew himself up and rendered the hand salute.

But afterward, Erica said, "I think we wasted the dose of pentathol on him, Jay, insofar as military information is concerned, anyway. But what he told us about his people, these Ganiks, is as fascinating as it is disgusting. I always felt and said that the twentieth-century ecology freaks were pure, certifiable nutcakes, and this distant descendant of some nameless bunch of them seems to bear me out.

"Also, I can now understand why this Jim-Beau became so violent and hysterical when the troopers stripped him and bathed him back there at the stream this morning. That word he kept screaming, 'plooshuhn'—what he meant was 'pollution,' Jay; obviously these cannibal scions of lunatic fanatics have become so fearful of polluting streams that they no longer wash either their bodies or their clothing, ever . . . not unless they get caught out in the rain or happen to fall into water. God, how can they stand themselves from day to day, much less each other?" She wrinkled her nose and shook her head.

Corbett nodded. "A very savage, primitive people. I hope we don't run into any more of the bastards, but from what little I could understand of this one's atrocious language, we would seem to be smack-dab in the middle of their stamping grounds and the track we're following is, he attests, one of their main north-south routes. Therefore, Doctor, I'm marching southwest for one day, then we'll head back due south. It may be a bit longer and a lot rougher trip, but, let's hope, a safer one.

"Without any sort of a track, it may be necessary to dismantle the horse litter and tie Dr. Braun into a saddle tomorrow. Do you think he can tolerate traveling that way? I don't want Sternheimer accusing me of killing one of his scientists."

She shrugged unconcernedly. "If Harry dies, he dies . . . but I don't think he will; he's too much of a bastard to do anything that would make me that happy, damn him. Oh, he'll suffer enough, sitting a saddle with that broken leg, and they once said that suffering was good for the soul, but there's not enough suffering in the world to do his soul any good. I'll see to it that he gets just enough painkiller to keep him from going into shock. He'll moan and bitch and scream and threaten, of course, but don't worry about it, Jay."

But of course Jay Corbett did worry about Braun's condition and kept him on his horse litter until it became crystal-clear that the column's further progress over and around the trailless, forested and brush-grown hills so encumbered was impossible. Then he had the warkak removed from his charger and placed upon the back of the best-gaited of the riding mules, figuring correctly that the high, flared pommel and cantle would afford Braun more support than the lower stock saddle.

Five or six kilometers into the second day's march, the column crossed another trail, but Corbett had them push on to the west of this one too, having the last few men erase from it all marks of their passage across it.

Finally, when they were into what appeared to be true wilderness, bearing no visible signs of man, he turned them back to the south, marching by compass bearing, the progress slow and wearing on both men and beasts. But not for two more full days was there any trace of mankind, any sounds other than natural wooded-mountain sounds of insect and bird and wild beast, any sign of lurking danger.

When that danger finally did manifest itself, it was with dramatic—and, for many of the marching men, deadly—suddenness.

Chapter III

After the first full day of cross-country marching, even Erica gave over urging speed. Speed was simply impossible, except on those rare occasions when the column chanced upon a deer trail or a shallow stream angling more or less south. Otherwise, the sometime vanguard—sore-muscled, sweating in spite of the chilly air, faces whealed and bloody from thorns and lashing branches—were compelled to hack a path through the thick brush of rhododendron and mountain laurel and red barberry with sabers and battleaxes.

Nor could even the hardened veterans keep up such exhausting labor for any length of time. Corbett found it necessary to split his small force into three sections, with one under Gumpner, one under Cabell and the third under his personal command, each section taking a two-hour stint at forging the trail. Only Erica, the prisoner, Dr. Braun and the other wounded were exempted from the hard labor, even Corbett taking a turn at hacking down brush and branches with his saber.

Since scattered areas were still burning, although mostly well west of the party, Corbett forbore adding the further hardship of cold camps, so the flagged men had at least hot food and light by which to hone new edges on their well-used weapons. Most had hot food, anyway. The prisoner, however, had refused to eat from the start, frantically forgoing any flesh—pony, venison or even rabbit—and making do with the raw roots of certain plants he dug or pulled up, spiced with the stray worm or grub or insect. This nauseating diet was his only sustenance . . . until the night one of the wounded men died.

Because of the utter dearth of signs of mankind since the second trail had been crossed and because of the state of complete exhaustion the trail-cutting caused, Corbett had mounted only perimeter guards at night, leaving all the rest to much-needed sleep around the coals of the cookfires.

He and the others were awakened near dawning by an enraged shout, followed by a shriek of agony, to behold a grisly sight. The hobbled prisoner lay at the feet of a perimeter guard who, his face mirroring disgust and murderous fury, was at that moment in the act of drawing his saber.

Corbett's order halted the guard, and a second order had fresh fuel added to the coals of the nearest fire, thus giving Erica and all the men a view of the grim tableau.

The lower face, the beard and even the front of the filthy shirt of the prisoner were running blood. His manacled hands were red from fingertips to wrist, and streams of the blood had streaked his hairy arms to the elbows. One of those gory hands clutched a bloody flake of stone and the other a shiny, gelatinous-looking chunk of tissue that Corbett at first failed to recognize. Even as they all watched him, the shaggy prisoner, still whimpering, brought that which he held up to his mouth, tore off a bit of it, chewed and swallowed. At this, the perimeter guard whirled about and doubled, retching.

When, shortly, Corbett saw the newly dead body of Corliss, with its abdomen raggedly opened and most of its liver excised, it was all that he could do to hold down his own gorge, and he deeply regretted having stopped the guard from sabering the savage cannibal.

Upon questioning, the prisoner sniveled, "Ah din't kill 'im. He jest died and ah 'uz *so* hongry."

"My God, man," replied Corbett, "you've been offered, *and flatly refused,* food every time the rest of us ate, so there's no excuse for what you just did. What kind of sick, unnatural creature are you?"

But the shaggy man clammed up, sullenly, and another shot of Erica's drug was required to get more out of him; then they were all half sorry they had heard what they had. It cost them all any remaining appetite for breakfast.

As the officer and Erica paced slowly, leading their fine horses side by side, in the wake of Gumpner's hacking, cursing section, Corbett shook his head, saying, "I still can't say I understand any of it, Doctor; these Ganiks wear the skins of animals, yet they can't or won't eat them, preferring human flesh, even the bodies of their own families."

Erica shrugged. "Possibly it's because you were a soldier

and seldom if ever ran up against the emotional basket cases that made up the environmental branches of the anti-industrial revolution, Jay. As a scientist, I worked for both industry and government and I had to face and debate more of the nuts than I care to recall.

"The ancestors of this creature were the types that delayed for years the construction of a badly needed dam in Tennessee in order to supposedly save the spawning area of a three-inch fish that, it later developed, was not only not endangered, but not especially rare, either. As cracked as many or most of those eco-freaks were, yes, I can see how their descendants emerged into the unprepossessing likes of Jim-Beau. And if they are all as incestuous as his family seems to be, you can see how any earlier-extant strains of insanity were bred deeper and wider with every new generation.

"It would seem that the catch words of that ancient, addle-pated movement have become gods and devils to their inheritors. 'Organic farmers' are become 'Ganiks,' their principal god, 'Kahnzuhvaishuhn,' was once 'conservation,' just as their most evil and most feared devil, 'Plooshuhn,' was once 'pollution.'

"I can fully empathize with you and your men, Jay, for I find everything about Jim-Beau disgusting, too. But nonetheless, he is a fascinating specimen that should be studied in depth at the Center; that's why I won't allow him to be killed. He'll have to be watched closely, of course, for the rest of the trip back. Corliss quite probably died naturally, in his sleep, from his injuries; but then too, our Jim-Beau, our 'hongry' Jim-Beau, just may have hastened him along into death, for his own personal gastronomic reasons."

Near dusk of the second day's march, Jay Corbett and his section hacked their way out into a track which seemed to meander in an east-west direction and was clearly too wide and well defined to be a mere game track. Also, there was a mound of fresh-turned dirt on the southern verge that looked suspiciously like a small grave.

And indeed it proved to be a grave, but a most singular grave. It was shallow and contained the almost-fresh carcass of a small deer, expertly flayed of its hide, but otherwise untouched.

"Now who," Corbett mused aloud, "would go to the trouble of stalking one of these chary mountain bucks, then take only the skin and leave so much good meat behind?"

All of the Broomtown men seemed equally perplexed, but Erica nodded and said, "Ganiks, of course, Jay. It would be of a piece with this weird bastardization of a religion they seem to practice. Don't you see? Over the centuries, needing hides and skins for clothing, they've probably rationalized to the point that the killing of wild animals isn't sinful, so long as they neither eat the meat nor leave the carcasses out in the open to pollute."

Corbett shook his head. "Well, if they don't want it, we sure as hell can use it. Gumpner, have that carcass gutted and cleaned—that's tonight's supper. Cabell, you're our best tracker; see if you can determine which way on this track the party that left that deer was moving."

To Erica, he said, "I'd hoped that these days of painful trailmaking had left those bastards behind; obviously, we're still in their territory, and moving deeper into it, for all we know. If we're going to have to fight them sooner or later, I'd much prefer to do it with men and animals that aren't all worn out from forcing trail, day after day, so we're going to use this track for a while until we strike a north-south one again. Whichever way the deerslayers went, we'll go the other."

East they marched, making very good time, even while sparing the mounts and pack beasts as much as possible; and early in the second day on the track, they struck a north-south track, whereupon Corbett headed south along it. They moved fast now, covering as many kilometers per day as the officer thought the animals and men could endure, but they moved warily, too, with all save Dr. Braun and the captive armed and alert from start to finish of each day's march.

On the morning of the eighth day after the eruption and quakes, gunshots from all along the camp perimeter awakened Corbett and the rest. In the gray light of false dawn, he and his men sprang up, grasping rifles, pistols, sabers and axes, only to find no one to fight . . . not then. One of the perimeter guards had taken a thick, short dart in the groin, and he bled to death before he could be gotten back to camp. Three dead Ganiks were found, and great pools or splashes of blood were to be seen in two more places.

Corbett took a strong mounted party out as soon as it was light enough and scouted out from the perimeter in a full circle, finally finding where the Ganiks had left their ponies while they came in afoot, to be unexpectedly greeted with large-caliber riffes firing explosive bullets. They found one more dead Ganik, too.

A bullet had obviously torn off a good part of the left arm of the savage, but that was not what had killed him. His throat had been cut . . . and his body had been stripped and butchered. Heart, liver and kidneys seemed to be gone from the cadaver, along with most of the flesh of both thighs, upper arms and buttocks. Moreover, the generative organs were gone and the head had been axed open to scoop out the brains.

While some of the troopers leaned from their saddles, gagging and retching, Corbett was engulfed by an ominous foreboding. Savages properly terrified of firearms and their deadly effect would not have stopped so close to those fire-spitting devices long enough to kill and butcher one of their wounded, and without the psychological advantage of advanced weapons technology, he knew that he and his small command had about as much chance of survival as a wet snowball in hell.

As soon as he and his force were back in camp, that camp was struck and the column moved out on the track southward. But it was far too late to escape their doom, and in his heart, Jay Corbett knew it. Nonetheless, he formulated contingency plans and issued the requisite orders to his remaining NCOs.

"Gumpner, Cabell, Cash, the most important thing is for someone to get back to Broomtown alive and in condition to lead a large force back up to the site of the disaster, where most of the pack train is buried, before rain and the elements have time to further damage those devices and books. The second most important thing is to try to get the two scientists—Dr. Arenstein and Braun—back to Broomtown, but do not—I repeat, do not—endanger the primary goal for the sake of the secondary one.

"I am now certain that we're surrounded, have been for days, and are being deliberately paced by a large force of those cannibals, so none of us may make it back, but I do not want it to be for want of trying, gentlemen. When the battle joins, as it will, soon or later, you and your men must make every shot count, but be certain to save the last one for yourselves. From what we've learned from that Jim-Beau, none of us must allow himself to be captured alive by these savages. If all else fails you, jam the point of your dirk or bootknife in under the angle of the jaw, here, at least an inch deep, and slash downward toward the front; the pain will be short and sharp and you'll be dead inside five minutes."

At the first rest stop of the day, Corbett had the loads of loot from the Hold of the Moon Maidens dumped at the side of the track, then the few supply loads and waterskins redistributed among all the pack animals, overriding Erica's objections brusquely.

"Doctor, it's another military decision; we'll most likely be fighting or racing for our very lives before this day is out, and I'm of the opinion that our lives are worth a bit more than a few pack loads of scrap metal.

"Oh, and don't give Dr. Braun any more drugs today. He may have to fight, too, and he can't do that doped up to the gills. Now can he?"

"No, he couldn't," she agreed, then grimaced. "But Harry is not going to like being denied his shot."

Corbett just shrugged. "Then let him take up the matter with me. I'm trying to save his life—surely that's worth some pain for a few days?"

Erica said, "To any other man or woman, probably, but you don't know how selfish, how stubbornly self-centered, Dr. Harry Braun can be."

With a long sigh, Corbett stated, "The only other humane alternative, Doctor, is simply to shoot him. *You've* heard Jim-Beau gloating over the hideous atrocities his kind inflict on helpless captives—cooking and eating them alive and all the rest.

"But he's still your patient, Doctor. If you have reason to think that the pain resulting from discontinuance of the drugs will put him into shock, tell me, and I'll put him down while he's still half-conscious."

She shook her head slowly and said sadly, "I wish now that I were a good liar, for I have a gut feeling that Harry is a . . . a jinx, that with him safely dead, we just might survive this predicament. But I'm not, Jay, I'm not a good liar, so I can't say the words that would doom him, irrevocably.

"Yes, he'll hurt like hell without a shot, but his injury is knitting nicely, so far. I doubt he'll go into shock, but if he does, you'll still have your pistol. Won't you?"

"I will, Doctor," was his grim-faced reply. Then he turned and led his armored charger back toward the van, now mounting up.

Corbett's worst suspicions regarding their untenable situation were confirmed within two hours. Two troopers were darted from ambush—one in the van, one in the rearguard. The first, the one in the rear, took the short, stubby, deadly missile at a downward angle just behind his clavicle and had bled to death before Corbett reached him. But the other was deeply pierced in the side, just below his rib cage; Gumpner put an end to the man's agonized screams with his axe.

Corbett left the two bodies where they lay, taking only enough time to strip them of their weapons and ammunition before setting the column back on the march toward their doom.

In a short stretch where rocky walls made the track too narrow for a double column, the end trooper simply disappeared, without a sound, apparently plucked from his saddle as he rode. His eyeless, tongueless head, impaled on a sharpened sapling, confronted the vanguard a few kilometers farther south.

At the next fairly open spot, Corbett halted, had each rider fill his canteen and his mount's waterskin, then dumped the remainder of the water. The supplies were portioned out as far as they would go, then the thin reserves of ammo were equally divided, and he gave his final orders to his force.

"They've trailed us and harried us, gentlemen; their next move will likely be a full-scale ambush or even an open attack, depending on how many they number, and it could come at any time now. According to the prisoner, they never fight in the dark, so if they don't hit us hard today, expect them at dawn.

"If it is an ambush, ride for your lives and don't take time to shoot unless you have a clear target and no option; it would seem that guns don't scare them, for some reason.

"If, on the other hand, they confront us in the open, immediately assume a wedge formation—wounded and noncombatants in the center—and we'll do our level best to blast our way through them. Once we are through them, Sergeant

Gumpner and Corporal Cash will be responsible for continuing on with the noncombatants and the wounded, they and one squad. Sergeant Cabell and I and the rest of the force, will turn back and hold off pursuit as long as possible.

"Sergeant Gumpner, choose your squad now and keep them together when we resume the march. You'll also take the only still-loaded animal—that's the medical supplies—and all of the spare animals, too. Remember my earlier orders and the priorities they contained.

"Good luck to you all, gentlemen, and God bless and keep you. In almost a thousand years of soldiering, you men were the finest command I ever had."

Corbett reined about and kneed his tall horse in close to Braun's mule. "Do you think you can stay in your saddle unaided, Doctor, at a fast gallop? Or would you prefer we tie you to that kak?"

Braun was sweating profusely; knots of muscle were working at the corners of his jaw, and the hate-filled eyes he turned to meet Corbett's were bloodshot and teary.

"You goddam sadist! You know I can't sit a saddle well or securely with a goddam broken leg. Of course I'll need to be tied on, you nitwit bumpkin! And don't you think for a minute I won't tell Sternheimer and all the rest how you and that bitch have tortured me in every nasty way you could, either. You may be the big dog, here and now, but just you wait until we all get back to the Center, you uneducated ape!"

Corbett called over a pair of troopers to see to strapping the infuriated scientist safely into the war saddle. Taking one of the spare sabers, he had the men buckle it in place on the mule's harness, then loaded and armed a pistol, before slipping it into Braun's empty belt holster.

"Dr. Braun, you may say anything you wish of me to the Director or anyone else. Those who know me—and you—well will recognize them for the peevish lies they are. Your difficulties with Dr. Arenstein are between the two of you, have been for centuries, and I want no part of them or of her or of you, once this present mess is concluded. If I am an uneducated ape to you, Doctor, you are to me an overeducated ass and utterly despicable. Despite that, I wish you sincerely the same luck I just wished the troopers."

Late in the afternoon, as the blaze of sun was just touching the western horizon, the van debouched into a small valley bisected by a broad but shallow stream. Milling on the near side of the stream was a mob—it could not, by even the loosest interpretation of the word, be called a formation—of at least two hundred Ganiks. All were, with their beards and uncropped hair and furs, as shaggy as their runty ponies, and even from more than fifty meters, the combined stench of them was gaggingly indescribable.

As the veteran troopers rapidly formed their wedge for the charge, the Ganiks began to screech and shriek and howl like the wild beasts they shamed in both filth and savagery. They lengthened their mob along the stream, readied darts and waved rude clubs, few seemed to bear swords or real spears.

At the point of the wedge, Corbett remarked to Gumpner, "The bastards are making their line shallower, which will make it easier for us to break through them. If they had any sense, they'd have massed on the other side of that brook, and let the water absorb some of our impetus before we struck them. We'll commence firing at twenty-five meters, concentrating around that big, red-haired bastard there, the one on the piebald pony, with the old saber; the brook looks shallowest directly behind him, and that's where we'll break through them."

"Sir," said the stocky sergeant, a bit hesitantly, "not that I mean to question the major's order, but . . ."

Corbett smiled and turned in his saddle to lay a hand on the bridle arm of the graying noncom. "Then don't do so, Gump. You've been given your orders, you have your responsibilities. Cash and I will fight the holding action . . . but I deeply appreciate the offer, old friend.

"Now, are we all formed up? Then let's *go!*"

Corbett had been secretly worried that the troop horse he now rode might panic when he began to fire a pistol from off its back, but the beast behaved well enough, galloping flat out with bared teeth that bespoke some measure of war training.

The Ganiks had seemingly expected their prey to try to by-pass them, ride around them, not charge directly into the thickest part of the mob. Nor had they expected the firesticks of which their ancient legends told to begin to kill at such long range. As the wedge scattered the mostly riderless ponies, trampling the victims of their fusillade and then splashing through the stream, precious few of the flanking Ganiks were close enough to do more than cast darts and howl in frustrated fury, so the wedge rode on unscathed.

They had time to climb the farther hill and start through the narrow defile at its summit before the bemused Ganiks had regrouped and set about a pursuit, in numbers now reduced by a good quarter part of the original mob.

Corbett had several of his best shots dismount and clamber to positions high up the two walls of the gap and set the rest to dragging up any debris they could find to partially block that gap and provide cover for the other riflemen. While they frantically labored, he rode on to make certain that Gumpner's party was safely on its way.

And it was well that he did so. He came up behind the tiny column in time to pistol down two Ganiks who, afoot, had just succeeded in dragging from his saddle a wounded trooper and were about to slash his throat. By the time Gumpner and two troopers came pounding back, sabers out and ready, Corbett was off his horse and helping the wounded man to remount.

Jay Corbett gasped, "Damn it, Sergeant, keep this column moving forward, southward; the tail end will just have to look out for itself. The amount of time that a bare score of us can expect to hold that mob back there is very limited, and you and yours are no longer strong enough to stand and fight them. You've precious little chance as it is now—don't lessen even that!"

He remounted, rendered an abbreviated horseman's salute, then reined his armored horse about and rode back toward the booming cracks of his men's rifles, where they were holding the mouth of the gap against vastly more numerous forces.

Sergeant Gumpner rode on south heedless of who saw the tears coursing down his lined, stubbled cheeks. Like generations of his forebears, he and the other Broomtowners had loved the gentle, patient, but infinitely knowledgeable man who had made soldiers of them, loved and respected him for the father he was to them. Now Gumpner knew that that ageless man was fighting his last battle in order to give a few of his military children a bare chance at survival.

"One of us *will* get back to Broomtown, too." The middle-aged soldier half-sobbed to himself. "I'll see to it. The major's last order *will* be carried out, come hell or high water!"

Farther back, in the twisting, turning, rock-walled defile, Erica found her well-bred, clean-limbed horse overtaking Braun's big mule. "Dammitall, Harry," she panted, "can't you get any more speed out of that animal? You'd better, because Gumpner's not going to wait for you or anybody else!"

Closer, she noted that his face was pale and twisted in what she took to be a combination of pain and pure terror.

"You . . . got to help me, Erica," he finally mouthed. "Got to . . . girth or something . . . saddle loosening, with me strapped into it . . ."

"Oh, all right, Harry. But after this, you're on your own, remember that." She glanced back along the track, waved a couple of troopers past her, slung the rifle she had been carrying diagonally across her back, then dismounted.

After a brief examination of the mule's gear, she looked up and angrily began, "You poor fool, there's nothing wrong with . . ." She trailed off when she found herself staring into the gaping black bore of Braun's pistol.

The face above that pistol was still twisted, but she could belatedly define that expression correctly. It was hate—pure, unadulterated hatred of her, with a gleam of triumph from the cunning, bloodshot eyes.

"You bitch!" he hissed. "You've robbed me and hurt me and humiliated me and even tried to kill me, but this is the end of it. I loved you, once, but you deliberately killed that love, giving yourself to anyone, everyone, except me, for centuries. Now I hate you, and I'm going to kill you as you almost killed me, back at the Center."

She knew precisely when he was about to pull the trigger—his lips thinned, his jaws tightened, and his eyes narrowed—but in the narrow passage, with her horse and his mule blocking her in, there was no way that she could have dodged, so she reached up and grasped his gun hand, forcing it and the gun muzzle upward. The booming explosion almost deafened her so that she hardly heard her own scream as burning flecks of gunpowder struck her scalp and arms.

Braun freed his good leg from the stirrup and savagely kicked her in one breast with the toe of his boot. Only then was he able to shake loose her grip on his wrist and once more level the big pistol.

But when he pulled the trigger this time, no buck and roar was forthcoming, only the click of the falling hammer. Furiously, he gripped the slide knurls and tried to draw it back, but it was immovable. So, in frustrated fury, he slammed the side of the heavy steel weapon with all his might across the back of Erica's bowed head, and as she crumpled bonelessly onto the rock-strewn track, he urged his big mule southward, shouldering aside her horse, thinking that a vengeance long, long delayed was the sweeter to savor and that he had served the treacherous, promiscuous bitch no less than she deserved.

He was to live to regret depriving his and Gumpner's party of the only qualified physician and surgeon.

The deadly-accurate fire of the picked sharpshooters lying or squatting on the high ledges served to keep the milling, noisy broil of Ganiks at a good, safe distance for more time than Corbett had originally figured. When those few of the cannibals brave enough or stupid enough to try to ride over the Broomtowners had all been spilled from their primitive saddles to flop onto the rocky ground with their life blood fast-flowing from the fearsome wounds inflicted by the explosive bullets, the others seemed wisely resolved to keep a goodly distance. But Corbett knew full well that it was only a matter of time before some leader arose to head up a full-scale charge against his flimsy defenses and/or flank his position.

To give at least a warning of any such flanking maneuver, Corbett sent two riflemen to climb to the top of the gap on either side and position themselves behind boulders at the verges. A single, booming pistol report from far up the defile brought all the men facing about for a moment, but when it was not followed by any others, all turned back to the work at hand—rolling and manhandling larger boulders up to both block the defile and form a breastwork from behind which the men might more safely fire whenever push came to shove.

A fortuitous find atop one side of the gap was a huge old tree. Recently uprooted, possibly by the earthquakes a few days past, it lay close enough to the verge that a squad was able, with ropes and cracking muscles, to topple it into the gorge below. But Corbett and the men had to leave it where it landed, just forward of the rude breastworks, for there simply were not enough men to manhandle it athwart the gap.

"But," thought the officer, eyeing the maze of cracked and shattered branches spreading from wall to wall and extending almost to the entrance of the defile, "any frontal assault is going to have to come in afoot, for no pony is going to allow itself to be ridden through that mess."

Then one of the sharpshooters called down from his high ledge. "Major Corbett, sir, some more of them just rode in from the north. Looks like fifty or sixty. Three or four are on real horses, and they and some others have helmets and breastplates and swords. Do I try to pick a few off, sir?"

"No, Pomroy," Corbett ordered, "wait until they're closer."

Slinging his rifle, the officer scrambled atop the huge mass of tree roots now resting upon and towering high over the breastwork boulders. Finding finally a precarious footing at the apex, he brought up and adjusted his big binoculars, fixing the field of the optics on the party of newcomers now splashing through the brook.

Aside from the few full-size horses, bits and pieces of steel armor and a scattering of swords, sabers and steel-shod pole arms, these Ganiks looked no whit different from the closer group. Their visible skin was just as grimy, their long hair and beards just as matted and their faces no less brutish; such cloth clothing as they wore was uniformly ragged and filthy; the animal skins and furs and cross-gartered rawhide boots were worn and shiny with grease.

But despite the nondescript appearance, the arrival of these reinforcements sent the mob of Ganiks milling just out of easy rifle range into a veritable frenzy of welcome. While uttering every sound of which human vocal apparatus is capable—along with some that, if asked earlier, Corbett would have said were impossible—they waved their primitive weapons with such wild exuberance as to knock a dozen or more of their fellows off their ponies, and Corbett noted that two or three of these remained where they fell.

"Christ," the officer thought, "Erica was right, these Ganiks must be lunatics; they're as dangerous to each other as they are to strangers."

After perhaps a quarter hour, when the Ganiks had quieted to some extent, one of the armored men on a real horse began to move his mouth and wave his long sword, but the distance and the slurred dialect made it impossible for Corbett to tell what he was saying. Shortly, however, two contingents—each of some thirty or forty Ganiks and each led by another of the armored horsemen—left the main body and set off to east and west.

"Flankers," the officer muttered to himself. "A three-pronged attack."

He unslung the padded case, slipped the binoculars into it and hung the case on one of the thicker root stubs, then climbed back down from his perch. On the ground he beckoned over Cash and the PFC who was assisting the acting sergeant. "Those men who just led the reinforcements in are obviously the Ganik commander and his captains, and he's a bit more intelligent or maybe just cagier than the bulk of them. He's sent a strong party, each under one of his officers, to either flank of our position. Now he seems to be pep-talking the rest of them into a frontal assault, and it's only a matter of time, the length of it dependent on how much we demoralized that first contingent earlier today, until they do hit us.

"Now, the abattis that that tree has formed has changed my strategy, Cash, for we are no longer vulnerable to a cavalry charge—not only is no horse or pony going to penetrate that splintery mass of branches, but even a dismounted force is going to be slowed up by it.

"Therefore, I don't want anyone firing down here until the bulk of the Ganik force are into that abattis. Understood? Yes, our primary objective is to hold off pursuit of Gumpner's party as long as possible, but our secondary objective is to cost those damned cannibals so many casualties here that when they do finally get by us or over us they'll be so understrength that Gumpner will have at least a fighting chance.

"So have the two highest snipers climb on up and join the men atop the sides of the gap. The lower ones can come down and join us; they'll be just too vulnerable where they are to darts or thrown axes.

"Put the rock details to gathering fist-size ones for throwing, now—no need to make the breastwork any higher than it already is. Get the mounts picketed back around that bend where they'll be safer; if some of us do live through this action, I don't want them to be trapped here for lack of mounts.

"Station a man up on those roots. I left the glasses up

there. He's to let us know the minute they start to move on us.

"Oh, and you might as well have the men fix their bayonets. There might not be time, later."

Chapter IV

Erica slowly, haltingly regained consciousness. There was the sound of voices, ebbing and surging, first loud, then dim as if with distance. At first, she could feel nothing, then, like a clap of lightning, the *pain* began.

There was no one place where it commenced, rather it seemed to encompass every cubic millimeter of her body, throbbing, seemingly intent upon rending her every cell apart. Her instinctive impulse was to scream, to shriek out her agony to the ears of all the world, but she could not. Try as she would, she had seemingly been bereft of control over her body, any part of it—neither her lips nor her jaws nor even her eyes would open on command, and not even a groan could she force from her throat.

The voices surged louder again. She could understand them, for all that the language—what was that language? It seemed that she should know well its name, but now she could not recall it—was slurred and much debased from its origins. They were, she knew, discussing her.

". . . tolt you it 'uz a Ahrmnee," attested Joe-Bob Lodge. "A mite skinny, he be, but betcha he'll cook up jest fine." He squatted and pressed his fingertips into the thickest section of Erica's thigh. "Be tender, too, betcha."

"He ain' daid, yet," Kevin Spottswood remarked. "He still a-breathin', may be, we kin mek 'im screech, back t' camp. Thet'll tender 'im up more, betcha."

The voices faded away, for Erica, as unconsciousness again claimed her and her breathing became shallower.

Kevin's horny, dirty palm held before the Ahrmehnee's nose failed to register respiration, so he knelt, leaned over and placed his ear against the chest, then sprang up with a start. "Thishere ain' no *he*, Joe-Bob, it be a *she*!"

Joe-Bob began to fumble with the length of rope holding

up his faded, ragged and filthy trousers, stuttering, "Le's . . . le's . . . le's fuck 'er now, afore the resta owuh bunch gits here. I . . . I . . . ain' *nevuh* been first on no took-female."

But the older man, Kevin, shook his shaggy head emphatically. "Somebody, he done axed opuned your haid and stuffed it with turds, boy, bound to, way you tawk! Thishere Ahrmnee bitch, she near daid, enyhow, you and me come to pole 'er, she gon' be *awl* daid, and you know what Long Willy'll do to us, then! The bunch'll be a-chawin' awn owuh short ribs afore night, an' you betcha ass he won't kill us quick, neither."

Joe-Bob began to tremble all over and big tears squeezed from the corners of his mud-brown eyes, to become lost in the matted tangle of his dark-blond beard. "But it jest ain' fair, Kevin. Ol' Long Willy, he gits him eny one the wimmens eny time he wawnts to, too. My turn, it don' come up fer more'n a week . . . and I'm so all-fired horny. It jest ain' fair!"

"It the way it is, boy," shrugged Kevin, resignedly. "It the way it allus been in the bunches. Onlies' way you can mek it diffrunt, is you fight Long Willy and kill 'im, opun and fair; then you'll be top dawg till somebody kills you."

Kevin went on, "Now you go back up top an' fork your pony an' go fin' Strong Tom. Tell 'im wher I be an' whut we founded, heah? I'm gon' git 'er out'n the sun an' see kin I keep 'er livin' till yawl gits back."

Gumpner had kept the party moving at a gallop or a fast trot for as long as his experience told him the mounts could safely endure so frenetic a pace, then he halted them, and he and his hale men were engaged in transferring saddles and gear onto the spare animals when first the riderless troop horse, then the big mule bearing Harry Braun caught up to them.

"They got Dr. Arenstein?" asked the sergeant, with a soupçon of deference, despite the press of circumstances.

His face a mask of agony, Braun just nodded, then, after a moment, gasped out, "My girth was slipping. Poor Erica had dismounted to tighten it for me when three of the stinking savages seemed to appear from nowhere. One of them smashed Erica's head with a huge club, while the other two

came at me. I shot one, but then my pistol jammed, so I
struck the other with the barrel of it, then the mule bolted."

"And probably just as well for you, Doctor, that it did."
Gumpner nodded soberly. "Give me your sidearm—maybe I
can clear it."

Shortly, the old noncom's bootknife and knowledgeable fingers had extracted a ruptured cartridge case from the
chamber of the big automatic. When he had recharged the
pistol, he placed it back in Braun's belt holster, then saw to
having the injured man and his horse harness transferred to
another mule. After removing most of its heavy armor, the
sergeant mounted the troop horse; then he led his party
southward again, at a fast, distance-eating trot, trying not to
hear the distant crackling of the rifles, the duller booming of
the big pistols, or to reflect upon how dear was the price of
survival of himself and the few accompanying him.

It was pure slaughter, butchery, not warfare, and Corbett
willingly gave credit where credit was due. It was certainly
due the Ganiks, for determination and raw courage in the
face of near-certain death. They just kept coming, wave after
screeching wave of them, even when they had perforce to
crawl over bloody, squirming piles of their own dead and
wounded even before they got to the hideous deathtrap of the
abattis.

And now ammunition was running very low; some of the
riflemen were in fact reduced to throwing rocks, or to casting
back the Ganiks' own rude axes or iron-pointed darts.

Up atop the gap, however, the threatened flank attacks had
failed to materialize, and Corbett now wondered if he might
not have been wrong in his estimate of the Ganik leader's
strategic sense. Those two contingents sent around the gap
might very well have been sent in pursuit of Gumpner, and
against even one of those groups, the sergeant and his small
force would be all but helpless.

Of course, there was nothing he could do about that dire
contingency, not now. But he could content himself to a
degree on the account of this main body. Their casualties had
been staggering—there must be easily five or six score dead
and seriously wounded Ganik bodies within and before that
thick maze of branches, with perhaps another dozen between
it and the breastwork. Even if they had been reinforced again

after the attack began, there were certain to be too few left to mount any sort of organized pursuit of the other party.

In the little valley just north of the defile, Long Willy Kilgore and his sole remaining lieutenant, One-ear Carson, were experiencing increasing difficulty in haranguing those Ganiks still alive and unhurt into further attacks on the stubborn defenders of the gap-mouth.

Not even the addition of the thirty-odd men of Strong Tom's as-yet-unblooded force had seemed to help, and Strong Tom himself had flatly refused to try to lead an assault, not wanting to leave the fine, rare prize his bunch had taken—a young, toothsome Ahrmehnee woman, unconscious from a clubbing and now bound belly-down across the rude saddle of a led pony.

But at last, having correctly pointed out that as only one or two of the fire sticks still were speaking—their magical fires apparently having burned out—Long Willy convinced some fifty men, most of Strong Tom's bunch, and all led by One-ear, to advance against the tiny band of warlocks. It was very bad timing, but Long Willy did not know that until far too late.

When the watcher atop the root ball informed Corbett of the return to the valley of what looked to be the entire eastern contingent of Ganiks, the officer had all three of the men atop the eastern verge climb back down and share out their full cartridge boxes with the men behind the breastwork. And before more than a third of that hundred and fifty rounds had been fired, One-ear Carson's grudging wave were all either dead, wounded or in full flight back to the safety of the vale.

Never a man to flog a dead pony, Long Willy Kilgore made up his mind quickly. "A'right, thet there bunch, they's jest too strowng fer us. We loses us enymore mens, we gone be easy meat fer eny damn Kuhmbuhluhn paddyroll comes alowng. So le's us jest git awn back to camp. We got us thet Ahrmnee gel, and one of them firesticks, them and a whole passel of stuff fer to 'vide up 'mong them as is lef'. Le's git!"

"How 'bout ol' Johnny Skinhead and his bunch, Long Willy?" asked Strong Tom. "Rackon we ought'n send an' let him know we going back?"

Long Willy just shrugged. "He ketches them othuhs, he

ketches 'em; ef he don't, he don't; eithuh way, he'll come back to camp, sometime 'r t'othuh."

Corbett didn't, couldn't, believe it at first. He could not bring himself to believe that the mob of Ganiks, who in one or two more frontal assaults could certainly have overrun his position, had simply ridden back north, out of the small valley, leaving all their dead, most of their wounded and a vast herd of riderless mountain ponies. So he kept his men standing to arms for nearly two more hours, crouched behind their stone bulwark, while wounded Ganiks whimpered and groaned and moaned and shrieked, while a veritable squadron of black buzzards swooped lower and ever lower above the stricken field, and noisy ravens crowded the ledges above the carnage.

At length, he led a half-dozen riflemen through the rough abattis which had served them so well, over the windrows of dead and dying Ganiks, he and his men giving mercy thrusts of their bayonets to those that happened to be in their path, and then down into the valley. They experienced but little difficulty in securing ponies from the herd the Ganiks had left behind, and the officer led them on a cautious patrol, scouting the former attackers' line of withdrawal. Not until he was fully satisfied that there was no subterfuge involved, that the smelly, savage adversaries had truly, astoundingly, simply broken off the engagement and returned whence they had come, did he lead his tired but exuberant patrol back to the valley.

Back at the gap, he took six fresh men and six more ponies, then followed the track of the eastern group of Ganiks, seeking a way to reach the floor of the defile from the mountains on that side, but there was none that a horse or pony could negotiate, although there were many places where agile men might go up or down.

Full dark had fallen before he once more returned to the valley to find Corporal Cash and the remainder of the force encamped a bit upstream of the ford. Inside a ring of rifle pits hacked into the stony soil with the rude weapons of dead Ganiks, the played-out troopers were feasting on chunks of spit-broiled pony steak.

"Did you remember the animals we left up the defile, Cash?" were Corbett's first words, upon dismounting slowly, with a cracking of joints.

"Yes, sir," the young man replied. "I had them led up as far as the breastwork, then had the men bring them armloads of mown grass and enough water to slake them. There's just no way we could get them through those tree branches, sir."

"Very good, Cash," Corbett nodded, "but you'd best detail a guard on them for tonight. Every predator and scavenger from twenty kilometers around is going to be converging on that pile of corpses before sunup."

· While the noncom went about choosing men for the horse and pony guard, Corbett stalked on stiff, aching legs over to the butchered pony carcass and employed his bootknife to hack off as much meat as he thought he could eat, then set about the cooking of the stringy stuff. Once his belly was full of half-burned, half-raw meat, the officer took a final turn about the encampment, then rolled himself in a horseblanket and fell promptly asleep.

Erica wavered in and out of consciousness for nearly a week. When, finally, she again became aware of her surroundings, she found herself in a dim, smoky and incredibly filthy, stinking hutlike cabin of unpeeled logs, chinked with clay and roofed with moldy thatch. Conifer tips stuffed the ill-cured and rotten-smelling hide on which she lay, and another of the rotting hides had been thrown over her naked body.

With the onset of full consciousness, however, came cold, crawling terror. Not only did she not know where she lay or how she had gotten there, but she could recall no event of her life, from birth to the present. She did not even know her own name! She whimpered without conscious thought.

But then she did begin to think. Closing her eyes, she earnestly sought memories, any memories. She could dimly see a figure mounted on a horse. No, a mule, it was, and the one so mounted was a man. She knew that she knew him, knew him of old, knew him well and should know his name, but she did not.

She recalled struggling with him for something held in one of his hands, then he hurt her. Seemingly of their own volition, her fingers sought out her right breast under the covering of stinking hide, finding it still sore to the touch. And, after that, there was no memory, nothing.

"But my name, I must have one." Unknowingly, she spoke aloud.

Immediately, there was a rustling in the far corner of the room. Shortly, a skinny, misshapen female shuffled across the floor of packed earth to squat before the woman on the hide mattress. The newcomer stank far worse than the rotted hides. Parting her lips to disclose gapped rows of discolored teeth, she began to speak.

"Looks like you'll live. Heh heh. I 'uz b'ginnin' to hope you'd die, 'r Long Willy'd git impatshunt and slice your gullet. Heh heh. Been right long sincet thishere bunch et a woman, and I be right fond o' some cuts o' female, I be. Heh heh." The harridan poked a stubby, stained finger into the swell of the bosom under the hair-shedding hide coverlet.

Then the stringy-haired creature arose, saying, "Bes' I gits Long Willy. Heh heh. Don'tchew go 'way, Ahrmnee gel, heah?"

The man who came back in with the stunted female was tall; his shaggy head brushed the thatch. Without a spoken word, he bent and stripped back the covering hide from the nameless woman. He kicked off a pair of shapeless rawhide brogans, propped the sheathed longsword he had carried in the near corner, then shucked his dirt-shiny shirt to bare muscular arms and body as hairy as an ape's except where old scars and several pus-oozing sores peeked through.

As he unbuckled a scuffed belt which supported one large and three smaller knives, he spoke his first words. "You feed 'er yet, Lizzie?" When the flat-chested creature indicated the negative, he went on, "Wal, soon's I'm done fuckin' 'er, you stir your scrawny stumps and git 'er a bowla stew."

After he had pulled two broad, stubby knives from their sheaths under the hides cross-gartered to his lower legs, he untied the length of rope holding up his pair of once-fine trousers and threw himself upon the naked, defenseless body of the captive woman.

A bony knee forced her thighs apart. His entry was immediate and violent, a series of short, powerful thrusts which drove his engorged organ relentlessly inward, deep into her dry, unresponsive vagina. She screamed in pain, tried desperately to push his bulk off her, but she was still too weak. He was ready for the fingernails she drove at his eyes, laughingly pinioning her two hands with but one of his own, while the other went about mauling her breasts.

He never tried to kiss her, rather held his head high up

from her, his eyes tightly closed throughout his protracted use of her body, ignoring her screams, her gasps, her moans and, finally, her pitiful sobs.

When, after eternities of endless time, he was done with her, had dressed and left, the nasty, cackling Lizzie returned. In one hand she bore a wooden bowl, and in the other a horn spoon. Despite the shock and pain of the abuse she had just been forced to endure, the nameless woman found the smell of the steaming fish broth mouthwatering, irresistible, after who knew how long without food. And no sooner had she swallowed the last drops in the bowl than she sank back on the rough mattress, oblivious to all that went on around her.

And much went on in the camp of Long Willy's bunch that night. As the captive's ravished body sank into sleep in the rude cabin, he who had so cruelly raped her sat in an old and scarred and oft-repaired seat that once had been a large and intricately carven chair; his longsword lay across his lap, and one of his hands held the shiny firestick that had been slung diagonally across the woman's back when she had been found by Kevin and Joe-Bob.

Long Willy was ambitious. He was determined to learn how to make one of the metal-and-wood devices spurt out the noise and the killing fire. Armed with so witchy a weapon, he knew that he could gather a much larger bunch, a bunch so large that the fearsome Buhbuh, even, would hesitate to try to force deference or a percentage of hard-won loot. Perhaps with a firestick he might even be able to slay the huge Kleesahk and thus take over ultimate command of all the bunches.

But previous experiments with captured firesticks had ranged from fruitless to disastrous. The first one, captured on the dawn when they had tried to attack the camp of the strangers, had seemed to be out of fire (actually, the trooper had emptied the weapon at the oncoming Ganiks before he had been slain), so torches had been applied to it at every single conceivable place, resulting in nothing but scorched wood and metal so hot that it burned Long Willy's hands.

The second had been taken from the garroted corpse of a trooper lassoed and lifted off his horse (although Long Willy, of course, had no way of knowing it, that had been a sniper rifle, the scope not in place, but still loaded with a single long-distance load). Long Willy's principal lieutenant, now deceased, had been covertly observing the strangers for some time and managed to convince his leader that he knew the way in which new fire was added to the sticks. So, holding the small end firmly against his flat belly, just over the navel, he had grasped it by the big, wooden end and held a blazing torch directly under the part that was of both wood and metal, intermixed.

So muffled had been the noise that those at any distance had been unaware of any untoward occurrence. Long Willy and his bunch had thrown the treacherous firestick away and then consumed most of their former comrade.

But Long Willy had learned from both episodes, being a trifle more intelligent than most of the degenerate folk he led. Thanks to his lieutenant's unintended sacrifice, Long Willy figured that he now knew just where to feed the fresh fire into the stick and knew, also, that the small, hollow end must be held away from the body, unless he who held it was desirous of becoming the main course at the bunch's next barbecue.

The next firestick captured (this one had contained one round chambered and three more in the magazine) he had placed with the big, wood end against his abdomen and, amid a circle of his followers, he had applied and held the flare of a torch to the central area, then waited for something to happen.

Something did happen. The chambered round cooked off, slamming the bronze-shod butt into Long Willy's belly with the force of a mule's kick, and the round thus fired blew off the head of the man so unfortunate as to be in line with the muzzle. Moreover, the recoil-activated mechanism chambered a second round, which the overheated metal of barrel and action fired off so close on the heels of the first that the two explosions of sound seemed but one, and this happened twice more, only ceasing when the magazine of the piece was empty.

In the close-packed throng of observers, all the bullets killed; one, which due to malfunction failed to explode, even killed two men, drilling through one, then the other, and speeding on to crease the rump of a pony. Even when Long Willy could at long last breathe almost normally, so fierce was the agony in his punished belly that he feared that he too would shortly die, to go onto the spits and into the stewpots.

The following day he gave an order that the next man bearing a firestick was to be captured alive if in any way possible. He had come to realize that he needed instruction from an expert in such esoteric devices.

But the expected man had turned out to be a woman, and now he was facing down the entire bunch and sat ready to violate bunch-law and bunch-tradition in order to gain his private ends.

Strong Tom stood before Long Willy, his face flushed with his anger, stamping his feet and shaking his knotty fists to add emphasis to his heated words.

"It be wrowng and you knows it, too! I tooked 'er and letchew fuck 'er fust, din't I? Thet's bunch-law. Now, me 'n t'othuh bullies gits to fuck 'er, t'night. You *gots* to brang 'er outchere, damn you!"

"You done tawkin', Strong Tom?" Long Willy demanded coldly, and when only a glare answered him, continued, "Then you lissun tight, 'cause I ain' gonna say it but the oncet.

"Onlies' way thishere bunch is evuh gonna git eny powuh is thishere firestick." He raised and shook the rifle. "And we-awl done learnt—leas'-ways, *I* done learnt—the onlies' way eny part of the bunch is gonna learn how you puts the fire back in thishere stick, is one the folks whut done used 'em fer to show us, or show me, enyhow.

"Now all them mens, they got away fum us, but we got us thishere woman, the Ahrmnee, and sincet she 'uz a-carryin' a firestick, seems likely she'd know how fer to put the fire back in it. Now, don't it, Strong Tom?"

Aware deep-down that the smarter Long Willy was deviously arguing him down, and not for the first time, the powerful but slow-witted lieutenant half-whined, "But, by Plooshuhn's hairy balls, Long Willy, we don' aim fer to kill the Ahrmnee cunt, jes' fuck 'er a few times. Dammit, *you* did!"

Long Willy, however, just nodded, "I did fuck 'er, Strong Tom, and that's how I knows how weak she be. Whoever clubbed the bitch dang near busted opened her haid . . . and if I thought fer one minute it 'uz thet dim-witted Kevin and Joe-Bob almos' kilt a young, purty Ahrmnee woman, whut had her a firestick, I'd be a-chawin' their livers for breakfas'.

"But, thet-all aside, she 'uz too damn weak to even fight

me eny, Strong Tom, and you done seed your own sef the way them Ahrmnee gels is fer the firs' few weeks we has 'em. So, weak as she be and all, I'm afeared you and eight 'r nine othuhs gits to polin' 'er all night, way you does, all she gonna be good fer come mornin's stewmeat. *Then,* who gonna tell us, show us how you puts the fire back in thishere?" He waved the firestick once more.

Seeing Strong Tom take a deep breath preparatory to more words, Long Willy forestalled him. "Strong Tom, I ain' sayin' you and the othuh bullies cain' *nevuh* fuck 'er, I'm jes' sayin' don' fuck 'er *now,* not till she's done got bettuh and, maybe, done showed me how fer to put the fire back in the firesticks. Cain' you git thet th'ough your thick haid?"

It was a *faux pas* of the first order to a man trying to avert violence in the camp, and Long Willy would never have been guilty of it had he not been tired, concerned for the safety of the captive and the precious secrets her mind held, and more peeved than usual at the stubborn Strong Tom. The subleader was a mountain of rolling muscles and a proven killer, but only his physical strength had elevated him to and retained him in the ranks of Long Willy's bullies. He knew that his wits were not as quick as most men's . . . and he had been known to kill or maim bunch members who made even the most lighthearted or innocuous reference to that lamentable fact.

The big man's flush became lividity. Snarling, he hurled his bulk at his seated tormentor. But when he crashed into the chair, Long Willy was no longer in it. Before Strong Tom could even think of arising from the splintered wreck on which he lay, his leader had twice clubbed his pate with the rifle butt, swinging the weapon by the barrel, like a mace.

And that ended the evening's council and discourse; the other bullies and the common Ganiks wandered off to their various cabins, huts or shelters, leaving the recumbent Strong Tom where he lay. If dawn showed him to be dead, they would all have fresh meat for breakfast.

With the rising of the sun, Corbett and his men, all laden with filled waterskins, bypassed the stinking mess left by a night-long feast of scavengers at the mouth of the gap. They rode ponies up the eastern hill to a low point in the wall of the gap, then climbed down to the floor of the defile after lowering gear and water with ropes.

The horse-guarding detail was glad to see them, to flop down and get a little sleep after a long, noisy night. Their shouts and other noises they made had driven most of the wild beasts back to the mounds of corpses. The only animals that they had been forced to expend bullets on were a skinny bear and a huge mountain boar, which later gave all of the men a satisfying breakfast of grilled pork.

But there could be no thought of camping at the site of the battle. For one thing, the stench of so much putrefying man-flesh was already unbearable, despite the chill of the preceding night, and was increasing geometrically as the rising sun warmed the area. Also, Corbett was almost frantic that the smaller party, up ahead, would be caught and killed—or, even worse, captured alive—by the thirty or forty mounted Ganiks now surely in pursuit of them.

When all the men were stuffed with greasy pork—the fat most welcome after many days of game and pony—Corbett had each man empty out his cartridge pouches to find that among twenty-two riflemen there were only two hundred and forty-six rounds. Grimly, he allowed two five-round clips to each man, including himself, with a third clip to each of the four best sharpshooters. The pistols were at least a little better supplied. Only he, Cash and six others of this party bore them, and the ammo supply for them was large enough to give each of them enough to fill four seven-round magazines, after which he and Corporal Cash each took six of the remaining rounds.

All men who had, during the previous day's battle, proved adept at casting darts he ordered to garner a supply of the missiles from the large stock available. Although crudely tipped and most primitive in appearance, the stubby javelins could be deadly at close range, cast by knowing hands, as mutely attested by his two battle casualties, both slain by Ganik darts.

With the mounts watered and saddled, Corbett and his force set off in the wake of Gumpner and his party, the officer setting as fast a pace as he dared, having but the two remounts available to him. He might, of course, have had his men run as many ponies as he wished or they could have herded them over the shorter, rougher hill route to join the column at the southern end of the defile, but his experiences with the shaggy mounts abandoned by his Ganik foes had persuaded him not to do so.

Although courageous and game enough, few of the weedy little beasts were in anything approaching good condition, the Ganiks apparently treating them as callously as they did their own kind. Nor did there seem to ever have been Ganik attempts to breed up the usual run of wild mountain ponies, such as had been done by the Broomtowners, the Ahrmehnee tribes and many another mountain race of folk, over the years.

But then, the appalling conditions of the ponies had also brought a measure of ease to Corbett's mind. The party of Ganiks that had ridden off to the west, apparently to track Gumpner's group, had had, he now recalled, only one mount per man, which would mean that if they tried to move too fast for very long, most of them would soon be afoot.

Unless . . . and that worrisome bit of unease continued to nibble at his mind, breeding fresh worry. Unless there were camps or villages of Ganiks ahead where the pursuers might expect to find fresh ponies and, God forbid, reinforcements. He just did not know all that much about these Ganiks. The captured Ganik, Jim-Beau, had been native to territory farther north and west of the place he had been taken prisoner, he had not seemed overly bright, and his knowledge of the overall numbers of the Ganik race and the size of the area they occupied had been hazy to nebulous. So, for all Corbett or any of his command knew, they could be riding into the very heartland of the savage cannibals.

Sergeant Gumpner might have relieved his officer's mind, somewhat. Although the track he and his group had been on since they had left the defile was fairly well defined, they had not seen any signs of a Ganik or any other human being.

Two of his best ponies had turned up lame, however, and following a brief consultation with Dr. Braun, the grim-faced noncom had kneed his mount over to Jim-Beau and ended the prisoner's life with his trusty battle axe. This sacrifice effectively replaced the two lost ponies.

That had taken place about the time that Corbett and his force had been stuffing themselves with broiled boar meat, the sergeant having kept his party moving throughout all of the preceding day, then all of the bright, moon-drenched night.

But Dr. Braun and some others of the wounded were suffering from the long, hard march, and that suffering was clearly weakening them; so Gumpner and the two men he had sent out ahead, on point, were on constant lookout for a safe campsite. The party would have to halt, he knew, and soon.

At length, one of the point riders came back to guide them into a tightly twisting defile, barely wide enough along most of its length for even a single rider and steeply rising, with a couple or three inches of clear, running water filling it from wall to wall. At the top of the incline, Gumpner found himself on a tiny, grassy plateau. A spring-fed pool at its center was the genesis of the stream that flowed down through the steep gap.

With the eye of military experience, Gumpner surveyed the location. If there were no more ways to get up to it, save the way he had come, he and his group should certainly be safe there for the couple of days it would take the mounts to exhaust the available forage. As high as the place was, fires would probably not be easily visible by night, especially on bright nights like that just past. And, if it came to that, two or three men would be able to hold that difficult defile against any conceivable number of the primitive Ganiks.

Nonetheless, cautious in every detail, as Major Corbett had taught him to be, Gumpner shepherded the column into the defile, through the thicket of stunted holly trees which hid the opening, then he, Sergeant Cabell and two other men carefully erased all visible sign of their passage, trying to give the appearance that the group had continued south, down the track.

That was precisely what the thirty-seven Ganiks, led by Bully Johnny Skinhead, Long Willy's eldest lieutenant, assumed when, some three hours later, they passed the clump of holly and splashed through the stream that cut across the track. Due to the fact that they had utilized shorter, though more difficult, cross-country routes rather than the main track, they would have come up to Gumpner's party a good hour before he had lucked onto his little hideaway had they not come across the body of Jim-Beau and stopped then and there for a meal.

Old Johnny was discouraged. That they had not caught their human quarry by this juncture meant, to his mind, that they likely would not ever catch them; for although his horse—lifted from a Kuhmbuhluhner steading, like most similar horses—seemed to be holding up well, few of the ponies were; some of the small equines were, indeed, tottering along, and there was no easy way to replace them. Not even the couple of hours of rest, while their riders had butchered and cooked and eaten the fresh-killed body of a strange Ganik, had done much toward restoring the fast-ebbing vitality of the ponies.

Getting fresh ponies up north was seldom a problem. Not only were there many Ganik farm families from whom ponies could be obtained by trade or force, but there were usually strays from the various Ganik bunches roaming the hills and valleys in ones or twos or small herds.

But as far as Johnny Skinhead knew, there were no Ganik farmers this far south, and, of bunches, Long Willy's was the most southerly of all. Nor had he seen any traces of equines since they had left, other than along this track.

Bully Johnny did not ride on much farther, for at the same time the trail petered out, no less than three of the drooping ponies saw fit to collapse, their prominent rib cages working like bellows, jerkings and kickings and cursing availing nothing toward getting them back onto their hooves.

"Piss awn it!" announced Johnny Skinhead. "Them strangers mos' prob'ly cut ovuh the ridges fer to hit the main track; I would, wuz I them—it ain' nowheres near's rough nor thisun be. And thesehere ponies wouldn' mek a hunnert yards up thet firs' ridge, by Plooshuhn. They may not evun mek it back up to wher we kin figger awn gittin' sumore."

"Long Willy, he ain' gon like us jes' comin' back, th'out ketchin' us summa them stranguhs," muttered one.

"You jes' let me do any worryin' 'bout mah boy Long Willy, Eskuh," snapped old Johnny peevishly. "Him an' me, we got us more brains in owuh peckers, nor you'll evuh hev in your haid!"

Bully Johnny Skinhead's very close relationship to the leader of the bunch would have been considered both most singular and shameful in the extreme among races of normal folk, although it was less than an unusual one among the Ganiks. He was Long Willy's father, but as he had gotten this

son—as well as at least two other children—on Crosseyed
Kate, his *own* mother, old Johnny was also Long Willy's half
brother.

Some years back, old Johnny, one of his more natural
brothers and Long Willy had returned from a raiding sojourn
with Buhbuh the Kleesahk's huge bunch to find that during
their absence, some other bunch had visited their family
steading, killed and eaten or taken away all of their kin and
driven off the livestock, then partially burned the buildings.

If not for that latter fact, the three men might have continued to live there between raids, eventually stealing a few
women to get brats on and to do the heavy work of farming,
but with matters as they had been, the three had simply
turned their ponies' heads about and taken up full-time residence with the bunches, finally being included in a few hundred sent by Buhbuh to form a southern bunch.

Then, five years ago, when Long Willy had attained to his
full growth, he had challenged, fought and killed the biggest
of the then-leader's bullies—which was one way of becoming
a bully himself. A few weeks later, he had called out and
slain the leader, Horsecock Coates, then the one other bully
unwise enough to indicate his antipathy toward this new leadership.

Few of the original leader's pack of bullies were still
around, after five years. Old Johnny had killed one in order
to take his place, and his other brother—he who had held the
muzzle of the captured loaded rifle to his belly while holding
a torch to its breech and chamber—had emulated Johnny's
murderous actions. One-ear Carson had died at the defile,
and now the only bully not of Long Willy's choosing was
Strong Tom Amory.

Back in the Ganik camp, Strong Tom lay as one dead for
hours after Long Willy had clubbed him senseless. At length,
the massive man commenced to whimper, then to moan, and,
with immense effort, finally got back onto his feet. He stood,
swaying, however, and pitched back down on his face at the
first step he essayed. At the end, sobbing noisily like a
whipped child, the bully crawled on hands and knees across
the camp to his hut.

Far to the south and east of that camp, old Johnny Skinhead and his men left the dying ponies where they lay, after

stripping off their gear, and led the party back up the track to that place he recalled where a shallow streamlet crossed it. He had decided that they would camp there for the night and rest the ponies before setting out for camp on the morrow.

But even before they traveled that relatively short distance, more ponies became unable to bear their riders, so that when they arrived at the projected campsite, some dozen of his Ganiks were trotting along afoot, while a handful of nearly foundered ponies trailed along far behind.

Corbett had pushed his command hard along the clear track, allowing only short rest periods for man or beast. They found the place where Jim-Beau's body had been butchered and eaten, but between the thirty-seven cannibals and the no less voracious wildlife, not enough remained to give them even a clue as to the being's identity, other than that it had been human.

Slightly relieved that the feast site indicated no trace of having been also a battleground, Corbett and his force pressed relentlessly on southward, down the hoof-scarred track. The larger, deeper impressions of the bigger, steel-shod mounts of Gumpner's group were everywhere overlaid by the smaller, shallower, but far more numerous ones of the Ganiks' unshod little ponies. And, ominously, the former seemed barely older than the latter.

Old Johnny Skinhead did not need to be told that a good number of equines were coming rapidly down the track from the north. He had felt the distant vibrations in the ground whereon he and the others lay, so he did not bother to even sit up when called to, saying only, "Cain' be nobody but thet slowass Strowng Tom, him and the fellers as come 'roun' t'othuh side. Somebody wake me up whinevuh they gits here. Heahnh?" Then he settled back down to sleep.

Dead certain that the only strangers were by now well east of his temporary encampment, the bully had posted no men to stay awake and watch the position—squarely athwart the track, on either side of the stream—nor had he set up a picket line, only hobbling the ponies and his horse that they might not stray, grazing, too far away.

Corbett's point riders did not return to the main column, they just waited in the middle of the track until the others came up to them. At their word, Corbett halted his command and, afoot, went up to view what they had discovered. On the day before, he had begun to nurture a grudging respect for the Ganiks, but most of it evaporated when he saw the careless disposition of the party of snoring cannibals.

Back with his force, he held a low-voiced conference with Corporal Cash and some of the others, accurately describing what he had seen up ahead.

"The whole damned passel of them are asleep, scattered up and down the track itself for some yards, and not a guard to be seen, anywhere. The ponies are hobbled, but they're even more scattered, grazing and browsing, and they all seem to have been unsaddled, too.

"Now we couldn't have gotten as close as we are to them without them being aware of it, especially since they were lying on the ground. So I suspect that they think we're the other horsemen, the ones that rode off to the east of that defile, then came back into that valley, back there.

"I counted about three dozen of the buggers, so order the men to save their rifles and ammo—after all, we have no way of knowing what dangers lie ahead of us, still. We'll keep up a fast trot until we come in sight of them, then charge. Sabers, axes and darts should be all we need on this bunch, unprepared as they are, and dismounted, to boot. Questions? All right then, let's get about it, men."

Chapter V

When the assigned troopers got Dr. Braun out of his saddle and laid out on a pallet of saddleblankets and sheepskins, one of them fetched over Gumpner, who set about examining the scientist as gently as possible.

He was truly gentle; nonetheless, Braun was screaming full-throatedly and gasping between screams, with tears bathing his face, before the examination was done.

Finally, the old noncom hunkered back, frowning, thinking, while the patient shuddered and sobbed. It was bad enough. The protracted cross-country trek in the saddle had not done the doctor a bit of good, and the more recent two full days and one night, almost without pause, had put the tin hat on it.

The entire leg—from crotch to toes—was immensely swollen and discolored. In several places, it was oozing clear or pink-tinged serum through the dirty, crusty bandages, while all of the toes and part of the foot looked to Gumpner to be in the earliest stage of black rot—gangrene. Harry Braun clearly needed the surgeon the party no longer had. A bright, multi-talented man, Gumpner could bandage wounds and set and splint broken bones, remove smashed teeth and their stumps, cut out missile points and stop the bleeding of wounds with fair consistency. He had done these various things many times, over the years, but he knew that he simply was not qualified to set about the procedures here required, and he deeply regretted the loss of Dr. Arenstein.

He had closely observed physicians in Broomtown, Major Corbett and, more recently, Dr. Arenstein administer the different types of injections—subcutaneous, intramuscular and intravenous—and he therefore felt certain that he could successfully administer drugs or antibiotics, but he could not differentiate among the host of small bottles and glass ampoules which were labeled only with combinations of letters and numbers, nor was he in any way certain just what amounts should be injected or how frequently.

As soon as he had quieted somewhat, the noncom matter-of-factly explained the situation and his own impotence in alleviating it to the scientist, withholding only his diagnosis of the lividity and lack of warmth in Braun's toes and foot.

"And so," he finished, "I'll be happy to give you something for your pain, Doctor, if you can show me which of the bottles to draw it from and how much to draw. But I'm afraid to try to open your leg and drain it, as it should be drained, I know. The condition it is now in, in fact, I'm even afraid to try to change those bandages."

The grizzled noncom's sincerity and concern were patent, and Braun was just then in too much agony to affect the open arrogance with which he usually masked his multitudinous fears of the world and most things and people in it. Weakly, he pointed out to Gumpner the bottles Erica had used before she had ceased dosing him against pain, then he indicated the dosage line on the barrel of the hypodermic syringe. He only whimpered once when the needle entered his flesh and, shortly, sank gratefully into the warm, feather-soft embrace of the drug.

Gumpner had placed a man among the rocks over the hidden entry to the narrow defile, another partway up the mountain, and a third up beyond the second; therefore, he had been aware that his pursuers had passed, headed south along the track, and then returned, and he knew that they were camping almost on the doorstep of his hideaway.

Consequently, he had slept but lightly, despite his own exhaustion, and was out of his blankets and pulling on his boots before the sentry who had dropped from the rock wall had trotted up to him.

"Sarge," panted the trooper, "Gibson flashed up a message that said that at least a score of men, not Ganiks, have come down the track from the north and attacked the cannibals that were camped at the stream. He couldn't be sure, of course, but he said that most of them looked like they had rifles on their backs, and they were all armed with sabers or axes."

Gumpner stamped the rest of the way into his boots,

checked his pistol and rifle, slung the latter, then picked up his axe. Then he turned to the other sergeant.

"Cabell, you're in charge here until I get back. Have a pony saddled for me, quickly, I don't want to risk the horse down that streambed in the dark. And one for Allison here, too; he's coming with me."

Corbett and his men came down the gradual curve of the track on a three-rider front that spanned the trace from one brushy shoulder to the other, sabers and axes—and, in Jay Corbett's case, a nicely balanced steel mace out but at the low-guard position, lest a glimmer of moonlight reveal that these riders were approaching the sleeping Ganiks on the attack.

At the place where the curve ended, where the track straightened out and widened, more than doubling in width, the officer waved the mace over his head. With practiced ease, the veteran troopers went from a three- to a seven-man front, roared a deep-voiced cheer and charged down the track upon the unprepared foemen.

A tall, large-framed man suddenly stood up directly in the officer's path. His bushy beard was either white or very pale blond—Corbett could not tell in the moonlight—but his bare head was completely bald and he was frantically tugging to get a sword free from an ill-fitting sheath or scabbard.

Although he could as easily have crushed that bare-skinned head with the heavy mace, Corbett slightly altered his aim and brought down the Middle Kingdoms weapon with all his might and all its not inconsiderable weight on the bald man's right shoulder. He rode on as the Ganik shrieked and began to crumple.

His reasoning had been simple and instantaneous. If the Ganik had a sword, he must be one of the leaders, and a leader of any group or race could be expected to have a better and more complete knowledge of events and peoples and territories than most of the followers, and Corbett still stood in dire and pressing need of reliable intelligence concerning the country that lay between this area and Broomtown base.

The action was bloody, savage and very shortly concluded. Corbett's force's casualties were negligible—one pony had been hamstrung and one trooper had taken a dart through his bridle arm, just below the elbow. Three or four Ganiks had gotten away, afoot certainly, and possibly wounded as well. With the exceptions of the bald Ganik and one another, the remainder of the cannibals lay dead on the track and along the stream, most of them never having gotten farther up than their knees before flashing saber blade or axehead hacked the life from their bodies and tumbled those bodies in the dust.

Corbett had fallen in love with the mace and resolved to carry it or one like it by preference in future. Unlike axe, saber or sword, there was no microsecond of dire danger while freeing a cutting edge from a body, and where stabbing was necessary, the short, broad finial spike provided ample utility for the purpose.

The officer dismounted a third of his force and himself joined them, leaving another third mounted as horse holders and the other third as security. The bald Ganik was on his knees in the middle of the track, rocking to and fro, barely conscious, his right arm hanging limp and useless from his crushed shoulder. With slashes of his field knife, Corbett cut away the man's baldric with its old, Ahrmehnee-style sword, and the waist belt containing a profusion of sheathed knives of varying lengths and shapes. After jerking out another knife peeking from the top of the Ganik's rawhide boot, the officer went to join his dismounted men in finishing off the rest of the Ganiks.

Corbett had just dispatched an already-dying Ganik near the stream and was swishing the gory point of his saber blade in the swift-flowing water when he sensed more than heard movements in the holly thicket to his left. Before he could turn, a stocky shape mounted on a pony emerged and from it came the *zweeep* of steel leaving scabbard, quickly followed by the flash of the moonlight along the length of a bared blade.

Corbett tossed the saber into his left hand, drew and cocked his big pistol, whirling to face this new attack.

It was well into the second week before Long Willy began to harbor any worries about the missing party and their leader, his father-brother, Johnny Skinhead. Even then, the worries were more for the thirty-seven Ganiks who had ridden out with the elderly bully than for the man himself, for the losses in the attacks against the strangers had been little short of catastrophic; Long Willy had left a good half of his men dead before that cursed gap.

All of the bullies, saving only old Johnny and Strong Tom, had been among those mangled corpses, but that had been no lasting problem; Long Willy had simply chosen the requisite number of bigger, stronger, meaner Ganiks from the remaining ranks of his depleted bunch and publicly announced that they were now his bullies and would remain so as long as they continued to please him and support him. Everyone knew, of course, that any man who felt himself capable of openly fighting and killing one of these bullies could expect to take his victim's place; that was one of the few laws of the Ganik bunches.

But although Long Willy was all-powerful in his own bunch, commanding the life or death of every man and woman in his camp, he, too, had and grudgingly recognized a suzerain, the Kleesahk, Buhbuh, whose bully he was by right of combat. And Long Willy knew well that Buhbuh's expected reaction to his loss of so many fighters for so negligible an amount of gain could be—and, he feared, would be—dangerous and deadly to him, personally.

Nor could Long Willy really blame the huge humanoid for his anticipated rage, for by halving his smaller bunch, he had also weakened by just that many fighters the larger bunch of which they all were a part. The attack on the strangers had seemed like a sure victory—considering how few their numbers had been—with promise of much loot, at least a dozen big horses or mules, and the thrill of prisoners to torture slowly to death, then eat.

However, despite the care he had lavished on the planning of everything, he had met with unmitigated disaster in all save the taking of the Ahrmehnee woman and her firestick. The pursuit party under Strong Tom had turned back because of that capture, and now Long Willy was sorry that he had not sent a rider to call back Johnny Skinhead, as well.

For there had never been anything approaching friendship between Long Willy and Buhbuh, for all that the Kleesahk had not disliked him enough to force him into a stand-up fight and kill him—as he well knew that Buhbuh could anytime he wished, for the partly human creature stood half again Long Willy's not inconsiderable height and was massive in proportion—he also knew that there were certainly Ganiks in this camp whose job it was to watch him for Buhbuh and report to that overall-bully any serious transgressions against the good of the bunches.

That Buhbuh had not already moved against him Long Willy ascribed to the fact that he had forbidden anyone to ride out of camp for any reason until the return of Johnny Skinhead's party, and had put his new bullies to the bloody enforcement of that edict. He wanted to face Buhbuh the Kleesahk in his own good time, and that time would not be until he knew himself capable of surviving the certain combat with the huge creature, which meant not until he had been instructed by the Ahrmehnee woman in all the niceties of the use and recharging of his captured firestick. Long Willy knew well that only that marvelous, deadly, esoteric weapon of the oldest Ganik myths and legends could give him the needed fatal edge over the monstrous, otherwise undefeatable Buhbuh.

But the captured woman remained weak, seldom able to even stand or walk without assistance, and neither he nor Lizzie nor anyone else seemed to be able to talk with her. She did not speak Ahrmehnee, rather did she babble on in some rapid, abrupt language that often sounded a little like Ganik but was not.

She was still lodged in Long Willy's cabin and was still tended and looked after by Lizzie Flat-chest, fed the best fare that the camp had to offer. Willy had, after having proved his strength and right to lead upon the bully's head, finally allowed Strong Tom to possess the woman, as was his indisputable right. He also had given each of his new bullies a brief session on the woman, but he had closely supervised all of these sessions and made certain that she was not bitten or otherwise injured and that she had several hours to rest between sessions.

But once these perfunctory and begrudged bows to bunch-law were done and over, Long Willy declared the interior of his cabin off limits to any uninvited man and placed a pair of his new bullies—a special pair, a pair who seemed much more interested in each other than in the Ahrmehnee woman—before the single door whenever he had to be away for any length of time.

In any case, Long Willy was not granted much time to worry about Johnny Skinhead and his group, for about noon one day, One-ball Sierrason came into camp on a barebacked pony, with his tale of the debacle on the moonlit track.

Long since intolerant of the constant jokes about his single testicle—it was all he ever had had and he knew of no way to grow another—One-ball had taken to the brush alongside the track to squat and had happened to be there when the host of strangers had ridden in to slaughter his erstwhile mates. He had managed to make it into the wooded eastern hills unseen. There he had found this pony, removed its hobble and, as his only armaments were his assortment of knives, had not gone anywhere near the track, but rather had ridden straight for camp.

"Whin we-awls fust laid down, you could hear them ponies awn the track, Long Willy, but whin sumbody he tole ole Johnny Skinhaid, old Johnny 'llowed he heared 'em, too. Thin he said won't nobody but Strowng Tom and his mens and not to wake him up no more till theyed done got there."

Long Willy sighed and shook his shaggy head sadly. "Wal, I must of got my brains awf my maw, 'cawse pore ole Johnny nevuh wuz too lowng in thet d'reckshun. Did you say whin you fust come in you'd seed ole Johnny go down, One-ball?"

The survivor nodded once and then spoke around the mouthful of catfish he was masticating gingerly, favoring his loose, rotting teeth. "He'd stood up and wuz a-pullin' out his sword. And I knows it wuz him, 'cawse I seed the light 'gainst his shiny haid. Enyhow, thishere stranger awn whut lookted like a Kuhmbuhluhn hoss rid up aside of him and basted him with one them iron clubs the Kuhmbuhluhn mens fights with lots of times. I din't see no more, aftuh thet, Long Willy, I skeedaddled. But Stinky Parsons, he laid low lownguh, he did, and he tole me ole Johnny, he wan't kilt outright; he said the feller whut had bashted him down come back aftuh everbody elst was done fer and sliceted ole Johnny up with a knife."

Long Willy looked around, then demanded, "Where be Stinky, now? He din't ride in with you."

With great effort, Sierrason swallowed the half-chewed chunks of fish, and replied, "Naw, Long Willy, soon's we two rode by where the firesticks kilt so many fellers, Stinky 'llowed as how he 'uz gonna cut wes' and head fer Buhbuh's camp. He wawnted me to come along of him, but it's two, three days longer a ride, and I 'uz *so* hongry. My pore teeths the way they is, I cain' eat roots and stuff no more, or nuthin' whut ain' been cookted."

While One-ball again filled his mouth with catfish, Long Willy sat in silence, thinking hard. So, that Plooshuhn-damned bug-tit bastard of a Stinky Parsons had been one of Buhbuh's spies all these years, and now was on his way to re-port the costly failure of Long Willy's folly to the Kleesahk. Which meant that there now remained only four, possibly five, days for him to learn the secrets surrounding the uses of the firestick. And he *must* learn, for strong and quick and deadly as he could be with sword or club or longknife, he freely admitted that the Kleesahk was more than he could take on and expect to live.

Although he had allowed the other men only one rape apiece, Long Willy himself had been making use of his prisoner whenever the mood struck him, day or night. So when he strode into the small, cramped cabin and jerked off the rotting deerskin covering her naked body, the dark-haired young woman cringed, whimpering, then sobbed and began to cry when she saw that another man was behind him. Nor did the demented, sadistic cackling of Lizzie Flat-chest, crouched in her corner niche on the other side of the cabin, in any way comfort the memoryless woman.

But when the tall rapist had taken from him the armload of burdens he had been bearing, the other man went back to stand just inside the open door. Trembling all over like a foundered horse, the nameless woman waited for this too-familiar man to remove his clothing and once more subject her to the horrors of his lust.

But he did not. Instead, he tugged her by one arm up into a sitting posture, jammed the butt of a smoky, sputtering torch into a ready-made hole in the dirt floor, then squatted before her, talking earnestly . . . and almost comprehensibly.

At length, he unwrapped from a cocoon of cloth and hide a vaguely familiar device. She knew that she should know just what the long, oddly shaped, shiny thing was called, knew that at sometime she had used this thing or something like it, but like all other memories, this one too eluded her grasping mind.

After talking on and on for some time, often pointing a

long, dirty finger at different parts of the object and at the torch, her frequent ravisher offered the nearly remembered object to her, signed that she was to take it into her hands. At last, as the shaggy man became more insistent, she took the long, heavy device into her hands and turned it over and over, studying the differing shades and textures of metals and wood, pummeling her unresponsive brain to try to dredge up some dim memory that might explain to her its function or utility.

The dirty, cracked-nailed finger of the man jabbed at a certain area of the object, and his speech became vehement. So she concentrated her tactile examination on that area, eventually crooking a finger about a rounded projection of metal and experimentally pulling . . . and the projection slid smoothly back, drawing with it the larger bit of metal of which it seemed a part. But then the rounded projection slipped from her hold and it and the larger piece all slammed back into the original position with a loud clanking noise.

At this, the man grabbed the thing back from her and spat out an excited-sounding stream of almost-meaningful words. He talked on and on and on, becoming more and more agitated of demeanor and, finally, almost shouting at her. Then, all at once, he jumped up, screaming something at the bewildered-looking captive. One big foot, shod in heavy hide, lashed out and sped toward her. The toe struck her between her breasts and slammed her back against the wall of unpeeled logs, and all the world exploded for her in a flash of white-hot pain succeeded almost immediately by black oblivion.

Long Willy excitedly handled the now fully charged rifle, for he was certain that he had seen a flash of yellow fire—actually, he had seen the momentary reflection of the torchlight on the brass cartridge case as the bolt fed it into the chamber—deep within the bowels of the firestick. Placing the larger, flat end against his belly, he thrust a forefinger through the metal ring below the place where he had seen the spark of fire and jerked it toward him, as he had seen some of the strangers do.

But no fire and noise resulted; pulling on the triggerguard does not fire a rifle. There was only a faint click as the pressure of his finger released the cross-bolt safety.

Snarling his rage and frustration, the Ganik leader took the piece by both hands gripped around the barrel and swung it with all his strength against the doorjamb.

And that was the end of the road for ambitious Long Willy Kilgore. The heavy-caliber explosive bullet struck him in the pit of the stomach and bored through the soft organs almost to his spine before exploding.

The woman stayed unconscious for bare seconds, then sat back up, her head filled with an all-encompassing agony.

However, there was now more in her head, much more, and that more boded deathly ill for many of her captors, those who would fall before the wrathful rage of Dr. Erica Arenstein.

Chapter VI

First to follow Long Willy into death was Flat-chest Lizzie, still cackling even as the exploding bullet turned her misshapen head and its contents into wall-festooning gobbets. The crone was followed almost immediately by Strong Tom, whose fatal error was to come through the low door as Erica turned from the body of Lizzie. Recalling in full just how cruelly he had used her when finally Long Willy had let him at her, Erica shot him in the groin, the force of the projectile flinging his solid body outside to flop and shriek in the dust until, after a time, he bled to death.

No other presences darkened that doorway, so Erica crawled—she still felt too wobbly to stand for long—back over to the foul and filthy mattress on which she had lain and suffered for so long. Part of the armload that had been brought in was all of the equipment that had been hung and belted on her body when Braun had clubbed her down there in the defile. From one of the pouches on her belt, she took a thirty-round magazine and used it to replace the smaller one in the rifle. Then she sat and waited for another Ganik to come in.

But the next ones to come, Erica did not recognize, for neither had availed themselves of the "sessions" that Long Willy had offered all of his new bullies.

Lee-Roy and Abner were brothers, and neither had ever had a woman, nor did they want to, for they had each other. Such as they were not uncommon among the Ganiks, among which race all sorts of mental and physical aberrations—rare among other races—were commonplace.

All of the bullies, along with every other living soul in the camp, had stood and watched Strong Tom slowly die of his frightful wound, assuming the whole time that it had been Long Willy who, finally having mastered the use of the firestick, had revenged on Strong Tom's blood that bully's long years of insubordinations. But when the bully was finally dead, the two brothers thought it might be wise to ask Long Willy if he wanted them to stand post at the door of his cabin. Otherwise, aroused as they both were from witnessing the dying agonies of their late associate, they were of a mind to seek out their own hut for a bout of lovemaking.

It was a distinct shock to them to see the body of Long Willy stretched out on the floor of the cabin as dead as Strong Tom. Their gazes locked upon their dead leader, they did not even take notice of the naked woman until she spoke to them in Ahrmehnee.

"Who the hell are you two bastards? I warn you, if you come near me you'll be as dead as that son of a bitch is!"

The threat was implicit, so neither man moved, but Abner said in atrociously accented and slurred Ahrmehnee, "We don't neethuh of us tawk Ahrmnee; cain'tchew tawk no Ainglish?"

"Far better English than you, you filthy, ignorant savage!" snapped Erica. Then, noticing that they did not seem to understand twentieth-century American English any better than they had the Ahrmehnee, she switched to the tongue known as Trade Mehrikan, a widely spoken dialect of English which while debased to some extent was not slurred as far from its ancient origins as the bastard dialect of these Ganiks.

At last, she seemed able to communicate. "Did you kill Long Willy?" asked Abner, apparently spokesman for the pair.

Erica thought fast, then answered, "No, my firestick slew him. My firestick slays anyone without Power who touches it."

Recalling the death of Long Willy's elder brother from an almost identical wound, Abner and Lee-Roy thought that her reply made sense, but inquired, "But you did kill Strong Tom, din't you?"

"Yes," admitted Erica, adding, "I killed him because he . . . he abused me while I lay sick."

Abner's eyes grew wide. "You means fer to kill everbody whut fucked you? Everbody, atall?"

Erica nodded, grim-faced.

"Hot damn!" Abner smacked fist to palm. "Kin Lee-Roy

and me watch? You won' kill 'em too quick, will you? I hopes you kills ole Six-fingers Allen the first!"

The other Ganik spoke up then, saying, "Yeah, yeah, kill ole Six-fingers first, huh?" He giggled. "Thin kill the othuh Allen, thet Julian, huh?"

Corbett crouched ankle-deep in the running water, his saber in his left hand, his cocked pistol in his right. In the shadow, the pony's rider sat dark against darkness, and there seemed to be at least one more mounted man behind him, so the officer leveled the pistol's muzzle at what seemed to be the chest area of the saberman, thumbed off the safety and . . .

"Hold on, there, Major," said a deep, familiar voice. "It's me, Sergeant Gumpner, me and Allison." Then, his voice cracking slightly, he said, "Thank God you're still alive, sir. I . . . we all thought you all was dead back there."

Corbett had his men cut the hobbles off all the ponies they could find and catch; the sole true horse he had them add to their own collection of animals, for, despite its poor condition, it appeared to be of a similar breed to his own big troop horse.

When all of the Broomtowners were gathered in the tiny, hidden plateau area, the sergeant rendered his report, then took Corbett over to where Harry Braun lay, feverish and babbling in delirium. The officer examined the swollen leg carefully, then wiped off his befouled hands and arose, frowning.

"I think you were right, Gumpner—he does appear to be in the early stages of gangrene. I don't know how much good I can do, if any at all. God, I wish Erica were here! But we can't move him the way he is, not even in a litter.

"So have another fire laid closer, over by that flat rock, eh? I'll sack out here, where I can keep an eye on him through what's left of this night, and when the sun's bright I'll do what I can to drain that leg."

Seated side by side on the stony ground, leaning against a pair of saddles, Corbett and Gumpner watched the delirious scientist, smoked their pipes and carried on a low-voiced conversation for a couple of hours. In addition to their official relationship, the two were close friends of many years' standing, and so, knowing Gumpner's innate curiosity, Corbett not only gave him an account of the battle at the defile, but told him just what decisions he had made and why he had chosen what courses he had from among other alternatives, freely and openly answering such questions as the noncom put to him.

In Gumpner's mind, it was continuing education at the feet of a man that he and all of the other Broomtowners all but worshiped. Of course, they deeply respected all of the other men and women from the Center. For how could they—ordinary, short-lived men, only a few generations removed from a savagery no less primitive than that of their neighbors—help but respect men and women whose lives were measured in many hundreds, not a few score, of years, men and women whose highly developed minds had lived since before that centuries-past war which had destroyed the fantastic-sounding civilization built by the distant ancestors of today's howling savages? But most of the Center people were at best cool, distant objects of deference who often behaved as if the Broomtowners were trained and mildly intelligent animals or, at best, retarded but usually obedient children.

Major Jay Corbett, on the other hand, spent a minimum of his time at the Center. There had been very few weeks during the thirty years that Gumpner had served in a military capacity when Corbett had not been either in Broomtown or out somewhere in the hills and woods with Broomtown men on a training exercise, a patrol, a reconnaissance or, more rarely, a short campaign against threatening tribes.

Where other men and women of the Center, especially the scientists, frequently were scornful and patronizing of the Broomtowners, in particular of the career soldiers of Broomtown who often risked and sometimes gave their lives to guard and protect these same Center folk on their expeditions into the territories of hostile tribes and races, Corbett had never been stinting in his praise of the Broomtown men who had earned such praise. Furthermore, Gumpner knew for a fact that Corbett not only had gone as high as the Center Director himself to see about reducing or eliminating punishments meted out to Broomtowners for supposed disobediences or insubordinations having to do with Center folk resident in Broomtown.

When the grizzled old soldier had ridden off, south from the defile, he had been a subordinate obeying the orders of his superior. But here, near the small fire, smoking and listening to the fatherly man, this patient, ever-understanding man, he thought that he at long last comprehended the true meaning and depth of friendship.

His late father, Sergeant Major Gumpner, who had served under Major Corbett for more than forty years before retiring to nurse his arthritis and old wounds, had once long ago tried to explain this very variety of emotion he now felt. Now, only after all these years, did Gumpner feel that he truly, truly understood what the old man had been trying to convey to him.

"One thing of significance that I noticed on the second patrol, that day, the one over the hills to the east of that gap—" Suddenly Corbett broke off short and leaned forward, his dark eyes on the twitching Braun.

". . . killed you, killed you, fin'ly killed you, damned bitch-dog, you . . ." Braun was mumbling, still delirious. ". . . all these years, cen'tries, been nothing but trouble, *tsuris* for me since damned day I met you, dirty cunt . . . rid of you at last . . . bitch on wheels . . . my *project*, took all the credit for *my* goddam project . . . you and that asshole Sternheimer, got him hot for you, you cooze, fucked him a few times and the shmuck let you take all the credit for my project.

"You tried to kill me, damn you, but I *did* kill you . . . nobody . . . never ever know . . . hope the Ganiks eat you! No-good whore, fuck anybody . . . everybody but me. Oh, Erica, my love, my love, why do you treat me this way . . ."

Then the unconscious man drifted off into a spate of meaningless mumbles, interspersed with moans, while his sweat-drenched face contracted, relaxed, then contracted again.

"Gumpner," said Corbett quietly, "you heard?"

"Yes, sir," the noncom answered just as quietly.

"Whether he lives to get back or dies before he does, you are not to breathe a single word of what he just said—not to any of the men, not to anyone back at Broomtown base, not to anyone from the Center, and especially not to him. Hear me?"

"Yes, sir. But, sir, if he killed Dr. Arenstein . . . ?"

Corbett laid a hand on his shoulder, looked him dead in the eyes and said slowly, "Yes, Gumpner, I am as certain as I am that I'm sitting here that Dr. Braun did do just what he said he did. Cowards can be highly dangerous, and he is a very intelligent coward. Moreover, he is cunning, and were he confronted with the words that just came from his own lips, he'd most likely swear that he was babbling in his delirium. He very well could have been doing just that, too . . . but I don't believe it.

"If he lives to get back, remember, he is a member of the Council of Directors, the men and women who run and have run the Center for centuries. Now, Dave Sternheimer doesn't like Braun any better than Braun likes him, but that wouldn't save your neck if it got about that you were slandering a member of the Council. Whether or not what you were saying was true doesn't matter. They'd see you dead, Sergeant.

"Please heed my orders, on this matter Gumpner. Your father and I were very close friends, and your granddad, too.

For Gumpner, there could be but the one reply—"Yes, this sorry secret to your grave, let your report parallel mine—Dr. Erica Arenstein died of unavoidable enemy action, period.

"Will you do this for me, Gumpner?"

For Gumpner, there could be but the one reply,—"Yes, sir."

With the rising of the sun, Corbett had one of the cookpots filled with water from the spring-fed pool and put over a fire to boil. Into it he dropped such of the surgical instruments as he knew how to use. When the water was boiling, he ladled off some of it into another pot, adding just enough of the icy water from the pool to enable him to immerse his hands in it. Then, with strong soap and a small, stiff-bristled brush, he scrubbed his hands and forearms thoroughly for nearly ten minutes, ending by waving them back and forth to air-dry, rather than using a possibly dirty cloth for the purpose.

When the pot had been boiling for a full half hour—this including extra time for the fact that more water had had to be added on two occasions—the officer used a long pair of forceps to remove the sterilized instruments onto a towel soaked with alcohol.

At his direction, Gumpner and Sergeant Cabell cut away the filthy encrusted bandages and removed the splints from Dr. Braun's leg, then swabbed it from crotch to toes with more of the alcohol from the medical packs.

Not entirely trusting the drugs he had early injected, Corbett had had long stakes hammered deeply into the soil in three places, then had lashed the ankle of Braun's good leg and his two wrists to them. In addition—for Corbett was experienced at performing vital field-surgery with little or no anesthetics available and knew what to expect from his patients—two brawny troopers had been assigned to keep the doctor's body still, and another to hold the ankle of the injured leg.

Major Corbett's first really good look at the shiny-skinned, terribly discolored and hideously swollen leg truly frightened him with the cold dash of realization of just how little he really knew of medicine or surgery. But he set his teeth and his resolve, rationalizing that Braun would assuredly die unless something was done. Even one chance out of a hundred that Corbett would fumble his way to the proper procedure must be better than no chance at all.

He began his incision as high up on the leg as the swelling and discoloration extended, glad that he had the foresight to strip to the waist and cover the front of his trousers with a linen apron when the incision commenced to gush foul, greenish pus. He also was glad that he had taken the security precautions, for despite the injected drugs and the stakes and lashings, it was all that the three brawny troopers could do to keep the shrieking patient still enough for Corbett to do what he must.

Seated against a rock, under the guard of a trooper, old Johnny Skinhead watched the procedure fascinatedly. He had fancied himself an expert at the refinements of torture until he witnessed this session. He could not shake off the grim presentiment that he would be the next man to be lashed out between those stakes and subjected to protracted torment at the bloody hands of the tall, beardless Ahrmehnee. He shuddered and unconsciously wet his tattered breeches.

When even hard pressure brought forth only blood and clear, odorless serum, Corbett sponged out the entire length and depth of the opening with hydrogen peroxide—it was either that or alcohol, for they were the only antiseptics remaining in the medical-supply packs—then began the long job of suturing closed the lips of the gaping wound.

But no sooner was he done than he made the discovery that in order to do a thorough job, in order to completely drain the leg, it was going to be necessary to open the inner surface of the limb as well. He debated resting for a while before undertaking the second part of the messy business, but decided it was best to get on with it.

Eventually, it all had been done. Both of the incisions had been swabbed out, sutured, fitted with drains and freshly bandaged. With the replacement of the splint, Corbett gave Braun another injection, had him untied, bathed—in the excesses of his agony, the scientist had befouled himself with both feces and urine—then bedded down warmly and left under the watchful eyes of a couple of troopers.

"He's in the hands of God, now," the weary officer told Gumpner and Cabell. "We've done all that we can for him." Silently, to himself, he added, "I just hope the bastard appreciates it, but he probably won't, knowing him."

Pointedly leaving Erica all of Long Willy's knives and the deceased leader's longsword, Lee-Roy and Abner dragged out the two bodies and dumped them near to that of Strong Tom. At her command, they found and toted over a battered armed chair, plunked it in front of the cabin which had been Long Willy's, then gently steadied the young woman until she was seated in it, cradling the rifle in her lap and clad only in her breeches, since they had not as yet located her boots and other clothing.

Then, one at a time, they ran down and dragged before her the other bullies, those who had accepted Long Willy's invitation to rape her. Erica shot each of the Ganiks, most of them either low in the belly or, like Strong Tom, in the groin. Two, who managed to tear free from Lee-Roy and Abner and try to run, she shot through the kidney.

The two brothers seemed to take immense and continuing pleasure from the executions, and, oddly to Erica's mind, so too did the crowd of assembled Ganiks, some of that crowd actively assisting the brothers to clap hands on their chosen prey, tripping up and holding fleeing men until the brothers got to them.

Erica had brought along the pouches of loaded magazines and stripper clips, expecting to have to kill many more of the Ganiks when they rushed her en masse. But they never did; rather they willingly accepted the fact that this sometime captive was their new leader.

At any other time, Erica would have been repelled by the conduct of the gathering. They dragged the suffering, dying victims of her bullets to spots where small groups of them could increase their agonies, torment them, further maim their bodies and mimic their cries and pleas.

The very last of the bullies, one Wall-eyed Duane, sidled away, out of the crowd as he became aware of just how this new wind was blowing, leaped bareback upon a wandering pony and set out across the clearing, his heels beating a frantic tattoo against the prominent ribs of the shaggy little beast.

Erica, who had always been a good shot, brought the rifle up to her shoulder and blasted the man off the pony's back. A knot of Ganiks ran over to where he lay in the dust, showing obvious disappointment when he died soon after they reached him, and then turned back to those victims still alive, still susceptible to added pain.

Throughout the next few days, Erica came to understand that she was in no danger from the remaining Ganiks. They all seemed to respect her, even to like her. With some dozen corpses to go around, all of them were better fed than was often the case, and it was amazing to her just how much human flesh these savages could consume at a single sitting.

When she had been offered Strong Tom's liver, heart and several juicy cuts from one of his thighs, she had wisely masked her revulsion and indicated her preference for a steady diet of fish. There had been no question, either spoken or implied, and her two bullies had since kept her well supplied with fresh-caught fish, probably taken from other Ganiks, since she had never seen either of the two fishing in the stream or pond.

Her demands for pots of hot water were always met, and when she closed and barred her door to strip and bathe, no one ever tried to enter. After the executions, all of her clothing and her boots turned up amongst the effects of Strong Tom and Long Willy, so she now went about both clean and clad, though still a bit bemused at how easily she had won over these revolting, primitive, savage but in many ways childlike Ganiks.

Her self-appointed bullies, Lee-Roy and Abner, were a boon. Not only did they wait on her, cater to her and respectfully coach her in the necessary functions and duties of

Ganik chieftaincy, but they willingly explained certain usages and customs when she seemed not to understand.

When, of a day, she announced that she wanted every man and the few women in the camp to troop down to the stream and there strip, wash thoroughly their bodies, hair and beards, then their verminous clothing, there was pure pandemonium in the camp, nor did the noise and agitation cease, despite the most sadistic efforts of the two bullies, until she had fired a shot from the rifle.

After a few moments of subdued muttering, one of the former coterie of Strong Tom shuffled out of the mob to face her. "Whutall you wawnts us to do, it ain' jes' ginst bunch-law, it's plumb sinful. Ol' Plooshuhn, he kills Ganiks fer thet!"

Erica shrugged and stated flatly, "You'd better take that risk, then. Because if you don't wash your stinking selves and soon, then I'm going to kill you for certain."

Old Kevin set his jaw stubbornly. "Wal, I ain' gonna!"

Erica leveled her rifle and, without another word, shot the Ganik spokesman down, the force of the charge hurling him back into the mob behind him. She ended by having to shoot two more, then her bullies beat another to death. But after that, the remaining Ganiks got the message and filed meekly down to the stream to indulge the singular whim of this strong and proven-merciless new leader. Like a pair of vicious dogs, the brothers rode herd on the throng, beating those who lagged, ripping the garments from those who did not strip fast enough for their liking, throwing in bodily those who hesitated at water's edge.

As the brothers stood panting and giggling on the stream bank, Erica gestured with her rifle, saying, "You, too, Lee-Roy, Abner." When the two just looked at her uncomprehendingly, she elucidated, "Strip and wash, you boneheaded apes!"

Still giggling, the brothers complied. For the next few days, they and the other Ganiks were far easier on Erica's nose. She was, in fact, considering forcing the bunch to burn down all of the vermin-crawling huts, along with most of the contents, when more Ganiks came riding in from the north.

Although most of the newcomers forked real, full-size horses, one who was mounted on a big pony separated himself from the knot soon after they had debouched from the wooded track and kneed his mount over to a ring of Ganiks, squatting about a fire and consuming their first meal of the day.

"Heyo, Stinky." One of the feasters raised an arm in greeting. "One-ball 'lowed as how you'd done gone up nawth fer to jine up with ol' Buhbuh."

The small, wiry, big-nosed man thus addressed just nodded. "Heyo, Fartuh, where be Lowng Willy an' the resta his bullies?"

The thick-lipped Fartuh Cartuh rolled onto a single buttock and broke wind loudly, then said, grinning, "We-awls been a-shittin' out the bes' parts of them ol' boys awl week lowng! Thishere bunch is got us a new leaduh, naow, Stinky."

The big-nosed man nodded, not looking at all surprised. "I knowed ol' Strowng Tom'd do fer ol' Lowng Willy soonuh 'r latuh. Sumbody cawl him outchere, heanh?"

With an even broader grin, Fartuh Cartuh let loose another blast of foul methane. "Thet 'un was Strowng Tom, Stinky, he's sayin' 'heyo.' "

At this, Stinky's dark eyes did widen perceptibly. "Yawl mean yawl done et Strowng Tom, too? Then who in Plooshuhn *is* a-leadin' the bunch?"

"I am, you smelly bastard," grated Erica, stepping into sight, the rifle held in the crook of her arm. "What are you and the rest of those pigs doing in my camp?"

Stinky stared at the Ahrmehnee woman in dull shock for a few moments, then reined about and rode back to the group of Ganik horsemen with whom he had ridden in. He spoke in such a low tone that none of Erica's people could overhear, and when he rode back, two of the horsemen accompanied him.

Dismissing the obviously inferior Stinky, Erica studied his two companions warily. Both were very big men—as tall as Long Willy had been, yet as broad and as muscular as the late Strong Tom—and well armed with swords, targets, axes and pieces of plate armor of fine quality and new enough that it had not yet started to rust of the customary Ganik neglect.

The one on Erica's right was as dusky of skin tone as was her own, current body, with hair and beard that were jet-black and curly under the matted filth, and a nose even bigger than Stinky's own beak; Erica thought that the man was at least half Ahrmehnee, Ganik or no, probably gotten upon some hapless kidnapped Ahrmehnee girl.

The other man, the one on her left, was possessed of a wild mop of brick-red hair but a singularly skimpy beard and a mere reddish fuzz rather than a mustache on his upper lip. "Hormonal imbalance," thought the physician Erica. "Likely, very sparse body hair, too."

On one side of the haired man's stubby, freckle-splashed nose, from the inside corner of the eye, diagonally down the face and across the square jawline, was a still-healing gash. It had been a deep, severe wound, for Erica could see the glint of teeth through the opening in the cheek.

Both of the men sat their big lowlander horses tensely, both pairs of eyes—the one black as sloeberries, the other a washed-out blue—looked as cold and hard as agates. The dark man bore an axe across his saddlebow, while the red man had a longsword gripped in one freckled paw, held with blade pointing forward at the level of his thick thigh. As she surreptitiously slipped off the safety of the rifle, Erica thought that if they had intended to give a menacing aspect, they had succeeded admirably.

The mounted trio reined up and halted only thirty feet from the woman, and the dark man cleared his throat, spat, then announced loudly enough for all to hear, "Ol' Buhbuh, he·be daid!" Then, to the shouting, wildly gesticulating throng of Ganiks, he roared, "Plooshuhn take you awl, jes' shet your moufs till I be done a-tawkin'!"

As the hubub subsided somewhat, he went on, "Naow, I be Black Jed Fando, and I done took ovuh Buhbuh's bunch and I'll be raht tickled fer to kill enybody don' lahk me bein' leaduh." He turned his head then and stared hard at Erica. "Mens or wimmens, eithuh, don' mek no nevuhmin'."

Erica contemplated shooting all three of the strangers then and there, but decided to hear the rest of what this arrogant, posturing jackass had to say.

Fando paused, waiting for a challenge, and when none seemed forthcoming, he continued. Taking one hand off the axehaft, he hooked a thumb over in the direction of the red-haired man. "Thishere be Baldfaceted Kirby, mah bully. I done d'cided he's gonna tek ovuh thishere bunch fer me." Turning to once more stare hard, provocatively, at Erica, he demanded, "Enybody don' lek thet?"

"Unless you two are determined to be entrees tonight," remarked Erica conversationally, "you'd be wise to take this dog-and-monkey show back where it came from."

She had unconsciously lapsed into archaic English of the twentieth century, so naturally no one understood a word she had said. But as her tone had not been threatening, Fando made an erroneous assumption and a fatal error.

Kneeing his big horse toward her, he extended a hand, "Gimme that there club, woman. I wawnts it."

From the hip, Erica shot Black Jed Fando just under the raised visor of his helmet, then did the same for the redhead and, for good measure, Stinky Parsons, too. Then, as calmly as she could, she turned her back upon her own and the new Ganiks and strolled back to her cabin, entered and slammed the door behind her.

The whoopings and shoutings went on throughout the camp for at least an hour, for normal conversation among the Ganiks, Erica had discovered, consisted of each one trying to make himself heard among and above all of the rest. At length, there was a tentative knock at her door. She removed the bar and stood a few feet inside, rifle again fully loaded and leveled.

But the first and second men to stoop and enter were the grinning, giggling brothers, Lee-Roy and Abner, bearing huge loads of weapons and segments of armor, which they dumped, clanking, on the dirt floor.

"What's all this junk?" snapped Erica.

At the end of a fit of giggles, Abner said, "Awl them their bullies down fum the main camp, they 'lows as how they lahks your stahl, Ehrkuh, and sincet you kilt thet Black Jed and his head bully, botht, they awl wawnts you fer the new leaduh of Buhbuh's bunch. But you *will* keep me'n Lee-Roy fer bullies, too, won'tcha?"

Although she had no desire to ride northwest, deeper into this primitive, savage land, farther away from the Center, she could see no option, at the moment, short of killing every living soul in the camp—not that she would have stuck at that to achieve her ends, but she did not have enough cartridges. So as soon as her three latest victims had been reduced to piles of inedible offal and well-picked bones, she slung her rifle, donned a helmet, belted on a sword and mounted Black Jed's fine roan gelding.

Flanked by the faithful, devoted Lee-Roy and Abner—
both now decked out in boots, armor, clothing and weapons
stripped from various of Erica's victims, with Abner on the
dead redhead's horse and Lee-Roy on Stinky Parson's big
pony—Erica set out to the northwest, leading a lengthy
column of Ganiks on their shaggy ponies.

Although she knew it not, Dr. Erica Arenstein had just set
out to take her place in legend.

Chapter VII

Even farther to the north, in the most southeasterly of the strongholds of the Kingdom of New Kuhmbuhluhn, a place called by the Kuhmbuhluhners Sandee's Cot, young Bili, *Thoheeks* and chief of Morguhn, had taken his oaths to the enigmatic Prince Byruhn of Kuhmbuhluhn and was preparing to lead part of his condotta out on their first patrol of the Ganik lands.

His was a most conglomerate command, this day. To his force of Confederation nobility, Middle Kingdoms Freefighters, Ahrmehnee warriors of two different tribes and the fierce Moon Maidens were now added old Sir Steev Stanlee—the new-made Count Steev—with a handful of his troopers and Pah-Elmuh, the Kleesahk, accompanied this day by two others of his semi-human ilk. Bili's two prairiecats had left some hour earlier to scout the route ahead.

Before noon of that first day, Bili and his composite force had already blooded their weapons in the cause of Prince Byruhn and New Kuhmbuhluhn. It was, it developed, but the sanguineous beginning to the longest and goriest campaign in which Bili ever took part.

Prince Byruhn's objective was no less than to drive all of the Ganiks—not only the bunches of outlaw-raiders, but the families of farmers, as well—out of the lands claimed by New Kuhmbuhluhn, and this was the purpose for which he had finagled the military services of Bili and his followers when the fires that followed the earthquake had forced the easterners to flee into the unknown lands of the western mountains.

At the end of his first week in his new service, he and elements of his force having taken part in no less than three patrols into and through various portions of the Ganik lands, Bili of Morguhn sat at meat in Sandee's Cot.

The scarred and grizzled Count Steev sat in the center chair, with Bili on his right hand and Rahksahnah, leader of the Moon Maidens, on Bili's right. Beyond her sat the acting captain of the Freefighters, Lieutenant Frehd Brakit. At the elderly nobleman's left were ranged *Vahrohneeskos* Gneedos Kamruhn of Skaht, who vice-captained the Confederation nobles insofar as anyone could do so; Vahrtahn Panosyuhn and Vahk Soormehlyuhn, the two senior Ahrmehnee in Bili's force; then the husky Moon Maiden called Kahndoot, who was Rahksahnah's lieutenant.

Kahndoot was with them at Bili's firm insistence. Although most of the other men did not like her—she was outspoken and brutally frank, openly contemptuous of most men and more than willing to meet any of them at swordpoint—Bili did. In the course of the past week's patrols and skirmishes, he had found the big woman to be highly intelligent, an accomplished warrior, a competent leader and a good follower; moreover, she had proved possessed not only of mindspeak abilities, but of medium-range farspeak, as well, and this last was of an inestimable value to a combat commander, especially to one leading troops over unfamiliar terrain.

Those at the high table had feasted well on lamb, boar and larded venison, a pasty of fish, roe and eggs with herbs, onions and root vegetables, filets of trout fried with tiny, highly spiced sausages, plus breads and other oddments all washed down with drafts of the fine ale produced locally.

While Bili and Kahndoot cracked nuts between their hard, powerful hands, most of the others nibbled dried fruits and sipped wines or more of the honey ale. When he had done and had divided the nutmeats evenly between himself and Rahksahnah, Bili turned and spoke to the old count.

"For all that we've taken a few casualties this last week, Lord Steev, none were killed or hurt so badly that Elmuh's wondrous skills could not quickly put them aright. I must say, here, that I like this mode of campaigning far better than that of which our lord, the prince, spoke. It sits better in my craw to fight armed, mounted men, rather than to raid and brutalize and burn out the farms and steadings of families."

"Yet, Duke Bili," the oldster gently pointed out, "that is precisely what you admitted doing against the Ahrmehnee for your sovran, High Lord Milo. How is this in any way a different, more objectionable campaign, here in New Kuhmbuhluhn?"

Bili frowned, admitting to himself that Count Steev was right, up to a point. After spitting out a bit of nutshell and sipping at a straw-colored wine, he nodded. "Aye, Lord Steev, you've made a good point. What we Confederation forces did to the Ahrmehnee was much alike to what the prince has outlined of his designs upon these Ganiks, but, too, there are differences.

"Primus," he held up a horny forefinger, "our only purpose in the despoliation of the Ahrmehnee lands was to break up the huge army of Ahrmehnee warriors gathered ready to invade the western *thoheekahtohn* of the Confederation, to bring them back to protect their homes and families; and this we accomplished, else Vahrtahn and Vahk and their warriors were not with me this night.

"But there is no such purpose to be served here. Not only would the outlaw bunches of Ganiks not lift a hand to protect their kin, these farmers, from us, but they will raid any we miss or overlook, and likely perpetrate far worse outrages than I would condone from my own troops.

"Secundus," he raised the middle finger to join the other, "those Ahrmehnee villagers fought back, fought hard. Despite our fine arms and armor, despite our big horses and prairiecats, despite our well-honed skills and years of experience, we took a decent number of casualties, considering we weren't faced with many men of warrior age. I have never before seen such matchless courage, such reckless bravery in the very teeth of impossible odds, and all this from the likes of ancient men, women and girls, even little children. They all fought us, and they all fought well."

Down the table, on Count Steev's other side, the two dark, bearded Ahrmehnee leaders nodded to each other and smiled grimly. Dook Bili had described accurately the ages-old valor of their stubborn, unconquerable race.

Bili went on, "But these strange people, these farmer Ganiks, the few whose steadings we have struck so far, are another bowl of beans, Lord Steev, as you know. Look you, man, any beast, even a mouse, will, if you threaten his get enough or corner him in his hole, fight you with all his power, even though he goes to his sure and certain death; this is the way of nature and of all things natural.

"These weird Ganiks, however, will curse you, revile you and lay upon you every sort of imprecation, but damned few of them will so much as shake a clenched fist at you as you butcher their wormy stock and burn down their huts. I don't expect simple farmers to keep full panoplies ready to hand—damned few do in any land or realm—but I have seen Ahrmehnee and others as well take up what was to hand and try to use it to defend them and theirs—scythes, hoes, spades, dung forks, even sickles and kitchen knives. What makes these Ganiks so strange and cowardly?"

Count Steev sighed. "I am a quarter Ganik, myself, Duke Bili, yet I cannot answer your proper question. All that I know is that it all has something to do with their singular travesty of a religion, one of their host of gods, this one called, I believe, 'Pazahfizm.' But be not deceived by events to date, sir—not all Ganiks practice that code. Of course, none of the bunches do, but a good number of the farmers are just as bloodthirsty and aggressive and dangerous as any outlaw you've yet seen or faced. But most of those Ganiks are in the north. They take all aspects of their ancient religion far less seriously than do those of the south and are, many of them, well on the way toward becoming good Kuhmbuhluhners, which is why our prince's warrant did not apply to them and their lands. They are fully willing *and able* to defend both themselves and their holdings, neither support nor even tolerate outlaw bunches, and even are beginning to accept arms training and service in the Kuhmbuhluhn army. I would that all Ganiks were alike to them."

Upon his departure for the north some weeks earlier, the prince had insisted that whilst he was absent Bili—being but two steps lower in hereditary rank than himself and, in consequence, the highest nobleman present at Sandee's Cot—and Rahksahnah, should occupy that small but comfortable suite of rooms customarily reserved for him on his visits.

Therefore, once the feasting hall had finally cleared and they two had made use of the semi-attached bathing house of Sandee's Cot, Bili and Rahksahnah lay snuggled together for warmth in the overlarge, feathersoft bed bearing the arms of Prince Byruhn. They were in converse, but silently, by way of that mental meshing known as "mindspeak," for neither ad as yet any appreciable command of the other's oral language.

"Poor Kahndoot," beamed Rahksahnah. "She has tried, ried hard to obey the dictates of the Silver Lady, but she has ot succeeded. Alas, I think me that she never will succeed; he ways of the Hold of the Maidens are just too strong in er.

"But, nonetheless, you have made of her a friend, my Bili. You are the first male friend she ever has had, and, you must now, she deeply respects you. Earlier tonight, after the meal, while you and Count Steev were closeted with Pah-Elmuh and the cats, Kahndoot and I had words. She thinks that you would make a fine Moon Maiden, were you but a woman, and there is no higher accolade in Kahndoot's mind."

Bili beamed, "Thank her for me, then. I consider her a doughty fighter, a fine officer and a good subordinate; such a sterling combination is uncommon and valuable for its very rarity. Also, her even rarer mental abilities aid me vastly in field operations. Now that she, and you, my love, are aware of and beginning to develop your latent mindspeak talents, 'd like you both to determine how many others of the Maidens possess these abilities. Do you think they will permit hemselves to be so tested?"

"Of course they will, my Bili," she replied, "particularly if hey are aware that you requested such, for they like you, despite an upbringing that taught them to scorn and despise all men, and despite the fact that Meeree—poor, suffering Meeree, who was my lover before the Lady gave us two each other—has endeavored to turn them against you.

"Believe me, Bili, I have spoken no single word of it, but hey all know, nonetheless. They know of how hard you fought your own officers to see Kahndoot publicly ranked among them; they all appreciate your unrequested effort on her behalf, and they honor you for it."

Bili shrugged. "Of course, I'm glad to secure the affection of troops I command, but I'd have done the same for any good—really good—officer of mine. You say that Lieutenant Kahndoot feels that were my gender different I'd make her a good Moon Maiden? Well, I say, and mean every word, just the way she is she has made and is making me a splendid officer, and I feel her to be worthy of every honor I thus far have seen fit to bestow upon her. Any other woman—or man, or even Kleesahk—who so distinguishes herself will receive of me equal consideration."

Her dark eyes gleaming, reflecting the dim light of the single as yet unextinguised taper, she nodded once. "And that is precisely why the Maidens so like and respect you, my own Bili. You accept all warriors as warriors, nothing more and nothing less, whether they be female or male, humankind or Kleesahk or animal. You are most good, my Bili, good and fair to all who serve you, and I agree with Kahndoot. Were you a woman, you would make a good Moon Maiden.

"Nonetheless . . ." Her hard hand, which had been pressed against his scarred chest, began to slide over the length of his belly with its ridges of hard muscle. "This particular servant of the Goddess is so very glad that you are not a woman, not on this night."

Although, with her elevation in status, Kahndoot might have been afforded accommodations in the more comfortable hall, she had chosen to remain lodged in the huge, lofty old tower-keep where lodged the bulk of Bili's force, along with the Kleesahks and the two prairiecats, Whitetip and Stealth. When she returned there after the conclusion of the feast, it was to find all of the former Maidens of the Moon Goddess gathered together in a third-level armory—standing, leaning, sitting or squatting amid or upon the racks of spare weapons and armor, and being addressed in their own secret language by another of their number, Meeree.

". . . must do is invent an excuse to all stay behind on a day when most of the men ride out against these Ganiks again. Then we can seize the gate and the watchtowers, with the one closed and barred and some good dartwomen occupying the others. I doubt me there be enough force in all of this New Kuhmbuhluhn to successfully storm and take this place.

"Now, true, we are but few, here; but remember, there are other women living now in this place. We can free them from their thralldom to the men, train the younger, stronger ones to arms. Those men who are biddable we will keep here to do the labor. Those who are not we will kill or blind or otherwise maim that they may not dispute our rule, our establishment of a new Hold of Maidens, the perpetuation of our Holy Race and the continuation of our ancient customs."

Flushed with her efforts, the wiry young woman turned to the tall, muscular officer. "What says our famous Kahndoot?"

Kahndoot looked at her levelly. "I say that you are a fool and a blasphemer, Meeree, and any poor, deluded woman who listens for long to your demented ravings risks becoming as demented and fanatically irreligious as are you!"

Fire flashed from the wiry woman's eyes and her hands felt, sought without conscious direction the hilts of the weapons she customarily wore. It was not such an answer as she had expected. She snarled, "Who are you to talk of blasphemy, sow? You have not yet taken up with a man!"

The bigger woman only shrugged. "No, I have not yet found a man to satisfy my tastes. But, in Her Own time, I believe that the Silver Lady will lead me to such a one. You see, Meeree, I still am faithful to Her, still abide by Her Will, Her sacred Will, expressed through Her hereditary priestess, the *Brahbehrnuh*, Rahksahnah.

"Can you say the same? Of course you can't, not without becoming a liar, as well. Do you think that you are the only woman here whom Her dictates deprived of a well-loved lover? Your selfishness has already led you into blasphemy and the agitation of treachery. Do not allow that immature selfishness to be the very death of you. Repent, bow your head to the Will of Her in all ways. The hold is gone. We all mourn it and its ways and the dear folk whom we never will see again. But the Goddess has lit for us a new and different path to ride, and, do we honor Her as did all our foremothers, we can but proceed along that new, strange way."

There were nods and murmurs of agreement around and about the room, but Meeree was not to be so easily mollified. She sneered, then said, "And just how do you know that the *Brahbehrnuh* truly spoke for Her, eh? How do any of us know that she did not simply develop an itch in her parts for this huge, strutting, hairless chunk of overproud manflesh, this Dook Bili? How do we all know that this perverse desire did not lead her to delude us who trusted her? How do we know that her tale of a new and evil way of life for us Moon Maidens was not a fabrication out of the whole cloth, out of her lust-crazed mind?"

Meeree was now almost shouting. Her face was purplish and her eyes gleamed with a feral light of rage and soul-deep hate. "And if it were true, if this perverted woman, who forsóok her own, true lover to go and live with a damned man, told the truth, then I think that we had best seek us out another deity. Even the gods of these Ganiks are, at least, consistent in their demands and prohibitions.

"We all knew, as I earlier said, that we had lost our *Brahbehrnuh* to her unfathomable lust for this ugly, hulking man-warrior, Dook Bili. Now, after tonight, it is become clear that we have lost Kahndoot, as well. It is passing strange. I never thought that the day would dawn when the mighty and most valorous Kahndoot, pride of the hold, would publicly become a lick spittle of a mere ma*aaaagh!*"

Despite her muscular bulk, Kahndoot could move like a bolt of lightning . . . and she did. The back of her hardswung hand splatted into Meeree's sneering lips and the force of the blow hurled her backward, frantically striving to keep her feet beneath her, until she stumbled over a pile of horse armor and fell back against the shield-hung wall.

Kahndoot stood, legs spread, her eyes fixed on Meeree. The bigger woman absently rubbed at the back of the hand—on which a bluish gouge inflicted by one of Meeree's teeth was beginning to sullenly ooze dark blood—but her broad, square-jawed face was calm; Kahndoot never fought out of rage, but used her quick mind to plan her aggressions and defenses.

Every woman in the room had risen to her feet. They all stood in silence, awaiting the outcome, for both Kahndoot and Meeree were noted warriors.

Meeree just lay there for a long minute, her eyes open but unfocused, then she slowly sat up and drew herself to where she could sit leaning against an old iron-mounted target. She drew the back of one trembling hand across her split, mashed lips and looked dully for a moment at the smear of blood. After working her tongue about inside her mouth, she turned her head to the side and spit blood in which glinted a white bit of broken tooth.

Coldly, she looked up at Kahndoot, and just as coldly, although in a tone somewhat slurred, she spoke the ritual words: "Shishter, you have drawn a shishter's blood."

Above the deep sigh which went around the room rose the deep contralto of Kahndoot: "And that same sister has drawn blood of her sister, as well." She held the back of her hand where Meeree and most of the others could see the red trail starting to creep from the deep toothmark. Then she asked, "Shall it be blood for blood, then, sister mine?"

Meeree spat out another glob of blood, then shook her head. She believed that without Kahndoot to oppose her, she could soon win over her other sisters to her plan to seize Sandee's Cot, make of it a new hold and thus regain Rahksahnah for her own.

Kahndoot nodded. "As you wish, Meeree. I do not fear you, so I will be fair. My preferred weapon is, as you know, the crescent axe, but while you are good at throwing them, you lack either the frame or the development for close-in work with one; therefore, I would say sabers and targets, but I will meet you with any other weapon, as well. Shortswords? Dirks? Mountain knives? Stabbing spears?"

"Shabersh," said Meeree, pulling herself slowly erect. "Shabersh and targetsh."

Kahndoot shrugged. "Again, as you wish. When? I suggest that we meet two days hence, when the patrol is returned."

"No!" Meeree snapped. "I want no Ganiksh doing my killing for me. Tonight! Now!"

Bili and Rahksahnah were young—he not yet nineteen, she a few months younger than he. They had been lovers for less than ten days, and so, responding to the driving needs of their bodies, despite the weariness from the week of riding and fighting, they had loved long and hard before sinking into a deep, delightfully exhausted slumber, still locked in each other's arms.

At the first crash of mailed fist upon the door to the princely chamber, Bili sprang up with such force that he almost threw the lighter Rahksahnah off the other side of the broad, long bed. Extending a hand unerringly in the dark, he gripped the wire-wound hilt of the unsheathed battle brand he habitually kept beside his bed of nights.

Swiftly and silently on his bare feet, he crossed the room from bed to door, the sword held at low guard, ready to fend off, to thrust or to slash. The heavy fist slammed against the thick door again, this time accompanied by a voice that Bili at once recognized, so he drew the bolts and opened the massive portal to see in the now-lit hallway Gy Ynstyn, his bugler.

The stocky young man with the full brown beard—all

Middle Kingdoms buglers wore beards, that among the generally clean-shaven hosts of warriors they might be easily recognized by commanders at a distance—was obviously very perturbed. His eyes were wide and his lips actually trembled as he spoke.

"Please, my lord duke . . . they, she . . . they're going to fight! Arming even now . . . won't listen to me or anyone . . . she . . . no chance, the lieutenant will kill her!"

Bili leaned the sword against the doorjamb, grabbed both of Ynstyn's upper arms in his big, hard hands and shook him savagely. "Make sense, man! *Who*'s fighting? And where?" But not even this seemed to help, so Bili soundly slapped the face of the bugler, then snapped in command tones, "Bugler Ynstyn, *report*!"

That worked. Years of professional soldiering in the condottas of the north brought the burden of ingrained discipline to order the turmoil in the man's mind. He came to attention and spoke in a controlled voice. "Your grace, Bugler Gy Ynstyn begs to report that Lieutenant Kahndoot and Trooper Meeree of the sub-squadron of Moon Maidens are in the process of arming to fight a duel, this night, in the main armory of the tower keep. Full-armed Maidens guard both the stairways and forbid entry to all men or Kleesahks, declaring that it is Maiden business and will be handled by them and only them."

"All right, then," said Bili brusquely. "You and those two guards bring a light in here and help me and the lady to arm. I'll put a halt to this duel foolishness, and that damned quickly, too. If they're so hot to see blood flow, there're still thousands of Ganiks out in the hills for them to put steel into."

Sir Bili, *Thoheeks* and chief of Clan Morguhn, with the *Brahbehrnuh* Rahksahnah by his side, and closely trailed by his bugler, Gy Ynstyn; Acting Captain of Freefighters Frehd Brakit; and *Vahrohneeskos* Gneedos Kamruhn of Skaht, strode purposefully across the expanse of lea separating the hall of Sandee's Cot from the grim old tower. His armor and weapons clanked and jingled to his stride, and the look on his face was as cold and menacing as the honed edge of the massive axe he bore in one powerful hand.

Up the outer stairs he went, then across the thick plank into the recessed doorway. The door swung open before him and he clanked on, wordless, through the first-floor entry foyer to where a flight of stairs led upward around the inner curve of the tower.

From somewhere above came the clash-clang of hard-swung steel on steel, along with the shuffle-stamp of combatants' bootsoles and the rattling-jingling of their armor as they moved. He did not pause, but put foot at once to the stone steps and started upward, trailed by his entourage, as well as quite a few more men from the first floor.

But around the first turn, his way was barred by a Moon Maiden. Armored, she stood, helmeted, a small, gleaming target strapped to her left arm and her shining saber held diagonally across her chest.

"No man passes until we be done with Maidens' affairs, above," she grated in a tone that brooked no argument. But then, finally recognizing just whom she now faced in the dim flare of the torches, she stuttered, lamely, "I . . . I . . . sorry, Dook Bili . . . not even you, you man."

Rahksahnah pushed around Bili. "And what of me, Ahbee? Am I, too, denied?"

Before the young woman could frame an answer, Bili simply reached his right hand forward and upward, gripped her right wrist and began to squeeze, easily fending off her attempts to use the edge of her targe, ignoring the kicks of her booted feet against his armored body.

Encased in that pitiless grip that could—and had—warped steel plates of armor, Ahbee withstood the pain, the grating of bone against living bone, as long as she could, then she was compelled to let go the worn hilt of the saber. At the ring of the weapon upon the stones of the steps, Bili released the Maiden's wrist and, pushing her ahead of him, climbed the stairs toward the sounds of combat.

It had been while Meeree, with the aid of two of the Maidens, had been arming that Gy Ynstyn had entered the small tower room they two shared. Still wearing his gambeson and helm, with his guantlets thrust under his dirk belt, he reached up for his scaleshirt, where it hung from a wall hook.

"What is it, Meeree? An alarm? Where is my bugle?"

Impatiently, she shook her head and stamped a foot. "Fool, keep you out of this affair. None of your man-silliness, this. I go to fight for my name, my honor."

He just stared at her for a brief moment, then lifted down

the scaleshirt, worked arms and head quickly through the openings and began to do up the side lacings with sure and rapid fingers.

"What do you, stupid man-thing?" she yelped. "Hear me do you not?"

Having done up the laces of the scaleshirt with the speed of the veteran warrior he was, Gy took down a plate cuishe and began to buckle it in place over his high boottop, speaking even as he worked. "You it is, lady, who said that your honor now is mine own, and mine yours. Has that honor been offended, we redeem it together. For are we not battle companions, now?"

"Senseless piece of masculine offal," Meeree hissed in rage. "*Maiden* duel, this is to be. To fight Kahndoot I go, and not even to see will you or any other man be allowed, so your armor take off . . . *now!*"

Gy's effort-flushed face abruptly paled above his beard. "Kahndoot? You . . . you go to fight Lieutenant Kahndoot, Meeree? *No!* You must not, my lady. She is bigger and stronger than some men. She will kill *you!* I will fight her, if one of us must; she and I are more of a size."

Both of the assisting Maidens were touched by the bearded man's obvious concern and unquestioning offer to take his lover's place against the undeniably dangerous opponent. But not the bitter, bloodthirsty Meeree.

"Filled with horse turds your misshapen head assuredly is, you fatherless cur-dog!" With deliberate malice, Meeree threw the secret—which he had imparted only to her—of his bastardy at him. "To fight Kahndoot, *I* go! No help I need, not from such as you, man-thing."

But Gy stepped forward, looking hurt and worried. "Meeree, are you ill? Feverish?"

"Get you out of my way!" she snarled at the concerned man, pushed past him and strode to the door. When he made to follow, one of the other two Maidens spun about, drew her sharp-honed saber and held the deadly edge bare millimeters from his throat.

Her voice firm, but her tone gentle, she said, "Good and most faithful you are, man-Gy, as any woman could be; true you are. But hold-custom served must be, even here. Please, to slay you do not force Ortha."

"Mad!" Gy raged in impotence. "Meeree must have, assuredly has, gone mad! You ... I ... we *must* stop her!"

Ortha sighed. "Perhaps mad she truly is become, man-Gy. But forced this fight she did on Kahndoot, so to be it now must."

The main armory, on the second floor, was big and high even for the outsized tower—which had been built by Teenehdjook and Kleesahk, few of whom stood less than eight feet tall and all of whom were of a proportionate breadth and girth. Had it been lower to the ground, in fact, it was of a size to have been almost large enough for a riding hall.

While Meeree and Kahndoot donned their panoplies for the match, the other Maidens had first set guards upon the stairs leading both up and down, then had set about shoving aside racks of weapons, armor and equipment so as to leave a long, wide oval of clear floor in the center of the hall. The broad, ancient flooring planks were gone over carefully to locate and roughen any slick spots on the stained wood, then more torches were fetched up and lighted so that every wall sconce was filled and the dueling-space was as well lit as it was possible for it to be.

Lieutenant Kahndoot was first to arrive, accompanied by the lithe Szehpee, who was her former lover-battlemate, and by Ahbahr, Kahndot's recently chosen sergeant-aide. The big woman seemed as relaxed and confident as she had earlier been. Meeree's reputation for fighting skills did not awe her; she knew herself to be as good or better.

Upon the arrival of Meeree and the pair who had assisted her to arm, Kahndoot again suggested that they two consider that blood had been shed for blood.

Meeree heard the bigger woman out with a sneering smile, then she crowed, "Listen to this, sisters—the great Kahndoot fears Meeree!"

If her purpose had been to anger her soon-to-be opponent, she failed. Kahndoot just sighed tiredly and shook her head, rattling the cheekpieces of her old-fashioned helmet. "You bemused fool, I do not fear you, I simply seek to save you from your own folly. There are few enough of us left alive. Will you then force me to kill or maim another of so few remaining Maidens? Give me your hand and kiss me as I will kiss you, in true, sisterly affection, and let us call this matter settled and done, eh?"

But Meeree coldly slapped aside the proffered hand, snapped, "Here is your kiss, you wallowing sow!" and spat full into Kahndoot's face.

Accepting the cloth offered by Szehpee, Kahndoot wiped the spittle from her skin, then lowered the cheekpieces and stood stock-still while they were buckled tightly under her square chin. When the swordknot was tight enough about her thick wrist, she drew her saber from the scabbard held by Ahbahr, then Szehpee handed the lieutenant her target and fastened the upper strap tightly, as she well knew Kahndoot preferred it done. Lastly, she checked to be certain that both the shortsword and the heavy dirk hung on Kahndoot's waistbelts were loose, easily available, in their scabbards, for were the saber lost or broken through mischance or weakness of blade, these weapons might be necessary.

As there had never been any formal set of rules governing the actual fighting of the duels between Moon Maidens, there was no need of a woman to enforce such a code. When each combatant could see that the other was ready, they moved out, toward the open center of the oval. They would fight until one was killed or too severely injured to continue.

Meeree at once took the offensive, moving in fast, her saber blade but a blur as she hacked and gouged at the bigger woman's defenses. But no matter how rapid her succession of blows and thrusts, no matter how shrewdly delivered, Kahndoot's targe was always there, waiting to turn or deflect them.

Round and round the two women stamped and sidled, Meeree tense and active, Kahndoot seeming almost relaxed, offering a splendid defense, but holding her own offense, awaiting the fatal opening that she knew her opponent would sooner or later afford her.

Absorbed as both were in their deadly pursuit, neither was more than peripherally aware of the sudden stir at and around the wide doors, which had been flung wide for ventilation. Nor did either but barely sense the tall, broad figure that relentlessly plowed a way through the throng of Maidens.

Not until a deep, masculine voice roared, "*Hold!* Lower your blades and back off, or I'll axe you both down where you stand, damn you!" was either cognizant that men now were within the armory.

Such was the ear-splitting quality of that voice within the confines of the armory that both women were virtually compelled to take pause and look over armored shoulders to the edge of the cleared space, at one side. What they both saw was not in any manner reassuring.

There, towering over and outbulking every other man and woman in the huge room, stood their chosen war leader, Bili the Axe. His suit of Pitzburk plate showed the hacks and dents and blemishes of long, hard campaigning, for all that it had recently been burnished to a high sheen that reflected the flames of the blazing torches.

His feet were planted wide apart, and both of his big, steel-sheathed hands gripped the metal haft of his mighty axe, so that beads of light glittered along the honed edges of the twin blades and upon the tip and fluting of the spike above those blades.

But his handsome face, visible under the opened visor, was what most awed and intimidated the combatants and everyone else who saw it. That face had paled under the tan, great stubs of muscle stood up just below and forward of the ears from the tight-clenching of his jaws, and the pallor had caused all of the many small scars to stand out far more prominently than was usual. His eyes were slitted and the fires of cold rage blazed out from the narrowed openings. Instinctively, veteran warriors—and none in that room were not—backed off from that glare, knowing that it could only presage violence or death.

"Neither of you sought or received my permission for this," Bili grated out. "I should axe you both down where you stand, but since you are but newly come under my command, I choose to grant you the boon of another chance. But I grant that boon only if you both case your steel, drop you targes, doff your helms, make apology to me and this company, then request leniency of me.

"If such courtesy goes against your grain," Bili said and grinned like a winter wolf and with no more humor, "then you both are full-armed and so, too, am I. You want to shed some blood, here, I'll help you shed more than you can afford to lose. Make your decisions, and *do it now!*"

For a long moment after he fell silent, there was neither

sound nor movement in all the hall, so that many men and women started at the noise of Kahndoot's targe dropping to the floor. With the hand thus freed, the big woman unfastened her chin buckle, snapped up the cheekpieces of her helmet and then began to loosen the saberknot from her wrist. As she bent to deposit helmet and saber atop her targe on the floor, Meeree moved.

With an inarticulate scream of pure, blood-lusting rage, the slighter woman flashed forward, her saber high and back for the basic downslash, clearly aimed at the now-unprotected head or neck of her sometime opponent. The blade blurred down.

And shattered like glass against the side of Bili's axeblade! "Lieutenant Kahndoot," he growled, "you've made your choice, the wise one, reinforcing my faith in your sagacity.

"This would-be back-stabber has made her choice, too, so someone give her another saber. If she's determined to kill or be killed, I shall see that she dies honorably, at least."

He took his left hand from off the axehaft and began to lower his visor for combat. And that was when Meeree, not waiting for a fresh saber, drew her broad, heavy shortsword and lunged at him, screeching the bloodcurdling warcry of the Moon Maidens.

It seemed impossible to many of the watchers that any man, even a man as big and powerful as Bili, could easily handle his long, huge and heavy weapon with but one hand; nonetheless, he did precisely that. He brought the head swiftly up, caught the slash of Meeree's blade against the finial spike and let the blow's own momentum propel the edge deep into one of the narrow slots between axebit and haft. The impact momentarily numbed Meeree's hand and wrist, and his practiced twist of the haft tore her hilt from her grip and sent the blade skittering across the floor of the armory.

While she backed away, holding up her metal-sheathed targe for defense and fumbling with still-tingling fingers to draw her dirk, her last weapon, Bili took up the axe in both hands once more and brought it high up for a sidewise decapitation stroke.

And then Rahksahnah's mindspeak beamed, "No, Bili . . . please, don't kill her. Yes, she deserves it for this night's infamies, but please, for me, don't kill her."

He had already begun his deadly swing, but at the very last moment, he managed to twist the weapon in such a way that the flat struck full on the face of the targe, rather than the knife-sharp edge on the neck. Meeree's stout targe of hardwood, leather and steel crumpled like so much rotted parchment under the powerful buffet, and although his axe touched not her flesh or even the chinmail guarding that flesh, still did the irresistible concussion of that blow shatter every bone in her shield arm, springing joints, tearing tendons and lacerating muscles and flesh. Such was the agony of the multiple injury that she lapsed into unconsciousness and sank to the floor in a boneless heap of clashing metal.

"Killed her, you should have, Dook Bili," stated Kahndoot, matter-of-factly. "That one will be trouble as long as live she does."

Eight decades and more of long years into the future, the old man that that young warrior was become could but freely agree with the statement of his decades-dead lieutenant.

"If only I had killed that murderous bitch Meeree then, how much bloodshed and sorrow and suffering I'd have saved, I then knew not."

Tears of loss and mourning flowed from the rheumy old eyes. But then the dying, drug-clouded mind went once more back to those tempestuous days of youth and love and war.

Chapter VIII

The brothers, Lee-Roy and Abner, had impressed upon Erica the fact that she would need far more bullies as leader of the main bunch—at least two score. The men with whom she was riding north to the camp of the main bunch had been, it was true, bullies to the dark man she had shot, but they also were the same men who had acclaimed her a worthy successor to her victim, so she decided that they could all be depended upon to support her. These, plus the brothers, gave her a round score of bullies; the rest she could choose when she arrived.

The plan of escape that she devised while traveling north was simple and, she thought, simple of accomplishment. The impression she had been given of the total numbers of the main bunch was at least four thousand and perhaps as many as six thousand. Of these, only a few hundred would be required to clear away enough of the rubble from the site of the landslide for her to locate and retrieve the Center transceiver and its powerpack; these new transceivers were virtually indestructible, especially so when enclosed, as the parts of this one had been when buried, in their waterproof, shockproof cases.

She knew that she was too far north for helicopter rescue, but she also knew that two or three hundred Broomtown men and Center personnel with modern arms, plentiful ammunition and some explosives could go through even the thousands of Ganiks like Grant went through Richmond. All that she needed to do was to have the transceiver and powerpack dug out and brought back to the main Ganik camp. She could hook it up and, some night at the proper time, she could report her situation to the Center, then just leave the set on so that the rescue party could home in on it with their own equipment; true, it might take them some time to organize and come up this far, but the powerpacks were good, so Sternheimer asserted, for a solid three months without recharging.

As she and her party rode north, Erica resolved to start laying the groundwork for her scheme immediately she had been formally empowered as high chief or whatever. But such was not to be.

The camp of the main bunch was a surprise in many ways to Erica. It was situated not in some forest clearing as had been the smaller one, but on a wide, deep shelf hard against the southern and western flanks of a mountain. Several large collections of huts and cabins were separated from each other and from a knot of larger buildings built of stone by acres of gently rolling grassland, with rocky upthrusts of the underlying mountain's bones showing through the soil only here and there. Herds of ponies and a few horses and mules roamed and cropped this expanse, and Erica saw a few spots that looked to have once been cultivated.

From a distance, it did not appear to be a very easily defensible location—she doubted that even ten thousand Ganiks could have adequately manned the running miles of verge— but up closer, as the column made its way along the track that wound and twisted its serpentine course at the foot of the shelf, the defensive advantages of the location became clearer.

There was but one incline up which mounted men could ride, and the aggregation of stone buildings crouched along the verge above it, the verge at that point being heightened by a dry-stone wall, tumbled in places, but mostly still some three meters high. In a host of other spots, strong, agile men could easily scale the sides of the shelf, but then would find themselves on foot against mounted, highly mobile defenders. Her bullies all assured her that since the shelf had been seized by the now-deceased Buhbuh some sixty years agone, it had never fallen to or really suffered much from storm or siege.

She had expected to be lodged in one of the stone buildings, but her escort passed among these structures, then angled to the north again. Skirting a long, narrow lake which was fed by small streams trickling down the higher slopes of the mountain among the roots of the black-green conifers, but which seemed to have no exit stream, they finally came to and set their mounts up a broad, shaly incline.

At the top of the incline was another shelf, this one perhaps fifty meters in width and fifteen or twenty meters in depth. Beyond this shelf, a cavemouth led into the stony bowels of the mountain. This cavemouth had been quite long at one time, but boulders and timbers had been so placed as to wall up all but a single entrance some two meters wide and three high.

The bullies dismounted outside, but led Erica, still on her fine horse, through the high portal and into the dim, cool cave.

Before a week had passed, Corbett found it imperative to move on. Not only was the graze expended, but the ponies had browsed away most of the rougher herbiage as well.

Harry Braun was, of course, in no shape to sit a mount, and there was no earthly way to maneuver a horse litter through the twisting, sharp-angled passage leading down to the track from the hidden plateau. But, Corbett decided, there was one other thing he could try, and if that failed, he would just have to leave a detachment behind, here, with the gravely ill Braun and push on to Broomtown with the main force.

He had gotten from the captured Ganik, Johnny Skinhead, a fair idea of what lay behind, but only hearsay and guesses of what lay ahead. He had not used pentathol, since he felt himself unskilled in that mode of interrogation, but there had been no need of it, in any case. The captive had seemed beside himself with terror that he would be subjected to the identical "tortures" that he had watched Corbett, Gumpner and the rest "inflict" on Dr. Braun, so Corbett was reasonably certain that the injured Ganik had spoken what he took to be the whole truth.

Later, after the officer had sedated the prisoner, after he and Gumpner and Cabell had performed as best they could under the circumstances to repair the damage done by the mace to the Ganik's shoulder, clavicle and humerus, and after the middle-aged savage was finally sure that he was not to be tortured, butchered and eaten by his captors, he became almost friendly and somewhat voluble.

Unlike Jim-Beau, this older Ganik had willingly gobbled

whatever was placed before him—game, pony flesh, wild tubers and the occasional fish. His explanation of this phenomenon was that there were three varieties of Ganiks—those like the late Jim-Beau who adhered strictly to the strictures of the old-time religion; an uncertain number of far-northwestern Ganiks who had drifted so far from that same religion that they now were, for all intents and purposes, heathen Kuhmbuhluhners; and then the vast majority of the free-roving, non-farmbound Ganiks, like Johnny Skinhead, who adhered to the religious customs only when and if said customs fitted their personal needs of the moment.

From Johnny Skinhead's descriptions of them, Corbett could only assume that these Kuhmbuhluhners must be a misplaced group of folk from the Middle Kingdoms who had, for reasons he could not imagine, filtered down through the mountains from the northeast to settle among and enter into endless warfare against the Ganiks.

Having traveled extensively in different bodies for the Center over the centuries, Corbett knew that there was a state called Kuhmbuhluhn—once a kingdom, it now was a duchy or an archduchy, he could not recall which, of the Ehleenee Confederation—and likely these mountain Kuhmbuhluhners were descended of settlers from that state. Thinking that they might make a promising project on the order of Broomtown, Corbett filed the knowledge away in his mind.

Johnny Skinhead seemed not at all loath to accompany the column south, for although he mentioned that with or without a mount he would experience little difficulty in making the journey back to the camp of his "bunch," he was not anxious to go back in his present condition; according to his stories, any save the most primitive doctoring was unknown to the Ganiks and most seriously ill or badly injured members of the "bunches" usually ended up in the stewpots.

Corbett had begun to develop a liking for the uncomplaining, outspoken old cannibal and at last agreed to his constant importunings and allowed him to accompany a hunting party, but only after the apparently ambidextrous oldster had demonstrated the ability to accurately cast darts with his left hand.

To Sergeant Cabell, who was to command the hunt, he said privately, "I think he can be trusted not to try to harm one of us now, but don't take any chances with him, anyway.

If he makes a break to escape, let him go. By the time he could get back to his people and lead them back here, we'll be well on the march to the south."

But Johnny Skinhead made no escape attempt; indeed, he was the first rider to ascend back onto the plateau. The carcass of a huge deer had stiffened draped across his big pony's withers, and a bulging sack of wild sweet potatoes jounced on the mount's back behind the cantle.

All of the hunters proved heavy-laden. Moreover, all were abrim with praise for the expertise and woods skills of the old Ganik. Most of the Broomtown men had lived off the wilderness for months at a time, yet Johnny Skinhead had made them look and feel like tenderfoot tyros at the art.

As Corbett and those who had not gone out stood with the dog-tired hunters eyeing the plentiful supply of plant and animal food gathered from this area which they all thought to be hunted out, Sergeant Cabell voiced the feelings of his group.

"That old bastard is a pure wonder, Major. He never forked that pony until today, yet before we'd gone three kilometers, he had him responding to knee pressure or something, because when he went after that big deer he darted, he sure as hell wasn't using his reins.

"Another thing—I think we ought to take him down to Broomtown and use him to teach classes on wild plants, 'cause he sure Lord knows more on that subject than anybody I ever met."

The officer nodded. "Okay, Cabell, we will. But for God's sake, see if you can get the old stinker to bathe again before we hit the trail, and his hair and beard could stand some soap and water too, as well as a bit of shearing. He may very well *be* a wild man, but he doesn't have to look and smell like one when we ride into Broomtown."

On the morning of their departure, Corbett sedated Braun heavily from the dwindling supply of drugs, then had him painstakingly strapped securely into the horse litter, hand-carried to the place where the outer slope began, then borne down to where he could be lowered with ropes to the shoulder of the track near its confluence with the stream that wound down from the hidden plateau. Once there, the troopers slung the litter between two of the pack mules, then squatted and waited while the rest of the column filed slowly down the twisting defile from above.

Although the attack and massacre of Johnny Skinhead's party of Ganiks had been only a week earlier, the efficient system of nature had left very little on or along the track to show for it—a fleshless skull peeking empty eyesockets from half under a bush, a few scattered scraps of coarse, stained cloth, bits and pieces of inedible equipment; that was all.

Under Corbett's direction. all of the iron-shod darts of the Ganiks had been collected from the site early on, along with the quivers for carrying them. Then he, Gumpner and those few troopers already adept at their use had overseen practice sessions on the plateau for those, the majority, who were not so good with the short, barbed missiles. Now, as they rode out and headed south, every man save only Dr. Braun bore a half-dozen darts in addition to his other weapons, for ammo was in short supply and they still had far to go through possibly hostile territory, and besides, it had always pained Corbett's thrifty heart to leave usable items of enemy equipment on a battlefield to rust and rot.

With only a faint twinge of worry, the officer had given back to Johnny Skinhead both his horse and his old sword, personally helping the Ganik to rearrange both baldric and weapons belt to facilitate easy access for the left hand, and as they all headed south, the sometime prisoner rode with the mounted wounded, differing from them only in his nonuniform clothing, his long, straight sword in place of a saber and his lack of a firearm.

While bullies with small parties of lesser Ganiks rode forth to summon to the main camp the leaders and senior bullies of the various smaller bunches, Erica and her two faithful bullies, Lee-Roy and Abner, undertook the exploration of the sprawling complex of interconnected caverns that had been Buhbuh the Kleesahk's home and headquarters for more than fifty years, prior to his recent death in battle.

The outermost portion of the complex had been mostly filled with horse stalls of stone and timber and storage area for bags of grain and bales of hay and straw. Erica abhorred rats and mice and expected the rodents in such a milieu, but was told upon inquiry of one of the bullies that a resident pair of semi-domesticated stoats had long since eliminated that problem. On a couple of occasions after, the woman caught glimpses in the light of the torches and fat lamps of the soft-brown, snaky creatures, with their glittering eyes and their sharp white teeth.

In the living area, most of the furnishings were vastly outsize—the frame of the bed sitting some meter and a half off the stone floor, its thick rawhide ropes supporting a hide mattress a good three meters long and almost that in width. With effort, she could get onto the bed, but the chairs and tables were an utter impossibility for her or anyone of average stature, and she resolved to see them either adapted or replaced.

Living quarters lay to the right of an entry foyer. To the left, a high, broad passage led into a gigantic, irregularly shaped chamber. The soaring ceiling of this chamber was invisible, being beyond reach of torchlight. About the floor, which sloped gently upward at the edges, was pile upon pile of assorted loot—weapons, armor for both man and horse, saddles and other horse trappings, trousers and breeches of cloth or leather or both, shirts, blouses and jerkins, boots and brogans, bolts of fabrics, an incredible profusion of furs and hides, tools and utensils of every type and usage, pots of iron or copper and of every imaginable size and shape.

Deeper into the mountain, beyond the three lofty chambers, were two passages and some dozen chambers far too regular in shape to have been wrought by nature. In the walls and floors of passages and chambers alike, round holes of uniform widths and depths told the story of heavy equipment once bolted in place.

Erica thought that the sizes and shapes of some of these rooms and the arrangements of some of the holes were vaguely similar to those that had been within the volcanic mountain in the Hold of the Moon Maidens; but the equipment had all still been in place within that uneasy mountain, and here it all had been removed who knew how long ago.

The ceiling heights of the rooms and the passages leading to them had been hewn to accommodate persons of average height and breadth—none was more than two hundred and fifty centimeters high or one hundred and fifty centimeters broad in the passages, although the rooms were relatively spacious—and she imagined that a creature of the Brobdingnagian proportions of Buhbuh the Kleesahk must have found any use of the complex uncomfortable, to say the least.

Nonetheless, all of the better, more intrinsically valuable loot was stored in the man-made rooms, most of it in massive wooden chests. No one seemed to know the whereabouts of the keys to the huge iron locks. One bully opined that the Kleesahk had always carried most of them hung around his neck, so they were probably lost for good along with his body. So Erica had Lee-Roy and Abner "open" the locks with a sledge and a crowbar.

The first they opened contained more weapons, but these were of faultless craftsmanship. The torchlight glittered on the colorful gems set in gilded hilts, on the acid-etched and silver-washed blades of axes, on slim daggers cased in sheaths of red-gold filigree. Another chest was elbow-deep with jewelry—finger rings, armlets, headbands, necklaces, earrings, nosestuds and lengths of flatlink chains, brooches and cloak pins; these were of gold, silver, electrum, copper, brass, bronze, tin, nickel, lead, and wrought iron, and most looked to be of Ahrmehnee design.

The other bullies seemed as amazed at these finds as Erica and her senior bullies, Lee-Roy and Abner. Clearly the late Buhbuh had considered these chests and their contents to be personal treasure to be counted and gloated over in private. But none of it meant anything to Erica, while the continued goodwill of these Ganiks did, so she invited them and all of the other bullies remaining in camp to help themselves to the long-hidden loot she and they had uncovered.

But Erica was granted only a few short days for such explorations of the caves and expropriations of the hoarded effects of her gargantuan predecessor, for certain of the groups sent out returned unexpectedly with grim tidings.

With the deduction of the necessary guards to man the towers and other defenses along the single entry to Sandee's Cot and of the inevitable handful of sick and wounded men and women, Bili's squadron and Count Steev's force numbered about three hundred effectives, plus the Kleesahks and the prairiecats.

After a couple of weeks of long-distance patrol sweeps with the entire available contingent, it was decided at the nightly officers' council to divide the force into thirds—one to be led by Bili and Rahksahnah, one to be led by Count Steev,

Robert Adams

and the last to be led by Acting Captain Frehd Brakit and Lieutenant Kahndoot. Count Steev's force would take two Kleesahks; each of the other forces would have one of the huge quasi-human creatures, plus one prairiecat.

It was also decided that at no time, would they separate beyond the farspeak range of the Kleesahks, thus making it possible for one or both of the other troops to come to the aid of a troop if it found itself beset with more of the outlaw Ganiks than it could easily handle.

So they began the meat of their campaign. Their initial targets were the widely scattered camps of the bunches of outlaw Ganiks, and when Bili learned that these preferred not to fight in the dark, he took to striking their camps by night, sending the prairiecat Whitetip and the Kleesahk Pah-Elmuh ahead to take out sentries and find and spring any man traps.

When he and his force were in position and mounted, with weapons out and ready, he would have his Freefighter archers drop fire arrows into the thatch roofs of the camp structures, wait for the resulting fires to drive the sleepy Ganiks out, then lead his heavy cavalry in to cut down the generally unarmed outlaws, the archers and Ahrmehnee dart men remaining around the perimeter to bring down any that tried to flee the carnage within the camp.

It was not his favorite mode of warfare, and the young *thoheeks* much preferred those occasions when they met or, more often, ambushed bands of mounted, armed Ganiks—when he could feel the shock of metal weapons on his armor, when the sounds that penetrated his helmet were the normal shouts and screams and warcries of real battle, not the despairing shrieks of doomed, helpless men being slaughtered like autumn hogs.

Game was plentiful, much of it having fled from the fire-ravaged areas to the east, so the columns lived off the country, absenting themselves from their base at Sandee's Cot for a week or more at a time while they sought out more camps of cannibals to burn and butcher, roving bands to ambush or chase to earth, Ganik farms and steadings to put to the torch, trying to terrify the resident families in to leaving the area entirely and fleeing south or southwest.

Bili and the officers had agreed that the forces should have one day of the peace and comfort of Sandee's Cot for each day they spent out on campaign, but such respites did not mean days of idleness. Bili was too astute a commander to permit such folly, even though he knew that the discipline exacted from Freefighters or the High Lord's Army of the Confederation would be impossible of implementation in this heterogeneous force.

But even so there were endless means of keeping the men and women occupied. There were horses and ponies to be cared for and exercised. There was equipment, weapons and armor, to be mended or cleaned and polished, repaired or replaced. The areas of habitation required daily cleaning. Four times in each twenty-four-hour day a detail of guards had to go out to take its turn on the outer defenses.

And then there was drill, both unit drill and individual. On the broad stretch of plain between the hall and the lakeside tower keep of Sandee's Cot, mounted units of men and women wheeled and maneuvered, the Ahrmehnee and Moon Maidens learning to recognize and differentiate between the ages-old bugle signals of the lowlanders, while these same lowlanders accustomed their perceptions to the bone whistles that the mountain warriors of both sexes used in place of the horn.

Various of the officers and the two Freefighter weaponsmasters supervised nonstop practice exercises with every weapon available to the force, while the single bowmaster saw to it that none of his archers lacked for practice.

Moreover, in the cosmopolitan atmosphere of the shared dangers, rewards, joys and sorrows, the vastly disparate groups—Kindred and Ehleen and Freefighter, Ahrmehnee warrior and Moon Maiden and born-Kuhmbuhluhner—began the process of coalescing into a unit.

Young Ahrzin Soormehlyuhn, after watching a dozen Freefighters desultorily chucking darts at circles painted on bales of straw, strolled over and asked if he might participate. From the quiver across his back, he withdrew one of his own Ahrmehnee darts and a peculiar pointless rod. Then, with a practiced flick of his thick wrist, he sped the dart into the center dot of the target, and with such force that it tore completely through the thick bale and flew on for several yards beyond.

After doing the same with all of his darts, Ahrzin soon was taking orders for hand-whittled Ahrmehnee throwing sticks from every lowland warrior in sight or hearing.

Dragooning the two blacksmiths resident in Sandee's Cot and shamelessly looting the armories in the tower keep, Bili saw to it that every man, woman and horse was provided with the most complete panoply that could be fashioned or adapted from the materials at hand. Generally, the additions and replacements were gladly accepted. True, a few of the older Ahrmehnee grumbled about the added weights and hindrances to quick movement when Bili insisted that their chainmail hauberks be fitted with plates at certain points, but when weapons practice showed them the added protection of these improvements, they shut up.

All of this was not, of course, accomplished in a single rest period, but by the time Prince Byruhn of Kuhmbuhluhn was able to make the time to return for a brief inspection visit, Bili was able to show him a formidable force and to detail an impressive list of accomplishments toward the prince's goal of completely ridding his father's lands of the dangerous and unpredictable Ganiks.

Old Count Steev of Sandeeland, a man of only average size, felt a little like a child among adults at that private meeting which preceded the prince's return to the north. Although Bili was a big, brawny man, Prince Byruhn was bigger, while Pah-Elmuh, the Kleesahk, was bigger than all three true men combined.

The prince leaned back, bringing a shrill squeak of protest from the sturdy chair set at one end of the conference table. Thrusting out his jackbooted legs beneath the table, he clasped his hairy-backed hands on his flat belly and from beneath the single thick eyebrow that ran luxuriantly from temple to temple he gazed at Bili, who sat at the other end of that table.

"You have done well, young cousin, as I knew you would, and my report to his majesty, my dear father, will give credit where credit is due. Too bad for New Kuhmbuhluhn and my House that you hold lands and obligations elsewhere, Sir Bili, for a nobleman like you is an invaluable asset to any sovran. Without any doubt, you will rise high in your own kingdom; I feel it safe to predict that your hereditary title is but the least of those you will hold ere death claims you."

Although he diplomatically kept his silence, Bili knew whence had come the prince's "prediction," for Pah-Elmuh had already told Bili that he would one day bear the same title as Byruhn.

Lying still on his deathbed in an opulent chamber of his sprawling palace in Karaleenopolis, old Prince Bili of Morguhn silently railed at Pah-Elmuh and at Fate.

"He knew so much, damn it, so very much of my future. So why did he not, why was he not allowed to know that which would have, might have, saved for a world that would have treasured her, for our little children who needed her, and for me, who so loved her, and has never to this very day of my imminent death ceased to miss her, my dear, ever dearest Rahksahnah?"

But there was none to answer that question; there never had been anyone that could.

Now horse- rather than pony-mounted, provided with plates to supplement their thick, beautifully wrought chainmail, and schooled in the shock tactics of heavy-armed cavalry, the Moon Maidens and Ahrmehnee warriors were easier for Bili to assimilate among his Freefighters, Confederation nobles and Kuhmbuhluhners. And although the Ahrmehnee often complained that the horses were less intelligent, less hardy, less nimble-footed and far less biddable than their familiar ponies, not even they could deny the distinct advantages given them against pony-mounted Ganiks by the bigger, heavier mounts.

The Maidens, on the other hand, had been horse-mounted to begin with, but their antique-style armor had been both scanty and light of weight since, like the Ahrmehnee, their style of warfare had been of the hit-and-run variety, lightning-fast attacks and speedy withdrawals, such as were the duty of the light cavalry in those organized armies of the east with which Bili and most of his officers were familiar.

Now they too had been fitted with supplemental plates, their caplike helmets replaced with full helms giving protection to nape and throat and face as well as pate. As was to be expected, there was abundant grousing, but only in the beginning, during the necessary drills, before the Moon Maidens experienced the exhilaration of their new power to easily wreak bloody death at close quarters without the high rate of casualties that must have resulted had they attempted such in only their traditional equipment.

Nor was the exchange one-way. Bili witnessed a Maiden lean from her saddle and send her sickle-axe spinning along no more than a bare foot above the ground until it met and tangled agonizingly with the churning legs of a mountain pony aboard which a Ganik was attempting to flee an ambush. With a shrill scream of pain and terror, the pony tumbled in a heap, sending the shaggy rider flying toward the hard ground and a broken neck. Bili made note of that woman, and throughout the days of the next rest period, she and those of her sisters especially adept at this feat were to be found teaching the art to the men, lowlanders and highlanders alike.

Slowly, gradually, the scattered small bunches were being cleared out by one means or another. Right often now, the wide-ranging cavalry came upon unburned but, nonetheless, deserted, tenantless bunch camps. Roving bands of Ganik marauders, too, were becoming fewer, although those that did materialize were now larger and warier, obviously aware that they were being hunted.

"Undoubtedly," stated old Count Steev at an officers' meeting on the first night of another rest period at Sandee's Cot, "the bastards have finally recognized the fact that they no longer have the free run of this country, that it no longer is safe for them to live in small bunches in the wildwood. Most likely they're fleeing to the camp of the main bunch, that camp which once was Buhbuh's, before our own beloved Sir Duke's mighty axe rid the world of that monster for good.

"With them there, we can concentrate for a while on the far less dangerous job of getting the farmer-Ganiks burned out and on their way southwest and out of our hair. As you all know by now, this strange and troublesome race breeds like barn-rats, and without them to provide a constant pool of replacements, the bunches will prove far easier to finally eradicate."

"But, Sir Count," Acting-captain of Freefighters Frehd Brakit asked diffidently, "why not immediately move against this larger camp of the paramount leader of these bunch-Ganiks? I would think that the longer we defer that move, the better prepared and stronger will be their defenses."

Count Steev grimaced. "Their defenses could hardly get

stronger, Captain. That camp is going to be a tough nut to crack, our losses will undoubtedly be heavy, barring some miracle, and the Prince wants as much as possible done on other fronts before essaying an assault and, thus, weakening this force."

"Thank you, my lord." The ever-correct Brakit nodded and resumed his seat.

And so, at the end of that period of rest and drill, the columns rode out again on their mission of terror. No matter how thoroughly they despoiled and burned and slew stock, they always left uninjured any ponies or draft beasts of the farmer-Ganik families, pointing out, promising, that if the victims rebuilt within the bounds of New Kuhmbuhluhn, they could expect the same or worse.

On their next return to Sandee's Cot, the prince again was in residence and awaiting them. Nor did the royal personage waste any time in assembling not just Bili and Count Steev, but all the officers, for a meeting to hear a report of his intelligence service.

"Gentlemen, Lady-Lieutenant," he stood before them entirely at his ease, rocking back and forth on his booted feet, "Count Steev, Pah-Elmuh and a few other trusted officers have been aware that I have had tame Ganiks from the northwest of the kingdom posing as outlaws down here for some years. As the smaller bunches have been so masterfully destroyed or driven in to join the main bunch at bay, I recalled all of these operatives I could reach. From their reports, I have some most singular intelligence to impart to you.

"That there is now a new paramount leader to replace the late, unlamented Buhbuh was to be expected. But all of my tame Ganiks declare that this new leader is a *woman*, an *Ahrmehnee* woman, an Ahrmehnee Witchwoman of awesome powers. They all say that her name is Ehrkah, although this is not an Ahrmehnee name, and that she was brought among the Ganiks as a prisoner and attained first to leadership of the small southerly bunch that captured her, then to the leadership of the main bunch, by exercise of these deadly powers.

"My tame Ganiks attest that she owns an oddly shaped rod or club—they couldn't agree which—of shiny metal which she can use to slay men at some distance with fire and thunder.

"Now, you all are free to believe this tale or not, as suits you. True, the Ahrmehnee do have Witchwomen, I understand, some of them said to be possessed of mental powers similar in certain ways to those of the Kleesahks, but I hardly think that any real Witchwoman would be captured by Ganiks in the first place, or voluntarily remain with the savages in any case.

"We all, here, know how hag-ridden and painfully superstitious these ignorant, bestial Ganiks are, and I think that these traits, combined with the fact that they are mostly of unstable mind and have so recently seen their traditional order smashed into red ruin and they, themselves, driven back to the very wall has bred in them some sort of mass hallucination.

"But be this matter completely false or formed around a kernel of truth, the time is not long before you must strike their main camp. I do not envy you that job, nor can I and my northern forces give you any additional force to do it, for we are even harder pressed by the Ohyohers, these Skohshuns.

"However, I have great confidence in you, as does my royal father, the king. With Duke Bili and Count Steev to lead and direct such brave and resourceful officers and troops, I can see only continued victory for New Kuhmbuhluhn."

Chapter IX

On the last few patrol sweeps, Captain of Freefighters Sir Fil Tyluh was able to rejoin the lowlander force. His skull had been cracked by the oak-and-stonechip club of a Ganik in the great battle on that plateau which had been called "The Tongue of Soormehlyuhn" and which had been shaken apart in the earthquakes.

Upon examining his comatose body, Pah-Elmuh had discovered a section of the skull pressing hard upon the brain sac, had surgically excised that bit of bone and then had used his vast and arcane mental abilities to set Tyluh's mind to the task of healing the body. This healing process had taken time, but as he watched Tyluh riding at the head of his column, Bili thought that he looked very fit for a man who, by all rights, should have long since gone to Wind.

The young *thoheeks* allowed the captain to retain the services of the man who had been taking his place during his convalescence, Lieutenant Frehd Brakit, for three weeks, then he took Brakit—for whom he had developed a fondness and deep respect—as his personal aide.

That was why, of a bright day, Brakit lay beside Bili in a clump of brush atop a hill, whence they and their escort could clearly view the camp of the main bunch of Ganiks, only some half mile from their perch. Twice since they had ensconced themselves here, mounted Ganik patrols had ridden almost over them, but the mental powers of Pah-Elmuh and the other two Kleesahks who had accompanied them out on this highly dangerous but vitally necessary reconnaissance had so clouded the minds of all those Ganiks that the hilltop had appeared to them deserted. It had been by this cunning method that the Teenéhdjook—huge, hairy, nonhuman partial progenitors of the Kleesahk, who were actually a hybrid race of Teenéhdjook and outsize humans—had for untold

131

eons of time protected themselves from aggressive, murderous mankind.

But Bili actually had two pairs of eyes available to him for this task, his own, and those of the prairiecat Whitetip, now crouched hidden in the thick growth of conifers on the higher and more rugged and precipitous slope of the mountain only a dozen yards above the place where slope met shelf. A part of Bili's rare mental ability was the knack of meshing his mind with that of the huge feline, thus seeing through his cat eyes, but this was a chancy talent and did not always work, depending upon many variables for success.

Because he had been careful to choose only mindspeakers for this mission, there was no need for oral communication between Bili and his companions. Now, he mindspoke his aide, Lieutenant of Freefighters Frehd Brakit.

"All right, you've seen, now. Do you think that the plan we discussed earlier is feasible?"

"Aye, my lord," Brakit answered just as silently. "To my way of thinking, it's the only plan that is, since you and we are not suicidally inclined. Yonder lies a natural fortification, and only a few hundred men who were both mobile and determined could easily hold it against the direct assaults of several times their own numbers; as it is, *we* are the few hundreds and the defenders there number at the least seven times our strength."

"Closer to ten times, I'd say, man-Frehd," put in Lieutenant Kahndoot, "if we include the strength of the two patrols whose routes crossed near to here and consider that there are likely six more such patrols at any one time to adequately cover all approaches to that camp."

"The woman is right," Pah-Elmuh beamed. "The others and I, we Kleesahks, can sense many mounted groups of Ganiks on the move through these woods, here."

Bili nodded once, unnecessarily, but by constraint of long habit. "So, then, all of you study that camp, try to memorize it and its surroundings; I want to construct a sand-table model of it when we get back to Sandee's Cot, so that all of the force will have a basic familiarity before we get here.

"Frehd, scout out what you feel would be the best locations for your specialty. Take one of the Kleesahks and move to another vantage point, if you think that will help. I'll mindcall you whenever we're ready to go back.

"Now, I go to the mind of Whitetip."

Bili first farspoke the prairiecat. "Is my cat brother in a safe place, one where he cannot easily be seen?"

The powerful beaming of the cat answered readily, "Yes, brother-chief, Whitetip is well concealed, yet still can he see much of the places below him. But he cannot stay here for long; the stench of those two-legs below is nauseating him."

As always, whenever he suddenly went from looking through human eyes to looking through the eyes of the cat or horse, Bili suffered for a few seconds from the lack of acuity of vision and the paucity of colors and textures, although a predator cat's eyes were better in all of these ways than those of the equines.

The big cat had chosen an excellent position, and a comfortable one as well. The deep mat of fallen needles cushioned his pads and body from the hard rocks studding the sparse soil beneath, while the thick dimness of the dense stand of gnarled cedars made a sighting of even as large an animal as Whitetip from any point below most unlikely.

Partially meshed with the mind and all of the senses of the prairiecat, Bili was also quickly aware that the female cat— one of the Confederation Army cats whose small size, relatively small cuspids and other deficiencies of mind and of body were the unfortunate results of interbreeding, over the centuries since the coming of the Horseclans to the lands of the eastern seaboard, with the native treecat—was farther up the mountain, guarding Whitetip's back and their route back over that mountain.

Whitetip was a purebred prairiecat, which strain was virtually extinct in the eastern lands. He and his sept—some dozen or so other cats, all related in various degrees one to the other—had but recently come into the Confederation lands in company with a Kindred clan of Horseclansmen, Clan Szanderz. All muscle and sinew and bone, he stood some ten hands at the withers and weighed three hundred pounds, well fed. His upper cuspids projected, slightly curving, to more than an inch below his lower jaw, when it was closed. His mindspeak was powerful and his farspeak could range farther than average.

The female, on the other hand, was of lighter structure, weighing only a bit over half of Whitetip's heft. Her cuspids were but little larger than those of her treecat cousins, and although her mindspeak was perfectly adequate for the military purposes to which she had been bred and trained, it was nowhere near as powerful or as far-ranging as was that of the purebred male prairiecat.

The two vastly disparate cats had fled the crumbling plateau during the height of the earthquakes along with the other cats who had accompanied Bili's original squadron of Freefighters and Confederation nobles. Somehow, in the terror and milling confusion of avoiding the scattered forest fire ignited by white-hot debris from the volcanic eruption that immediately followed the quakes, they two had found themselves together well west of any other cats or humans, in company with only a couple of big Ahrmehnee ponies.

After much wandering, Whitetip's farspeak had finally contacted Bili's familiar mind and the cats had reached his emergency camp just before Prince Byruhn and his force arrived.

Although the female cat was in unabashed awe of her huge companion and constantly deferred to him, he despised her small size, lack of endurance and stunted dentition; nor did he try in any way to disguise his belief that she was a sorry specimen of retarded, misbred cat. Why, she did not even bear a real name, only the designation of her regimental assignment in the Army of the Confederation—37th Regiment, Scout-cat #Q19.

Bili had quickly rectified this last deficiency, calling the friendly, biddable feline "Stealth." Then he had set about attempting to change the big male's attitude toward her, soon discovering, however, that Whitetip was almost as stubborn as was Bili's big black stallion, Mahvros.

"Brother-chief," the big cat had sulked in mindspeak, "how can Whitetip be expected to treat as an equal so runty, stupid and stunted a creature? Whitetip has seen wild spotted cats of more intelligence and basic ability than this nameless number-cat. Had she been in any way distinguished, her previous two-leg brothers would surely have given her a name."

Bili had sighed in exasperation. "Cat-brother, you have seen, have experienced in this last year, how prone are the men of the Confederation Army to slap numbers rather than real names on everything and everyone. It is a sickness of the two-legs, and the cat, Stealth, should not be blamed for their folly; a truly wise cat-chief would not be so narrow in his outlook.

"Nor can she in any way help being smaller, finer-boned and lighter than you. Not very many prairiecats that came east with God Milo and the forty-two Kindred clans stayed for long; most journeyed back toward the Sea of Grass, singly or in groups. With so few remaining and those few widely scattered, they could not always find mates of true, pure prairiecat stock, so most of them eventually interbred with tame or even wild treecats, and, as you know, treecats are mostly even smaller than Stealth. But her prairiecat strain is very distinguished, Whitetip. I have it of the Undying High Lady Aldora, herself, that both Steelclaws, the mighty cat-chief Horsekiller—he who led the Clan of the Cats for the forty-two Kindred clans—and the redoubtable, justly famous cat Dirktooth are all in this small cat's pedigree."

"Little credit she is to her forebears, then," Whitetip had declared flatly. "Her mother should have not wasted good milk on such as she, she should have pushed her away to go to Wind—that, or eaten her. Why, brother-chief, that useless female creature cannot even run a full mile without having to be given a horse or a pony to ride upon, lest her heart fail. Please cease to bespeak Chief Whitetip on such meaningless topics, brother. This thing you choose to call Stealth has never been, can never be anything more than she is—retarded of both body and mind, almost useless. And Whitetip treats as his equals only those creatures that truly are his equals."

Then the huge cat had stalked away in all of his lordly, feline disdain, leaving Bili to grind his teeth in anger and frustration. But the chief of Morguhn was stubborn, too; he had kept trying and, gradually, he had begun to win over the monstrous prairiecat. Not that any of it had been easy; in fact, sometimes, he had been upon the verge of clubbing the head of the arrogantly obtuse cat with the flat of his great axe. But, as time passed, Whitetip had slowly come around.

Dr. Erica Arenstein knew the full meaning of utter frustration. Not only could she not persuade a requisite-size group of Ganiks to journey east with her and shift enough of the tumbled cliff line for her to reclaim the transceiver that would allow her to summon rescue units, but she found her own movements increasingly restricted; only within the warren of caves was she ever allowed to be by herself.

She soon discovered that leaders of the main bunch did not exercise much real power over the bunch. She gave her "orders" to her bullies, but it was their sole option when, how and even whether to carry them out or see them carried out by the lesser Ganiks. She had soon discovered that she had worried needlessly about acceptance by the full bunch of Ganiks; her acceptance by the most of the bullies had ensured this, for very few of the Ganiks who ever expressed opposition to the promulgations of the ruling bullies lived long afterward.

Very shortly, she was aware that the leader of the main bunch was little more than a slightly deified figurehead, not even expected to go on raids unless on personal whim. It was the leader's unquestioned right to choose bullies to perform the actual governing of the main and the satellite bunches, and leaders were expected to be accomplished killers, but it ended there. She was hailed as "Goddess," just as her predecessor had been hailed as "God," but that term only signified that holders of the title were the personified "luck" of the Ganik bunch, not that they were expected or imagined to possess godlike attributes.

At last, as the months passed, Erica had to resign herself to the facts, She was as much a prisoner here as ever she had been in the cabin of Long Willy Kilgore, the two significant differences being that no one raped her now, and her prison was larger.

When she had first arrived at the main camp and the bullies had ridden out with their escorts to spread the word to the far-flung bunch camps and bring back the leaders of those smaller bunches to meet with their new paramount leader, one of the units had returned quite early and bearing shocking tidings—an entire camp had been found by them to have been burned to the ground, with all of the folk of that bunch slain and the ponies wandering aimlessly in and around the carnage.

Hoofprints of big horses and large ponies had been found all over the clearing, and this had meant but one thing to the Ganiks; Kuhmbuhluhners. The thousand or so then living in the main camp had almost all ridden immediately out to track down and wreak hideous vengenace upon the perpetrators of the foul murders (although, from what she had learned of the Ganik bunches and their methods, Erica thought it likely they had simply been paid back in kind by folk tired of their constant depredations).

The avengers had come back a few days later, and a draggle-tailed, thoroughly frustrated lot they had been. They had found a trail and followed it, reckoning that the party of Kuhmbuhluhners numbered no more than a hundred or so, but then that trail had joined with the trail of another party of equal size and then, farther on, with still another. Still the blood-mad Ganiks had followed the Kuhmbuhluhner marauders . . . until it became apparent to them that the force was headed straight for a place they called Sandeeskaht.

From their descriptions, Erica assumed this Sandeeskaht to be an impregnable Kuhmbuhluhner fortress, before the defenses of which many Ganiks had fallen over the years and which was, consequently, held to be a place of very bad luck.

So the mob of resident Ganiks at the main camp had fumed and fretted and erupted several times into huge, vicious brawls which had ended in several dozen dead or fatally injured Ganiks. After two of her bullies had been slain while trying to break up the last one of these unhallowed melees, Erica had felt constrained to ride down onto the plain and blow the shaggy heads off five of the brawlers—which maneuver had brought the fight to a screeching halt.

The main camp enjoyed a couple of weeks of comparative peace and quiet in the wake of that episode, but then the survivors—many of them wounded and/or afoot—started to trickle in from bunches now exterminated or from bands of roving raiders ambushed and slaughtered by the inordinate numbers of armored Kuhmbuhluhners on their big horses, aided and abetted, if the tales of the fugitives were to be believed, by bearded Ahrmehnee warriors and even Moon Maidens.

In conference with most of her bullies in the spacious foyer of her cave-home-cum-palace, with a twenty-gallon barrel of an old and potent fruit wine broached in the center of their circle and battered cups, goblets or flagons in each Ganik's right hand, Erica posed a question.

"Why are you all so flustered at the thought of Ahrmehnee and Moon Maidens joining with Kuhmbuhluhners to make war on the bunches? Since you have always raided both Ahrmehnee lands and Kuhmbuhluhn territories, it seems only logical that the two would eventually join to combat you. I can but wonder that they waited so many years to do it."

Senior bully Abner just shook his head. "But don' no Ahrmnees never come wes' their stompin' groun's, not never."

Observing her look of puzzlement, Horseface Charley, who had been first appointed a bully by Buhbuh the Kleesahk, then elucidated.

"Lowng, lowng, time agone, afore the Kuhmbuhluhners come down fum the nawth an' not evun us Ganiks had done been here fer lowng, a whole dang passel of them Ahrmnees an' Moon Maidens, they come a-ridin' in fum the eas' and looked like they's a-fixin' fer to kill ever pore Ganik whut wuz. But the Kleesahks, they wuz owuh frins then and betwixt usuns and them, we kilt and et so dang miny them fuckin' murdrin' bastids thet they all done been plumb, flatout scairt fer to come back."

Charley upended his jack of old, cracked leather and, Erica thought, poured as much of the wine into his already sopping beard as he did down his working throat. Then he went on.

"Sincet we knows ain' no livin' Ahrmnees and Moon Maidens a-gonna come this far wes', us bullies is done figgert them whut has been seed mus' be ghosties of them whut owuh granfolks kilt, away back whin. See, them Kleesahks, they kin raise up ghosties and awl kinda bad critters fer to kill folks with. And them Ahrmnees and Moon Maidens whut wuz kilt, back then, they wouldn' hev them no cawse fer to hate eny them Kuhmbuhluhners, naow, but you kin bet they shore hates awl o' us Ganiks; and b'sides, bein' ghosties and awl, they'd hev to do whut the Kleesahks whut brung 'em back tolt 'em to do."

Erica listened in silence. She had learned that trying to talk even these somewhat superior Ganiks into rationality was on a par with trying to persuade her horse that it could fly. How or when or why these Ahrmehnee and Moon Maidens had decided to join their swords to those of the Kuhmbuhluhners in scourging the Ganiks into death or flight, she did not know, but they obviously had done so.

"And perhaps," she thought, listening with half an ear

while the increasingly drunken group of savages talked on in their slurred, vulgar dialect, "this is the only way I'll ever be able to escape these despicable swine. If they ever assault this camp, too, maybe, in the certain confusion, I'll be able to get away. Because if I have to spend the life span of this body here, I know I shall become as insane as any other of these congenital lunatics."

It was a few days after that "conference" that, while on her continuous exploration of the cave complex, she found a possible means of escaping her captivity, with or without any help from the Ganik-slayers of Kuhmbuhluhn.

As she gazed up the height of the narrow airshaft, she could see the regularly spaced round holes drilled in the living rock, with rings and streaks telling the tale of iron or steel rungs removed some time in the long ago. Again, judging by the mute testimony of rust-stained bolt holes, a fan or some other sort of air-sucking device had been mounted at this lower end of the shaft, but it too had disappeared, where or when no one could say.

More days were required for her to locate the materials needed—short lengths of strong hardwood of near to the proper diameter. These she found in a cache of spare shafts for the wicked Ganik darts, which, she had learned were but crude copies of those used by the southern Ahrmehnee tribes.

Additional days she spent at painfully trimming the dense, well-seasoned wooden dowels to the exact diameter of the rung holes. She needed twenty-three of these rungs. She also took the time to drag several of the bulky, unwieldy hide mattresses along the hallways and up the sloping ramps to stack them at the foot of the shaft, for should she chance to fall, she wanted something much softer than stone to land on.

Then one day, she made her way back and up to the higher levels of the man-made portions of the caves, with dowels, trimming knives and a short-handled sledge hammer wrapped in a hide and slung, pack like, over her shoulders with thongs.

By standing on the matresses, she could stand in the shaft with its lower edge at about the level of her hips, which fortunate fact made installations of the first few rungs easy enough. But the higher ones were correspondingly more difficult, for the shaft was very narrow—she doubted if the late

Buhbuh could even have gotten his head up it, even if he had chanced upon it—and gave her little room in which to work.

Twice she dropped the little sledge hammer and had to go back down to retrieve it before she thought—and silently cursed herself for not thinking earlier—of winding a length of thong about the haft, then looping it to her wrist. Once a flawed rung cracked cleanly in half under her weight and only her firm grip on a higher one prevented a fall.

She was bathed in salt sweat by the time she got close enough to the top to perceive that the way was blocked by two rusted screens. But so far gone in oxidation did these prove to be that she had only momentary difficulty in smashing her way through them with the little sledge hammer, though she clotted her hair and festooned her clothing with centuries worth of debris in the process.

But with the bursting of the last screen, she was able to thrust her head, shoulders and upper torso into the clean-smelling, wondrously cool mountain air. She was facing, she decided, almost due north and could see very little save trees and rocks. To either side, her view was equally scant, so she worked her body around in the shaft, that she might look uphill . . . her heart jumped into her throat!

There, crouched on a rocky ledge no more than ten meters from the shaft opening, was the largest puma that Erica had ever seen. The huge cat's long, thick tail was lapped about its forepaws, and it was regarding her steadily, its yellow-orange eyes never blinking, its red-pink tongue tip protruding slightly from between winking-white incisors too long to be housed completely within its mouth.

Breathlessly, Erica clasped the haft of her hammer—her only weapon, up here—the tighter and felt with her feet for the next-lower rung, although she well knew that the cat could easily be on her before she could retreat into the relative safety of the shaft.

The cat, however, made no move to attack, but neither did it seem to fear her; so slowly, very carefully, never taking her eyes off the huge predator until her head was fully within the stone walls of the shaft, Erica retraced her way back into her mountain prison. Next time she climbed up, she would have her rifle.

The barely willing "goddess" of the Ganiks had anticipated great difficulty in finding or making enough time alone to bear back up to the foot of the old ventilation shaft the items she would need was she to go who knew how far afoot through the mountains until she could chance across one of the roaming herds of semidomesticated ponies and then strike one of the tracks leading southwards. But she was immediately gifted almost two full days, while the bullies were gleefully occupied down by the lake, torturing to death several of the lesser bullies who had led out patrols on the very day that Erica had ascended the shaft. Patrols on the following day had found clear traces that Kuhmbuhluhners had spent a measure of time on the brushy crest of a hill less than a half mile from the foot of the shelf and the camp thereon. Furthermore, there was equally clear evidence that no less than three of the crisscrossing patrols had ridden almost over the spot, yet not one of those patrols had reported aught amiss.

Even had she not had work to do, Erica would have retreated deep into the caves, for the earsplitting shrieks and animal-like howls of the tormented men set her teeth on edge and her nape hairs aprickle. But as it was, by the time that the expert sadists finally allowed their viciously maimed victims to die and set about butchering their tattered cadavers for the feast, their "goddess" had transported all that she thought needful, save only her rifle and her dwindling stock of ammo, to the inner opening of the shaft that led upward onto the northern face of the mountain.

Now all she needed was a major diversion which would serve to occupy all of the bullies—for the lesser Ganiks never set foot in the cave—for long enough to let her get out and a fair distance from the camp on the other side of the mountain.

That particular wish was soon to be fulfilled.

Immediately they returned to Sandee's Cot from their reconnaissance, Bili and his companions set about forming a replica of their recollections of the Ganiks' main camp on a huge sand table erected within the largest room of the tower keep—the main armory, wherein Kahndoot and Meeree had dueled. When once the model was complete and as exact as their combined memories could render it, Bili summoned Count Steev, all of the officers and sergeants of the composite force, the two cats and the Kleesahks, wishing all to be familiar with his plans for finally exterminating the bunch Ganiks.

Once all were gathered about the big table, Bili said, "If our lord Prince Byruhn was correct in nothing else, he was at least correct in this instance; the main Ganik camp is assuredly going to be a tough nut to crack.

"At no point along the edges here"—he indicated the low line of cliffs that fronted three of the sides of the shelf—"is the level of the plain less than forty feet above the track that meanders along below it, and in some places it rises as high as sixty feet. At no point is that slope gradual enough to put horses or ponies up it, although dismounted troops could likely climb it easily enough, did they leave most of their armor behind.

"At only one place, here on the eastern face, is there an ascent for horsemen. It's only wide enough for about two abreast, though, and above its full length, the Ganiks have raised some twelve feet of wall—a rather rude wall, being of naught save fieldstone and rough timber, but as effective as any better would be at that point. Too, there are several stone-wrought buildings at the top of that ramp; they may be simply the large huts that they look like from a distance, but I would wager they are fortified, some of them at least.

"As you can see"—he moved the tip of the sword he was using as a pointer from place to place—"there are other clusters of huts and cabins scattered on the plain; too, there are some aggregations of what look like rude tents and lean-tos, these probably providing housing for those Ganiks we drove up there. Estimates vary, of course, but I feel safe in saying that we will be opposing no less than two thousand, five hundred of the bastards and . . ." He paused until the comments ceased, then added, "Possibly, as many as three thousand."

Only the old count and his officers and sergeants who had been sending out patrols of dozens or, at most, a few score against bands and bunches numbering in the hundreds seemed unimpressed by the odds they would soon face. The Freefighters, Ahrmehnee and Maidens exchanged looks, and Bili could sense the many mindspeak communications passing silently about the room.

The young *thoheeks* went on, "Now, everyone knows that a force attacking a fortified position like this one must be at least somewhat stronger than the force which is defending that position. But, unfortunately, this is not and cannot be the case with us and these Ganiks.

"Had I even a number of troops equal to the numbers of the Ganiks, I would await a dark night, range my archers along that track and use fire arrows to fire as much of that plain as I could—there's been little rain, of late, so that grass should go up like fine tinder—and then I'd feint a frontal assault somewhere down here near the southwestern corner and, as soon as enough Ganik force was committed at the site of that feint, I'd lead the bulk of my force up the eastern flank, here, and then sweep from one end to the other."

He sighed. "But if wishes were horses. . . . Therefore, the only plan that I can devise which does not smack of suicide is the one I now shall detail to you."

Chapter X

Although fairly shallow and sun-warmed along its shores, the long, narrow lake between the upper reaches of the shelf and the lower, grassy plain was apparently quite deep and of an icy coldness toward its center. After Lee-Roy followed her out too far one day and nearly drowned, Erica had taught her two senior bullies to swim, and, observing the three of them cavorting in the water on hot, stifling days, numerous others of the bullies had pled for similar instruction by their new leader.

Of course, a few of the more religious and/or superstitious had remained too fearful of the terrible demon Plooshuhn to take part in these frolics, but there were not many of these among the ranks of the bullies. So soon, though it was still a gagging experience to be near or even downwind of a mob of the unwashed lesser Ganiks, Erica found her constant entourage of bullies to be at least bearable.

As Erica continued to share out with them the treasured loot that Buhbuh the Kleesahk had hoarded for himself for so many years—especially the barrels and kegs of assorted spirits—the bullies made a practice of gathering several evenings each week in the foyer of the caves to drink and converse with their goddess and each other. And as she slowly came to know them better, the woman found many things about them to truly admire.

For all their basic savagery, their nasty brutishness, their universal and sadistic delight in witnessing or inflicting human suffering and death, and the grim travesty of a religion that a few of them still practiced, even so could she find things to admire about her lieutenants.

She realized and admitted to herself that these men were, of course, the natural leaders and, as such, superior in every way to the howling, gibbering horde of cannibals that followed them. In order simply to retain their places in their primitive hierarchy, they had to be stronger, more intelligent and of greater mental flexibility than the unwashed throngs they led. Like attracts like, and that was why she made it a point to fill the occasional vacancies in the ranks of the bullies with choices recommended by the existing ones.

For all their announced status as "senior bullies," Lee-Roy and Abner really only functioned as her personal staff. The real senior bully, Merle Bowley, was a highly intelligent, quick-minded and innovative man. He was not the largest— Horseface Charley held that record; Erica was certain that the man towered two meters, or very close to it, and could not have weighed much less than ninety kilos—but he was without doubt the most dangerous of them all. Even when he was smiling and outwardly jovial, that aura of deadly danger radiated outward from him, easily recognizable to those properly attuned.

Bowley was not short by any means, compared to most of the Ganiks—who all seemed too have been subjected to malnutrition and serious protein deficiency almost from birth. He was a sizable man, though some thirty centimeters shorter than the towering Horseface and correspondingly lighter. Erica reckoned his age to be mid-thirtyish, and there was as yet no trace of gray in his dark reddish-brown hair and full beard. When she had first come among them, his speech patterns had been identical to the slurred, vulgar, much-debased dialect spoken by all of the Ganiks, but soon thereafter, she had noted that he was beginning to ape her own speech. Now, after her months with the main bunch, Bowley was much more easily comprehensible to her than even the faithful—but not really too bright—brothers, Lee-Roy and Abner.

Bowley's aide, Owl-eyes Hewlitt, was a younger version of his senior. His sinister killer aura was there, if not yet as pronounced as Bowley's, and his mind was easily the equal of Bowley's. He was a bit taller, though not as broad and bigboned, and his hair and beard—once he'd taken to swimming frequently, he and Bowley having been the first two to request instruction in the esoteric rite—were of a glossy blueblack, although his eyes were a piercing dark blue. Like Bowley, whom he clearly much admired and aped in many ways, Hewlitt had taken to copying certain of Erica's speech patterns and pronunciations.

Another bully who really stood out in Erica's mind was Counter Trimain, short, broad, incredibly powerful, but always jolly. There was never a time when Counter was not laughing and joking . . . even while he was engaged in his specialty, protracted and bestially insensitive torture. He had impressed Erica with his deep knowledge of anatomy; this knowledge enabled him to keep the spark of life in his most unfortunate victims even while maintaining them in indescribable agony. Counter was also the closest thing to a surgeon or physician the bullies had had, prior to the coming of Erica.

The common run of Ganiks received no medical help or treatment of any nature. If they became seriously ill, badly wounded or incapacitated with age, their fellows quickly killed and butchered them for the ever-ready stew pots.

Bullies sometimes went that same merciless route, but the ones valued for some reason by the senior bully or the leader could usually depend upon at least a modicum of treatment at the skilled—if bloody—hands of Counter. In the two or three procedures Erica had undertaken since arriving in the main camp, Counter Trimain had proved himself to be an exceptional, if very unorthodox, assistant.

One early evening, as Erica and some score of the most important bullies sat or hunkered in the torch-lit foyer with their drinking vessels and yet another barrel of the late Buhbuh's tipple—this a sweet honey wine of amazing potency—Erica said, "Merle, where did your people, the Ganiks, come from? As I recall, Horseface said that you had been in this area for only a short while before the folk of Kuhmbuhluhn arrived from the north."

"Wal, Ehrkah," he replied, "I'll tell you jest whut-all wuz tole to me, back whin I 'uz a younker, afore I jined up with a bunch, atall. You's free to b'lieve whut of it you wawnts to, heahnh? It's a whole lot of it I don' b'lieve, no way! But eny-haow. . . .

"Away, way, waaay back, it wuz folks a-livin' awl ovuh, could do thangs cain' nobody do no more. They awl had waguns what din't need no oxes or ponies fer to pull 'em, and they had waguns whut could *fly*, if you kin b'lieve it, fly like birds. Whole passels of them folks lived close to each othuh, all ovuh the place, and they dirtied up the rivuhs and lakes and all so much all the fish come to die out'n ' em, and a man'd git real sick or die wuz he to take nary a sip.

"And evul demons had put them folks awl up to puttin' pizens in the dirt they growed their corn and beans and awl in, then a-pourin' more, diffrunt pizens awn 'em, too. Thet's whin the firstest Ganik farmers come along, Ehrkah, they wouldn' use no pizens in the dirt, nor none enyplacet elst. And thet flat pisted them pizen folks awf! They commincted a-persuhcutin' them pore, raht-thinkin' Ganik farmers sumthin awful, a-robbin' 'em of their land or a-tryin' to make 'em a-pizen too, lahk the rest wuz a-doin'.

"So them ole Ganik farmers, they tuk awl their wifes and their younkers and they lef' and went to places din't none of the pizen farmers wawnt fer to live in. And thet be why, whin the pizen folks started a-fightin' and a-killin' eacht othuh, wan't none of the Ganik farmers wher they could be easy got at.

"Fer a whole lowng tahm aftuh them pizen folks had done mostly kilt each othuh awf, the ole Ganiks farmed raht and lived raht and done raht by the land and the gods. But then the get of the get of them pizen folks whut had lived th'ough the killin' and awl started a-movin' in awn the ole Ganik farmers, and they din't see nuthin' wrawng with it.

"'Cept, them new folks, they wouldn' live raht. They awl dirtied water, won' no kinda animal they wouldn' kill and eat, they evun was a-tearin' up the land, a-diggin' up some kinda black rock whut they say will burn, lahk wood. And whin them ole Ganik farmers they tried to tell 'em whut-awl they wuz a-doin' wrowng by the land, the demons got 'em so riled up they commincted a-beatin and evun a-killin' them pore ole Ganiks. And sinct it wuz more demon-lovuhs then it was Ganiks, it won't nuthin fer to do but fer to move awn to find new lands whut din't have no get of pizen folks awn 'em.

"But seemed lahk everwher us Ganiks settles us, 'long comes mo' demon-lovers, lahk them Kuhmbuhluhn fuckuhs, afore lowng. And naow them Kuhmbuhluhners has done took to a-diggin' up them black rocks, up nawth, I hear tell, too."

"But, Merle," asked Erica, "what is wrong with digging and burning coal? That's what these black rocks of yours are properly called, you know."

Soberly, Bowley replied, "First, Ehrkah, it be a crime 'ginst the great god, Kahlohdjee, to dig enythang 'ceptin' food and wawtuh outn' the land. And secun', the black rocks wuz one of the pizens of the ole demon folks; burnin' them rocks pizens the air and, then, folkses innards and they dies."

Having within her ancient mind clear recollections of the various fringe-element movements—organic farming, ecology, the pollution fanatics, vegetarians, back-to-nature types—Erica dug more deeply into the singular practices, beliefs, customs of the Ganiks on subsequent evenings and soon came to the conclusion that the Kuhmbuhluhners were doing the only thing that any halfway sane and reasonable group of normal humans could do with the Ganik ilk—drive them out or kill every one of them.

Though she had decided on the ride north that rather than starve or seriously endanger her health she would partake of human flesh, she had quickly found that such a drastic step was unnecessary in the main camp. Not only was the lake full of fish and large frogs, with abundant crayfish in the feeder streams, but the bullies were always hunting, bringing back their kills by night, so as not to cause conflicts with the religious fanatics.

In any single week, Erica and the bullies might feast on venison, wild pig, the flesh of feral cattle and sheep and goats, hare, raccoon, opossum and a variety of fowl. The quantities and selection of plant foods—fruits, berries, roots, tubers, leaves, sprouts and seeds—was to her impressive. The Ganiks apparently knew every edible thing that grew in these mountains, and utilized most of them in their diet. Grain and beans for both man and beast came from raids upon the farmer Ganiks, and there were vast stores of these in the caves, the presence of which kept the resident stoat colony busy and well fed on marauding rodents.

The lunatic strictures of the Ganiks' perverted religion denied them consumption of the flesh of any warm-blooded beast, all of which were supposedly under the personal protection of the god Ndaindjuhd, who did seem to mind the animals' being killed by Ganiks and others—for such things as hides, furs, horn and sinew—just so long as the flesh was not eaten but, rather, reverently buried with a prayer of apology to the dead beast and to Ndaindjuhd. This restriction applied to wild and domestic beasts alike; the only things a farmer Ganik was allowed to take of his livestock were milk, eggs, wool or hair, dung and labor.

Most disgusting to Erica of the promulgations of Ndaindjuhd was that one decreeing that Ganik hunters should all either copulate with the dead bodies of their quarry or, if that prey was small game, at least ejaculate semen on its carcass before burial, supposedly in order to indicate to the god that they recognized and respected their own kinship to the beasts.

Moreover, she was freely informed, on the Ganik farms bestiality was performed often and openly by both men and women with the various species of livestock for the same holy purposes. That non-Ganik folk not only did not perform these rites but were horrified by and murderous toward those who did had always been one of the principal reasons that the Ganiks had never found themselves able to coexist with non-Ganik populations. Even the bullies, who mostly had strayed quite far from the tenets of the Ganik faith, always expressed anger at the patent intolerance of non-Ganiks for Ganik religious practices and reverence for the land.

The warped and exceedingly peculiar faith of the Ganiks did, however, allow them to eat human beings—which species did not fall under the protection of Ndaindjuhd—all matter of a vegetable nature and any non-warmblooded creature, including fish, amphibians, reptiles, worms and insects. And the protein-starved Ganiks ate every one of the latter category they could catch, and they ate them *all*—heads, skins, bones, organs, guts and even the contents of those guts.

But they were not allowed fish or frogs or anything else out of the main camp's lake or feeder streams. At sometime in the past, someone—either Buhbuh or one of his senior bullies—had astutely recognized the fact that the large numbers of lesser Ganiks would quickly exterminate the populations of the waters, were their hungry depredations allowed to go on. So the lake and streams were now and had for long years been the sole bailiwick of the bullies and the leader, lesser Ganiks being permitted to use it only for drinking water and for watering animals.

This practice meant that the trail side bank area was almost always roiled and muddy, so Erica and the bullies did all of their swimming and fishing from the less-troubled other side, which was, in any case, nearer to the cave. So, on a sun-shiny morning in August (at least, Erica thought it August; there was no way she could be certain of dates), she, Lee-Roy and Abner, having sun-dried their bodies after swimming, had dressed and were just casting their lines into the water when they heard it.

From afar it came. The distant tock-tock of hard-swung axes biting into wood, with another sound that Erica thought was the sound of one or more saws, these noises interspersed from time to time with the resounding crash of falling trees, the lowings of oxen, creaks of ropes and of harness and occasional sharp reports like the crack of whips.

Looking questioningly at her companions, Erica was somewhat reassured when Abner shrugging, said, "Soun's is hawd fer to place, Ehrkah—they comes down the hollers awn the wind, raht awftun. Them could be summa them Kuhmbuhluhn bug-tit bastids thirty, forty miles away."

But when Merle Bowley rode his long-legged horse in from the central area of the shelf-plain some hours later, Erica could tell at once from his expression that something was dreadfully amiss. Nor did he keep her long in the dark, only taking time to dismount, hitch the horse and throw himself flat to dip his sweaty face in the lake before relating his news and his hunches.

"I thanks we 'uz wrowng whin we hurtid them boys to death, naow, Ehrkah, and I had me a hunch we wuz whin we done 'er, too. Reason is, it be a whole passel of Kuhmbuhluhners is a-hewin' and a-fellin' great big ole trees, 'bout three ridges out f'um the camp, then they's a-snakin' them timbuhs closuh to us, to-wards us, like.

"Naow, a body kin *see* 'em, see 'em clear, f'um lotsa places awn the edges ovuh the track, but whin ole Horseface he taked a bunch and rode out fer to kill 'em, *he couldn' find the damn fuckuhs, nowhers*!

"I tell you, Ehrkah, I watchted him my ownsef; him and his bunch rode almos' ovuhtop of the bigges' bunch of them Kuhmbuhluhn bastids, they did, no more'n three, fo' yard fu'm 'em, lookted like fu'm heanh, but they plumb couldn' see 'em. So it cain' be but the one thang—them damn Kuhmbuhluhn Kleesahks is a-workin' Teenéhdjook magic out thar. Mos' likely, they wuz a-doin' the same thing back whin them pore boys we all hurtid to death din't see nobody nei-ther."

"But why," asked Erica, "would the Kuhmbuhluhners be felling trees so close to us, here? Surely they knew we'd see and hear them."

Merle's thick shoulders rose and fell in a shrug. "Lawdsy, Ehrkah, I don' know *why*, they jest a-doin' it. But you can bet the reason they a-doin' it don't bode no good fer us Ganiks."

She asked another question. "Merle, what is this Teeneh . . . Teenéhd . . . this magic you say the Kleesahks are working?"

The story that she got then was an exceedingly strange one, one that she did not know whether to believe or not. But she listened, making no comments, withholding judgment until she had heard all of it.

As Merle Bowley told it, when first the Ganiks had fled into this area of the mountains from the last place out of which they had been driven, willy-nilly, by intolerant non-Ganiks, there had been no real men resident, only a small number of huge, hairy human-shaped beasts called Teenéhdjooks. Though they varied in size and coloration, according to age, sex and individual differences, most of them were two or more times the height of a full-grown man and proportionately heavy. Nonetheless, they were able to keep their presence in the land unknown to the Ganiks—who were, even then, no mean woodsmen—for many years, up until some type of disease carried off most of their females of breeding age.

Among the Ganiks, in those long-ago days, were a few families of vastly outsized humans, and to one of these the Teenéhdjooks first showed themselves, seeking friendship and females. This family's surname was McCoy, and from the matings of their women with the Teenéhdjook came the first Kleesahks— which term denoted a hybrid of Teenéhdjook and human, an often sterile hybrid.

These huge, hairy hominids, these Teenéhdjooks, unless prematurely killed by accident or disease, lived much longer than humans—three or four hundred years not being uncommon among them. Although the hybrids they generated did not live that long, still they lived longer than men, some of them reaching an age of two hundred or more years, which fortunately served to keep their population fairly stable despite their low birthrate and the frequent sterility of the Kleesahks.

The Teenéhdjooks were hunter-gatherers, according to Merle Bowley's description of their preferred life-style, dwelling by choice in caves in the higher elevations of the mountains or deep within the thicker stretches of forest in oval or circular shelters made of hides stretched over wooden frames and placed atop pits dug in the ground. Also according to Bowley, the Teenéhdjooks had not progressed beyond the Stone Age, for while some of their tools and hunting weapons had been beautifully fashioned, all had been of stone, bone, wood or antler and they had had no knowledge of the bow—wooden darts with fire-hardened tips and what Erica recognized from the description as a *bola* being their only missile weapons, aside from flung stones.

Despite their clearly manlike traits, the Ganiks had decided that the Teenéhdjooks and Kleesahks came under the protection of Ndaindjuhd and, as the pelts were not to Ganik liking, they had lived in relative harmony with the hominids.

Then, in what Erica supposed was a response to repeated incursions or raids by the Ganik bunches, the warriors of the Ahrmehnee *stahn* had invaded in force, aided by a large group of Moon Maidens. In a great battle, early in the invasion, the fierce Ahrmehnee had virtually exterminated the then main bunch of the Ganiks, then had pushed on westward.

The Teenéhdjooks—such few of them as still remained—and the Kleesahks, who considered pure man to be incurably and incredibly savage in nature and who always tried to avoid any part in his constant squabblings and slaughterings, would most likely have retreated to their wilderness fastnesses, leaving the Ganiks and the Ahrmehnee to fight it out between themselves to the bitter and bloody end, had not some group of Ahrmehnee point riders captured and then coldly murdered two Kleesahk youngsters.

After that, with the priceless aid of the uncanny abilities of Teenéhdjooks and Kleesahks, the Ganiks were enabled to hound and harry the largest proportion of the huge invasion force to their richly deserved deaths, to capture and the Ganik torture frames and, eventually, to the Ganik stewpots. It was thought that some few of the invaders had escaped back whence they had come . . . but not many.

As Erica understood it, the "magic" of the manlike beings was an ability to cloud men's minds so that they either could not see things and beings which lay within clear sight or saw things which did not, in fact, exist. As if those abilities were not enough, they were possessed of incredible strength, could see in light far too dim for even the sharpest-eyed humans, had much keener senses of smell and of hearing and could communicate with their own kind and with a few humans by what she would have called telepathy.

On exactly how the Ganiks and their hominid allies had drifted apart, Bowley seemed less than sure, saying only that the Kuhmbuhluhners had "won the Kleesahks over" soon after they had entered Ganik territory. Then, when the Kuhmbuhluhners turned against and began to persecute the "raht-livin', land-lovin' Ganiks," the fickle Kleesahks chose to side with the newcomers against their own co-religionists, it seemed, for Bowley often spoke of the turncoats most disparagingly, calling them "phony Kuhmbuhluhners" and "rat finks"—which last was a term Erica had not heard used in hundreds of years.

Some years after the hominids had gone over to the Kuhmbuhluhners, Bowley had continued, an extended family unit of pure-blooded Teenéhdjooks had wandered down from the mountains to the north. They had possessed even more remarkable mental powers than had their predecessor hominids, and their arrival had thus vastly strengthened the Kuhmbuhluhners, who had responded to this strengthening by increasing their holdings at the expense of the Ganiks.

As more and still more farmer Ganiks had been dispossessed, had been offered the bitter choice of giving up their old-time religion, customs and time-hallowed practices or quitting the fertile valleys and glens to try to scratch out a meager existence on stony hillside farms, the bunches had mushroomed in size and aggressiveness. They had quickly learned, however, the utter folly of trying to meet the Kuhmbuhluhners—with their vastly superior weapons, long years of training, discipline and big, predatory horses, all too often aided and abetted by the wiles of the Teenéhdjooks and Kleesahks—in open, man-to-man battle.

So, generation after generation, the way of the bunches had been one of total outlawry, of raiding anyone and everyone—Kuhmbuhluhners, Ahrmehnee and even their fellow Ganiks—of sometimes dodging and sometimes ambushing Kuhmbuhluhner patrols, of a mean and nasty and brutish and often short existence that still seemed to most of them a better life than they would have had amid the never-ending drudgery of the farms whereon they all had been born and reared.

Then had come a few years of glory for the bunches. With the arrival of a renegade Kleesahk, Buhbuh, and his bloody ascendancy to leadership of the main bunch, the tide had seemed to turn . . . briefly.

Apart from his size and his longevity, Buhbuh had had, it seemed, few of the rare talents of his ilk, being far more manlike and, to judge by many of his actions over the years, more than a little deranged. A son of one of the leading Kleesahks, he had arrived among the Ganik bunch in his mid-teens, already seven feet tall, riding a stolen Northorse—the oversize draft-type horses used mostly by traders to draw their wains and wagons—and wielding a Kuhmbuhluhner greatsword easily with but one hand.

Within a month or so, he had hacked his way to the overall leadership with that sword, a leadership he was to retain until his death in the course of the great rout of the Ganik main bunch on the Tongue of Soormehlyuhn, a total of between sixty and seventy years.

One of his earliest acts had been the leading of the massed Ganik bunches in the taking of the area where the present main camp was situated. This area had been held by a vassal of the King of Kuhmbuhluhn and his retainers, who had been for some years engaged in stripping the rearmost caves of many hundred-weights of steel, iron, copper and sundry other metals. Pressed back and back by the swarming horde of the Ganiks, the defenders had finally taken refuge in the areas of the caves from which had come the metals. Yet when Buhbuh had at length pepped up his bunches to go in after the Kuhmbuhluhners, no living defenders were to be found, and none had ever known how they had escaped the Ganiks.

Erica thought that she knew the answer to that particular question, however. For large as the complex of man-made caves had been, one airshaft would not have been sufficient; two or possibly three would have been needed. Clearly, no one had used the one she had found, else there would have been rungs already in place within it, but that still left others.

And so Buhbuh had established himself in the caves, using them for home, stables, storehouse and treasury. He had personally led one or two big raids each year, sometimes on the

Kuhmbuhluhners, but more often against the Ahrmehnee. In addition, he had demanded and received first choice of all loot taken by any of the bunches. Most of the inanimate loot had disappeared into the recesses of his caves. Women had always been turned over to his bullies, for the huge part-human had been apparently of an asexual nature, never having been known to have shared his caves and his monstrous bed with either woman or man in all of the long years he reigned.

Not contented with the Ganik men and boys who straggled in from time to time to join the bunches, Buhbuh and his bullies had taken to riding among the hill farms of the Ganiks and persuading—which word Erica read as "impressing"—any likely-looking men and boys to ride away with them, also using these forays upon their own folk to acquire anything that appealed to them or that seemed to be of value, as well as to kidnap or lightheartedly gang-rape any likely female they chanced across.

When Buhbuh took over, the total of all of the bunches—main and satellite—had been between two and three thousand. At the moment of his death, however, that total had swelled to more than six thousand outlaw Ganiks. So many had there been that in order to minimize interecine warfare, existing bunch territories had had to be strictly assigned and the borders clearly marked. Then, too, more and new territories to the south and the southwest had had to be opened and new-made bunches assigned to them. The bunch that had captured Erica had been one of these.

With such overwhelming numbers at his beck and call, Buhbuh had kept the Ahrmehnee borders in a state of almost constant turmoil, nor had he ignored the hated Kuhmbuhluhners. Many of the fertile valleys and glens seized by these non-Ganiks had been rendered untenable due to the constant raids and incursions from year to year. The few that remained in Kuhmbuhluhner hands were those that had been massively fortified and garrisoned with seasoned warriors. Bowley noted that the base of the current persecutors of the bunches, Sandeeskaht, was one of the strongest such places.

When the news had reached Buhbuh that the vast majority of the fearsome Ahrmehnee warriors had been summoned to assemble in the far northeast and that even the grim Maidens of the Moon had ridden to join with them, he had speedily gathered thousands of his own men and mounted a larger raid than had ever before been launched against the ancient enemy.

There had been but little resistance during the first few weeks of the incursion. The bunches had merrily murdered and raped and pillaged and tortured and burned, filling their bellies with stolen grain and Ahrmehnee flesh, while sending back to the main camp long pony trains of assorted loot.

But then the first disaster struck. A contingent of the Ganik raiders, over a thousand strong, had unexpectedly met in the course of a swing far to the east some hundreds of heavily armed non-Ahrmehnee warriors and had been almost annihilated by them—would have been, had not another Ganik bunch about equal in size to the first chanced upon the battle and swung the victory in the Ganik favor.

Then Buhbuh and his personal force had discovered that they were being tracked, pursued, by a force of Ahrmehnee warriors. He had deliberately led them and the Moon Maidens who had subsequently joined them out onto the plateau known as the Tongue of Soormehlyuhn. There he had ambushed them and driven them to bay against the face of a low cliff, gradually whittling them away with attack after attack of his thousands. There had been but few of them remaining, and many of those were wounded, when Buhbuh led the Ganiks in another full-scale charge that would surely have ended the affair.

But then the second disaster struck the unsuspecting Ganiks. A line of bowmen who looked nothing like Ahrmehnee, but somewhat like Kuhmbuhluhners, appeared atop the cliff against which the Ganiks' prey were ranged. These proved to be master bowmen, and very soon their black-shafted arrows were slaying Ganik after Ganik, knocking them off their ponies' backs to be trampled to death.

Then, down a steep and shaly slope to the right of the charging Ganik thousands, came rank upon rank of steel-clad men on big, armored horses and armed with lances, axes, longswords, sabers and iron maces. When they reached level ground, they so maneuvered that they struck the Ganik mob—poorly armed by any standards and pony-mounted—from both the right flank and the rear.

Most of these strangers fought and rode their way completely through the horde of Ganiks, then formed up on the left flank of the now-halted and milling bunches and struck them yet again. From Bowley's description, Erica could be confident that the Ganik losses had been appalling, to say the least. When Buhbuh had reined about and set his Northorse at its fastest pace—a lumbering trot—toward the southwest, the battered Ganiks had quickly streamed in his wake.

Bowley himself had not seen Buhbuh die, but he had had the account from several who had. The Northorse had been seriously hurt in the first onslaught of the strangers and had at length fallen, sending Buhbuh tumbling. The Kleesahk had then doffed his barrel helm, dropped his quiver of darts and even his huge sword and set off at a run almost as fast as a pony's. But a big armored man on a large black stallion had spurred up behind the fleeing leader and split his head to the eyes and beyond with an oversized battleaxe.

The survivors of the battle had fled at their fastest speed—ahorse, afoot, on hands and knees, any possible way to escape their blood-mad pursuers. Erica thought that that must have been the very gang of barbarians that she and Jay Corbett and the Broomtown men had watched coming off that plateau as if the hounds of hell were hot on their trail.

The fearsome strangers and the Ahrmehnee and Moon Maidens had broken off the pursuit at the edge of the plateau, and the battered and bemused and by then leaderless Ganiks were just beginning to stop and think and gather and try to organize the tattered remnants when the third disaster struck.

Chapter XI

Along with the written rendition of the strategy he had outlined to his force, Bili of Morguhn sent to the prince a request for the loan of as many more of the Kleesahks as that portion of the kingdom could spare. Prince Byruhn sent him an even dozen, along with a wholehearted endorsement of his plan.

The usual week-long rest period lengthened into two, then three weeks; it took that long for the blacksmiths to finish fashioning the massive hardware items that Bili had ordered to specifications drawn up by Lieutenant Frehd Brakit and Pah-Elmuh.

Once completed, the order was loaded onto a two-ox wain, which took its place in line behind other wains loaded down with scores of wood axes of various types, saws, crowbars, sledges, wooden mallets, chain and cordage of differing sizes and strengths, adzes, planes and assorted other tools of the carpenter's trade. In addition, there were spare weapons, tents, buckets, supplies for man and horse, all the impedimenta necessary for the establishment of an encampment intended to house in excess of three hundred warriors for an indefinite period of time.

The distance between Sandee's Cot and the Ganiks' main camp, which Bili and his reconnaissance party had traveled in only two days, required more than six days for the column. Once, long ago, there had been a true wagon road between the present location of the Ganik stronghold and a spot just east of Sandee's Cot, where it had intersected with the Royal Road. But that had been more than fifty years past, before the late and unlamented Buhbuh and his horde had driven out the small Kuhmbuhluhn garrison and themselves occupied the shelf.

All of the logs of that road had long since rotted away.

Brush and even trees had grown up to narrow it to little more than a pony track, so long hours of hard labor had been required to widen sections of it sufficiently for the wains to pass along it.

Finally, however, almost a full week after leaving Sandee's Cot, the huge, patient oxen drew the huge, creaking wains into the area chosen for the campsite. That was about noon. Only three hours later, Brakit and Pah-Elmuh already were choosing and marking trees for the woodcutters, then selecting and marking the routes along which the felled and trimmed trees were to be snaked to the points where the artisans would take over. Since there were two of these points, fairly widely separated, it was decided to do most of the felling at a place an equal distance from both, or as nearly so as possible.

Work began at all three sites the next morning, even while two more teams of warriors-cum-laborers hewed and hacked and sweated and cursed and slowly cleared the paths for the logs and the oxen that would drag them into place. There were two Kleesahks with each working party, not including Pah-Elmuh, who stayed close to Brakit at all times. The huge hybrids quickly proved their worth when a mob of several hundred Ganiks came down from the shelf, armed to the teeth, riding fast, clearly bound for the woodcutters, who perforce working atop a ridge, were clearly visible from the Ganik camp.

But at a mindspoken signal from Pah-Elmuh, all of the Kleesahks dropped whatever metal tools they were using and stood in silence, unmoving as so many massive statues. Then the screams and warcries of the oncoming mob of Ganiks suddenly became cries of consternation, shouted questions and scarce-believing curses. The shaggy, smelly multitude passed within bare yards of the woodcutting party, looked directly at some of them, yet saw them not.

And almost the same thing occurred as the baffled Ganiks swung around and headed back for their camp. Their chosen path took them directly across one of the lanes being cleared for snaking the logs, and they rode their little ponies between two groups of the warrior-workers, yet obviously could not see the men who could have easily reached out and touched them.

In the days that followed, these occurrences became almost

commonplace and the workers quickly became accustomed to freezing in place, doing nothing that would make a noise, as larger or smaller contingents of Ganiks searched for them in vain. Of course, this invariably slowed down the work, but Bili and the other officers were well content to lose hours or even days of work time rather than find themselves in combat against the vastly overwhelming numbers of the enemy at a place and a time not of their choosing.

But Bili also knew that the Ganiks were going to have to be nibbled at to put them in the proper mood so that when the time was ripe his plans might work smoothly, with full Ganik participation, if not willing cooperation. But he had already formulated schemes to that end, nor was he much longer in putting those schemes into operation.

"Them damn Kleesahks and Kuhmbuhluhn bastids is flat a-scarin' the shit outen the fellers down ther, Ehrkah," Merle Bowley informed Erica the Goddess one night, adding, "Ain' hardly none of 'em too lowng awn brains, nohow, so they's allus a-scairt of enythin they don' unnerstan' . . . and it's a whole lots they don' unnerstan'."

It had been bad enough, thought Erica, when Horseface and his hundreds had been unable to find a fairly large group of foemen that watchers on the shelf could clearly see. That had even shaken the placid Horseface for a while, until Bowley and a couple of the older bullies had patiently explained to their bemused comrade that it was simply a case of hominid magic, such as had confounded to death the Ahrmehnee invaders of long years ago.

Then, for almost two full weeks, there had been alarms—dozens, sometimes—every day and some nights as well. So many cliffside sentries had sent their companions galloping back with word of large bodies of Kuhmbuhluhners advancing across the ridges, or marching east or west along the track or even in the process of scaling the cliff faces, that the Ganiks and their ponies had been run ragged dashing hither and yon. Usually, moreover, when the mobs and the bullies reached the supposedly threatened areas, it was to see no trace of the purported threat and to hear only the witless babbling of the sentries about how the armored Kuhmbuhluhners had suddenly just vanished into thin air.

Merle had at once suspected that hidden Kleesahks, down

below, had addled the sentries' minds, convincing the hapless men that they really saw what they thought and reported they saw. He countered this wily tactic—more or less—by posting roving groups of a bully and a dozen or so men on a route that ran along some hundred yards behind the line of sentry posts. Their orders were to find a high point away from the edges and see if *they* could spot whatever the men directly on the edges reported. Sometimes this had worked, other times it had not.

Then, half of a patrol had ridden back in from a circuit of the surrounding hills. All of the Ganiks in that hundred, even their leader, a bully named Weasel Welch, had been nearly out of their wits, literally white with fear. It seemed that at one minute the second hundred had been strung out behind them, and in the next minute they were gone, ponies and all!

Merle had been gathering and mounting a force to go out looking for the men when they appeared to sentries along the cliffs. Bursting out of the woods, the other half of the patrol whipped their ponies along the track, riding in silence but with many a backward glance, as if old Plooshuhn himself were hot on their heels. Nor did one of them even so much as slow until all were back up on the shelf.

The various versions of their story were all disjointed and vividly colored by their superstitious terror of the living dead, but by the expedient of taking a scrap from here and a bit from there, Merle was able to piece out the whole fabric of the fantastic tale.

At one and the same time that the group behind had become invisible to the group ahead, so had the group ahead vanished from the sight of the group behind. What had replaced the leading group had been at first a wavery, unstable patch of smoky fog. As the shaken men had watched, this cloud had grown wider, higher, denser, and then out of it, mounted on his big, familiar, dappled Northorse, clad in stained and hacked and dented armor, had ridden the ghost of their dead leader, Buhbuh the Kleesahk!

His contrabasso voice booming from within his closed helm, waving his six-foot sword in emphasis—as he always had done in vehemence—so violently that the long darts rattled in the case slung across his back, he had warned them all of the terrible fate awaiting them should they not heed his advice and flee the shelf to follow the farmer Ganiks south and west, but rather should try to fight this host which now opposed them. Many of this host actually were, he assured the terror-struck men, ghosts like himself, murderous and unkillable ghosts of those killed by the Ganik bunches over the years.

The gist of the warnings had been that, should the bunch continue aggressive movements against the host now opposing them, many would die and many others would simply disappear . . . forever, snatched to an eternal death of torment by demons. Also, rocks and fire would fall from the skies as they had so fallen on the very day Buhbuh had died. Others who did not heed his warnings would have the earth open beneath them and swallow them up, entire.

Some attested that Buhbuh had then just disappeared, but most claimed that the apparition had reined about and ridden back into the dense cloud of smoky fog, which then had slowly become smaller and more wavery before dissipating altogether.

Being a rational man, Merle naturally did not believe a word of the tale. Of course, he recognized the possibility that it was another instance of Kleesahk witchery, but it did not smack of any illusions he had ever heard of Kleesahks casting. He thought it far more likely that, their weak and unstable minds already roiled by the occurrences of the last few days, this group had commenced to lose the stomach for fighting the Kuhmbuhluhners and Kleesahks and had convinced themselves and each other that the spirit of a respected leader had now given them firm grounds for running.

He felt just then like either killing them all, then and there, or telling them to get on their ponies and skeedaddle, but realizing that either course might be a mistake with the other Ganiks so agitated, he set the tone by laughing at the men who claimed to have seen and heard Buhbuh, mocking them, making light of their fears. Loyally, the other bullies had emulated him . . . in public. Privately, however, they were all worried, confused and more than a little frightened. So, too, was Merle Bowley, but he confided in only one person: Erica.

Soon after Bowley had taken up swimming and had discontinued the common Ganik practice of wearing clothing until it rotted off his body, Erica had become aware of a physical attraction to him and, never having seen any reason to stay chaste for long, had begun sharing her huge old bed with him, now and again. With hundreds of years of experience in lovemaking, Erica was a good teacher, and Bowley had proved to be a quick learner, so quick that both soon were deeply satisfied one with the other and Erica, for her own part, found herself constantly postponing her departure and even trying to think of ways to persuade him to accompany her when depart she finally did.

Even in his primitive state, she had found Merle Bowley to be an admirable man, and that was *before* he became her lover, she took pains to remind herself. Could he enjoy the benefits of a proper education, of long exposure to a more sophisticated culture than the general brutishness of the bestial Ganiks, what wonders might come of his native intelligence, his rare innovativeness, his natural quality of leadership?

Of course, his present body was already encroaching on middle age, but with her to sponsor him, to twist and to wheedle Dave Sternheimer as only she knew how, there was not a thing to prevent Bowley from receiving a new, young body and learning to transfer his mind to it. Other exceptional people had been brought into the Center in just that way, over the centuries. So why not Merle Bowley?

But first she had to get him away from here before his present body was chopped into catmeat by either the grim Kuhmbuhluhners or the increasingly hysterical Ganiks. Try as she might, she still could not blame the men of Kuhmbuhluhn for what they were doing, for the more she was around the common run of Ganiks, the more she felt that if any race fully deserved extermination, it was assuredly them.

Carefully following in Pah-Elmuh's footsteps in order to avoid becoming the first victim of the various defensive mantraps ranged about the area, Bili examined the siege engines designed by Frehd Brakit and assembled under his and Pah-Elmuh's supervision. They were without a doubt the largest specimens he had ever seen, of a size to dwarf him and every other pure-man on the site.

Looking at the towering pile of monstrous boulders that had been gathered for missiles, he was glad that he was not on one of the engine crews.

"They're all ready, then, Brakit? Both here and at the other site?"

"Awaiting but your order, my lord duke. Within a quarter hour of receiving your word, the first boulders will be in the air," was the quick reply.

"Very well, Brakit," Bili nodded. "We won't need you today, but stand ready from dawn tomorrow."

Then, turning to the huge Kleesahk, he mindspoke, "Elmuh, I'll need you and all of the Kleesahks, tonight."

Leaning on his long stabbing spear and listening to an endless story being recounted by Herb Cantrell, the mounted sentry who shared this dark and isolated post with him, Ratface Coulson was taking sensual pleasure in the cool breeze blowing from off the ridges and ruffling his hair and beard; the day just past had been a scorcher.

Herb had just reached an interesting portion of the tale when his pony, tethered a few yards behind them, began to whuffle and snort and stamp. Cantrell broke off, muttering "Naow, whutinell's done got inta thet damn, dumb-ass pony, enyhaow? You rackon I awts to ride fo' the p'trol, Ratface?"

"Sheeiit," was the scornful reply of the spearman. "You's nervouser nor a ole hen, Herb. Mos' likely thet crazy critter jes' got hissef a good whiff of treecat, is awl. It's one out ther, and the wind be raht, raht naow."

Clenching and reclenching his hand on the shaft of his own spear, Cantrell tried to keep a quaver from his voice. "You . . . you *sees* a treecat? Is . . . is he *close*?"

"Aw, don'tchew got gettin' your dang bow'ls in no uproar," Herb chided. "Naw, I ain' seed no treecat, but I did see me tracks of one, a big 'un, too, day afore yestiddy, awn p'trol' out ther."

But it had not been a treecat that had spooked the pony. Rather had it been the thirty men and women and the twelve Kleesahks who had scaled the cliff face not ten feet from the sentry post and filed away in the darkness toward the nearest huddle of huts and tents.

Stealthily, the party had crossed the succession of ridges and hollows, using the trees and brush to help mask them and their movements until they were close enough to the shelf for the Kleesahks' mental projections to cloud the minds of the sentries on the verges.

But the Kleesahk talent could hide only sight, not sound; therefore, none of this party wore armor of any description, and their weapons had been padded with folds of cloth or leather. Also, every member of the group was a mindspeaker.

Across the four hundred feet of rocky grassland, the men and women and Kleesahks moved almost as soundlessly as ghosts. They were clad from head to foot in cloth or soft leather in shades of black and dark green or brown, the angles of their faces darkened with streaks of soot. Because their mission was one of silent murder, none bore sword or saber. Daggers, dirks, a few hangers, short-handled belt axes, wire garrotes and a cosh or two—these were the ideal weapons for the grisly task that lay before them. Their tall, human leader carried the only other item which might, by stretching the meaning of the word, be classed as a weapon: a fist-sized chunk of yellow sulphur.

The gory job was done quickly and efficiently, and in only an hour, the dark, silent group made their way back toward the cliff-line. On the return, however, several of the huge Kleesahks bore the bound bodies of unconscious Ganiks slung across their broad backs . . . and Bili no longer carried his chunk of sulphur.

Major Jay Corbett had not liked the idea of another long halt, for all that they had seen no slightest trace of human life or passage, for all that Johnny Skinhead Kilgore assured him that they were well south of any of the Ganik settlements. Something deep in his mind had warned him to keep moving, fast. But he had had no option; it had been either halt for an indefinite period or stand ready to bury the corpse of Dr. Harry Braun, shortly.

Despite all of the drugs lavished on him and the care with which he had been handled since they had left the small hidden plateau, the injured scientist not only had not shown any signs of improvement, he seemed to be getting worse. When not comatose, he was more often raving than rational, and his confessed murder of his associate, Dr. Erica Arenstein, was thus no longer a secret privy only to Corbett and Gumpner. The entire command had heard it at least two or three times over.

Consequently, when old Johnny and the hunters chanced onto a reasonable site for a long-term encampment, Corbett first looked it over himself, then went back to lead the rest of his column to it.

If halt he had to, the location was good—more than two kilometers off the track, with three high ridges between it and the track. The valley was fairly broad as such valleys went, with more than adequate water and with many weeks' worth of graze. Moreover, the spot he had chosen for the camp offered splendid defensibility, especially if the defenders were his Broomtown riflemen.

Within a couple of days, the veteran field soldiers had established a reasonably comfortable camp of lean-to shelters complete with soft and fragrant beds of blankets spread over close-packed conifer tips. Game had proved to be both plentiful and much easier to approach than it had been in the relatively heavily settled areas to the north.

Corbett had ridden out with both hunting and reconnaissance groups and, like all of them, had detected no traces of man except back, along the track, and even these had looked to be a year or more old. Old Johnny maintained, and the officer was more and more inclined to believe him, that those few who did ride south for whatever reason almost always used the wider, easier track farther east, along the border of the Ahrmehnee *stahn*. Nonetheless still tugged at by a vague unease, the major posted guards on the perimeter by day and by night.

In sharp contrast to the failing Braun, the middle-aged Ganik appeared to be the picture of health, despite his more recent injury. Although he had ridden every step of the way in the saddle of his horse, chatting and joking and cursing along with the troopers, and even had ridden along on several hunting parties, the bones of his arm and clavicle seemed to be knitting nicely, and after the first few days on the move he had declined Corbett's offer of painkilling drugs.

"Aw, naw, them stickin' thangs meks me sleepy, mos'ly. 'Sides, I don' need 'em no mo'—yestiddy awn the hunt, I founded me a whole bag fulla toothache roots."

"What," demanded Corbett mildly, "in the hell are toothache roots, Johnny?"

Wordlessly, the Ganik dropped the reins over the pommel knob, thrust his good hand into a narrow bag hung from his belt and then held the open hand out for the officer's inspection. On the broad palm rested a half-dozen thin, grayish, stringy roots.

"Try you sum, Majuh, they's good fer enythin' whut hurts you, enytahm it hurts you, and they don' mek you sleepy, lahk them stick-you thangs does, neithuh."

Corbett accepted the proffered roots, but postponed trying them until a later time. However, from then on, he could save the almost expended supply of drugs for Braun.

Burdened with the still-gnawing presentiment of trouble fast approaching, Corbett decided that the unit would remain for a week, maximum. If Braun showed no improvement in that time, they would pack up and push on, regardless.

But, strangely enough, once the officer and his assistants had again gone through the long, hard, nauseating procedure of opening and draining the scientist's leg, Braun did begin to improve . . . if longer and increasingly longer periods of lucid consciousness filled with whimperings, free-flowing tears and querulous, nagging complaining about anything and everything could be classed as improvement.

Despite the almost-constant annoyance, however, Corbett did consider Braun improved. He still was running a low-grade fever, but the officer thought that most likely was to be expected for a while, at least until he could get the injured man back to where he could receive the benefits of medical treatment by a real doctor.

Jay Corbett intended to find an excuse for promoting the two troopers—Thurston and Farmer—who had been sharing the nursing of the whining and petulant scientist; they showed the patience of Job. What with keeping their patient and his bedding clean and dry—Braun pissed himself several times each day, claiming that his intense pain robbed him of all control, but Corbett, who had been in rather severe agony himself at various times, believed not a word of it and wished that he had the materials and knowledge to catheterize the selfish, childish bastard—cooking for him and themselves, feeding him, and seeing after their own mounts and the two that carried Braun's litter on the march, the officer wondered just how and when the two men managed to get any sleep at all.

Toward the end of their second week in the valley camp, with the swellings noticeably subsiding in the visible portions of Braun's injured leg, most of the discolorations beginning to show signs of fading, and Braun himself becoming restive and all but unbearable to be around, Corbett had some of the men rig a padded seat and backrest under a shady tree near the bank of the swift-flowing stream and had the doctor—screaming and sobbing that they were killing him—borne down to and installed upon it.

As trooper Thurston gently tucked a blanket around the scientist's legs and lower body, Braun raised his head, looked up at Corbett with teary eyes and said, between his snuffles, "Why can't you just shoot me and be done with it, Corbett? Does torturing me this way give you a charge? You know, surely, that if I do get back to the Center alive, you and the rest of these pigs will rue the day you hurt and humiliated me, don't you?" After a very long sniff and a swallow, he added, with a measure of his old arrogance and pomposity, "You know, even if these half-civilized bastards don't, just how powerful I am on the Council and the Board of Science, and I . . ."

Jay Corbett used his command voice to the troopers. "Very good, men, thank you and dismiss. You, too, Thurston—I'll call you if I need you."

When the men were gone beyond easy listening, the officer squatted before Braun and said, "Doctor, you are right about one thing: I don't like you, I never have liked you, even in the happy centuries when I didn't know you very well. Now that I've come to know you far more intimately than I'd have ever preferred, come to know just what a rotten excuse for a human being Dr. Harry Braun is, my dislike for you has doubled, in spades! I think I've hidden that dislike of you from most of these men, but your own inexcusable behavior has eroded every bit of respect they ever had for you, and along with it, I'm afraid, went a good deal of the mystique that once surrounded all of us from the Center. Any day now, now that your ravings and tantrums have shown these sepoys of ours that our feet are clay, we can expect them to recognize us for the exploitive, parasitic vampires we really are and hoist us on our own petard. And you know, Braun, I can hardly wait for that day of final reckoning."

Braun's face had paled to as light a hue as the dark Ahrmehnee skin would fade. "If such a day ever does come, you damned traitor, you won't be there to see it. You've just sealed your fate. When Dave Sternheimer hears what you just told me . . ."

Corbett smiled coldly. "Ah, but he won't, Braun."

"Oh, yes, he will," Braun snapped. "The only way you can prevent it is to kill me outright, stop torturing, degrading me, humiliating me in front of these trained apes of yours."

The officer shook his head, his lips still bent in his frigid smile. "After all I've been through and put many of my men through to get your living carcass this far, Braun, I mean to see that you get all the way back alive . . . alive enough, at least, to be able to transfer to another body before this one dies. Oh, yes, my good Doctor, you'll get back alive, because I have a use for a living Dr. Harry Braun, back at the Center. Oh, and you'll not be saying a word against me to Dr. Sternheimer or to anyone else . . . ever."

Braun sniffed disparagingly. "There's not a thing you can do to stop me, once I'm back, Corbett."

"No, there isn't, really, Braun," Corbett agreed, but then added, "However, if you do say more than is good for *us*, then I would find it necessary to tell Dr. Sternheimer of some of your misdeeds, you see. I know Dr. Sternheimer and his values quite well, Braun, and I know which of us two would get the really dirty end of the stick from him. I have *said* some things, agreed, but you, Braun, you have *done* things."

"What are you talking about, Corbett, Center rumors? Fagh, not even an undereducated yokel like you could be stupid enough to think Dave Sternheimer would believe—"

"Just shut up, Braun, unless you'd like to hurt—really hurt—for a while," Corbett snapped, then returned to his softly mocking tone. "No, Braun, no rumors these, but facts. You've been raving from fever for weeks now, when you weren't babbling under sedation. During that time, you've told me some very interesting things, Dr. Harry Braun. If Dr. Sternheimer and certain others knew of some of those things . . . well, I'll leave it to your mind. I think your imagination is likely more vivid than mine."

"I . . . what . . . what did I . . . you can't think anyone would believe anything I said in . . . in delirium?" spluttered Braun.

"No, not really," agreed the squatting officer blandly. "But Dr. Sternheimer might decide to try pentothal or hypnotism, or maybe both together, and the things I'll tell him—if you force me to tell him—would give him some questions to ask, a place to start from.

"As to exactly what you told me, that is my—rather, *our*—secret, unless, until, you force me to make your various misdeeds public knowledge. You have been a very busy, very amoral, very malicious, backbiting, back*stabbing*, self-serving, utter bastard, over the centuries, haven't you, Braun?"

He paused, studying Braun as if he were some rare, loathsome insect impaled upon the point of a pin. "All right, in case your cesspool brain is churning up the thought that I'm just trying to delude you, that I really know nothing of any value or importance, I'll tell you one of the little dirty secrets you detailed to me.

"I am aware, thanks to your babbling, that you murdered Erica Arenstein, back there in that defile. You lured her into dismounting to help you, then you tried to shoot her. When that didn't work, you caved in her head with the barrel of your pistol. Then you just left her there where she'd fallen, rode on to catch up with Gumpner and the others and concocted a fable about her having been killed by Ganiks.

"Now, Braun, you know, I know, the whole damn Center knows, how Dr. Sternheimer feels—felt—about Erica, not that he ever would publicly admit it, for reasons I won't here enter into. But I do not think that he would be at all merciful to the man who coldly murdered his secret light-o'-love and left her body to be found and eaten by cannibals. Do you?"

"All right, damn you, I believe you," said the tight-lipped scientist. "What's the bottom line? What do you want? There's no possible way I can get you a seat on the Board; you're not a scientist or physician, not even a psychologist. And you're already on the Council. So what?"

Corbett shrugged. "Just some cooperation, Braun, that's all. A little friendly cooperation is all that I want from you. I want your vote on anything I propose in Council, from now on, for starters. I want to know that I'll also have your voice speaking for my interests at meetings of the Board."

He paused, as if about to add more, then smiled—really smiled, this time—and, patting Braun's good leg gently, said, "But we can go into all of this another time, old man, when perhaps you'll be feeling better. We don't want to overtire you on this first day out of bed, do we?"

Chapter XII

After a very early and very urgent summons had taken him from her bed, Merle Bowley returned a little before midday, his face drawn with worry. After two full goblets of one of the strongest of the old wines Erica had found stored far back in the warren of cave rooms, the senior bully slumped into a chair and gave her the shocking news.

"More'n two hunnert of Crushuh Hinton's bunch is a-layin' daid in they cabins, Ehrkah—throats cut, haids bashted in or choketed. Ole Crushuh hissef, 'long with everbody was in his cabin, is *gone*, no trace of 'em nowher, and it stinks so bad of brimstone in ther a body cain' hardly breathe fer it."

Erica wrinkled her forehead, trying to make some rhyme or reason out of all of this. "But Merle, why in the world would he have killed all his men in their sleep? Could he have just flipped out?"

Bowley shook his head forcefully. "*He* din't kill 'em, Ehrkah! It was a bunch of Kuhmbuhluhners and Kleesahks musta come up the cliffs las' naht, you kin see wher they come up, not a dozen feet fum wher the dang sentries wuz at. And they tracks goes raht crost of the ground inta the bunch's camp, then back the same way they come in—twenny, thutty mens and mebbe twenny Kleesahks, too."

"I can see why they'd kill those Ganiks, Merle," said Erica. "After all, they are at war with us. But why carry any away?"

He sighed deeply, and his worried frown deepened. "I shore don' know the answers yet, Ehrkah . . . but I got me a plumb awful feelin' we-awls gonna fin' out damn quick-like."

The bodies of the murdered Ganiks were, of course, not allowed to go to waste, but were equally divided among the other bunches of Ganiks. It was while One-ear McNamara's bunch were butchering their share that a nearby herd of the ponies suddenly tore off at a mad, terrified gallop, and when a brace of One-ear's subordinates loped out to try to find out what had spooked the small equines, their discovery was grisly and frightening.

The terribly burned cadaver of one of Crushuh Hinton's bullies lay upon the rocky ground. In addition to the profusion of savage burns, the body seemed not to possess an unbroken bone, and, moreover, the skull and body had burst open, as if it had fallen from a considerable height.

Then, even as they were running at top speed back to tell of this horror, the similarly charred body of another of the missing bunch leader's bullies plunged from out of the clear sky to slam onto the ground a few yards ahead of them.

Borne by white-faced men with trembling lips riding lathered ponies, the news of these upsetting occurrences was still being spread throughout the scattered camps on the shelf when the only patrol that had ridden out that day came up onto the shelf at a hard gallop to gasp out to everyone within hearing that dead Buhbuh had appeared to them as to the previous patrol and reiterated his warnings. The ghostly Kleesahk had informed them that demons had taken earthly forms in order to kill most of Crushuh Hinton's men and carry off for the demonic purpose of fiendish and endless torture that bully and his followers. He had gone on to say that there remained but little time for the Ganiks to safely flee southward. Those unwise enough to remain would know, when the stones and boulders began to fall from the sky, that very soon the earth would open to swallow them up.

Then, as with the other patrol so visited, the apparition had reined about and ridden slowly out of sight into the misty haze that had produced him. The patrol had reined about, too. Frightened out of their wits, they had raced pellmell for the relative safety of the shelf camps.

Sometime during that night, between four and five hundred Ganiks gathered their meager possessions, mounted their ponies and filed down the single trail to head south along the main track, having clubbed down the bully commanding the trail guards and persuaded those guards to accompany them south.

When the murder and defections were discovered early the next morning, Horseface, Counter and several others were all for mounting a sizable force, chasing down the deserters and either killing them or bringing them back for torture, but Merle would not hear of it, saying that the Kuhmbuhluhners would like nothing better than to witness them fighting amongst themselves.

"Let 'em go. They wuz awl the weaklin's, the scairtycats, enyhaow. Weuns is bettuh awf 'thout 'em."

But despite his nonchalant facade, Erica could tell that her lover was shaken, deeply shaken by the shattering series of events. It was to get worse . . . sooner than anyone thought.

For that night rocks began bombarding the length and breadth of the shelf. They ranged in size from chunks about as big as a clenched fist to monstrous boulders weighing two or three hundred pounds. Almost every camp was hit by some of them, and roofs were holed or smashed in entirely, walls were splintered and knocked askew, Ganiks were killed and injured. And the words on almost every lip in the unsleeping camps were the dire predictions of Buhbuh the Kleesahk's ghost.

And when the sleepy, nervous patrol rode out the next day, that was the last anyone saw of them. Merle and the other bullies could not make up their minds whether the patrol had been wiped out by the encircling Kuhmbuhluhners or had simply deserted and ridden south. Merle himself suspected the latter, reasoning that if the patrol had been ambushed and massacred, at least a few of the ponies—many of which had been foaled and reared among the herds on the shelf— would have wandered back, even if no men had survived.

"We've whittled the odds down a trifle, now," Bili of Morguhn, smiling broadly in high good humor, remarked to the gathering of officers of his heterogeneous force. "I have no way of knowing how many of the stinking savages the rocks killed or incapacitated last night or how many they are getting this night, but close on to six hundred of the Ganiks have ridden south along the main track. And I don't doubt but that more of them will leave after that prisoner, Hinton, has serenaded them a few times tomorrow. Pah-Elmuh has so worked on the bastard's mind that I think he really believes that he's being tortured by demons. His screams will lift the hairs on your nape. Let's just hope his voice and heart both hold out long enough to do us some good, to wreck the nerves of some hundreds more of those superstitious buggers."

The tall young nobleman took a sip of ale and went on, "Now, I know that the men and women are getting a bit tired of digging pits and ditches and felling trees and hacking at brush."

There was a chorus of grunts and other indications of a fervent agreement. Bili waited for the noise to subside, then continued, "I know they're wondering just when we'll get in some fighting. Well, I shouldn't think it will be long now. We've stung them cruelly, we're doing more of it at this very minute, we'll do still more tomorrow. More Ganiks will ride south, undoubtedly, and at that juncture I feel certain that whoever is commanding will see the necessity of striking us while he still has the strength to give him a chance of victory over us. Another week, at most, will see it done, one way or the other, that's my feeling."

All the while that Bili spoke, the assembled men and women could hear from the near distance the creaking of ropes, the solid-sounding *thunnks* as massive, hard-swung timber met equally massive thickly padded crossbeam, indicating that one of the oversize siege engines had sped yet another load of stone to arc down upon the main camp of the unhappy Ganiks.

Lieutenant Frehd Brakit and his hard-working engine crews kept at it through most of the night, only halting when they had expended the last of their stones. Then they sped off one more load—another well-charred corpse—and stood down for a few hours of much-needed rest.

Erica, Merle Bowley, Horseface, Lee-Roy, Abner, Owl-eyes Hewlitt and a dozen more of the bullies rode from end to end of the shelf the next morning, assessing the damage . . . and the carnage. It was not until they were riding back that they saw the corpse floating in the lake. At Bowley's command, two of the better swimmers went out and towed the burned and much-battered thing back to shore.

"Enybody thank they knows 'im?" asked Bowley. "Be he anothern of ole Crushuh's bullies?"

"Yeah," nodded Horseface slowly. "I thank he be the one called hissef Bawlbustuh Engel. Looks lahk sumbody he done burnt thet pore man's bawls raht awf, his peckuh, too."

"Shitfahr!" exclaimed Bowley angrily. "Sumbody jes' tell me how in tarnashun is them Kuhmbuhluhn bastids and them fuckin' Kleesahks a-gittin' tortured-to-death bodies and a half a mountun wortht of rocks a night to come down awn us?"

"They've obviously got a battery or two of catapults—rock-throwing devices that are usually used against besieged cities—out there somewhere on one of those ridges," said Erica. "They must be the world's biggest catapults, too, to heave rocks the size of some of the monsters we've seen back there. And that's probably what the Kuhmbuhluhners and the Kleesahks were felling trees for when they first arrived, to build those catapults. Engines that big couldn't have been easily dragged overland to get here—it would've been far less trouble and labor to build them on the spot they were to occupy."

Merle nodded glumly. "I done heerd 'bout thangs lahk thet afore—thangs whut thows rocks and fahrbawls and big ole spears and awl. Probly ain't none the scouts seed 'em cawse of them damn Kleesahks a-hidin' 'em fum 'em. But why in hell ain't we-awl seed 'em fum up heah?"

"They probably have them camouflaged during the day," Erica said, then, noticing the blank looks, elucidated, "Have them covered with leafy branches, things like that, so the positions look just like part of the ridgeline from this distance. That also may be why they only use them by night. That way, we can't see where exactly the rocks are coming from and so we won't know which area to send our men against.

"That's what is going to have to be done, you know, Merle. We're going to have to send a strong force out there to find and to burn those catapults before the damned things pound every living thing on this shelf into blood pudding.

"If whoever did it only hadn't managed to thoroughly bollix up my rifle scope, I might be able to do some terrorizing of my own against those sons of bitches, but . . ." She shrugged.

Merle turned in his saddle. "Owl-eyes, Horseface, yawl git back down ther and git three, fo' hunnert mens—*good* mens, too, none of them shithaids, heanh. Don' brang nobody whut cain' see good at naht, neethuh. I wawnts 'em strung out awl lowng of the top edges of the shelf, tonaht. Moon's damn neah full, t'naht, so sumbody they oughta see wher them fuckin' rocks and awl's a-comin' fum.

"We comes to know wher they a-settin' at, we'll tek us the whole dang bunch and go burn 'em up, then we'll stomp them fuckin' Kuhnbuhluhn bug-tits flat. Naow git!"

They got, and at moonrise Bowley's commands had been carried out, with nearly four hundred Ganiks standing or kneeling or sitting or squatting all along the winding, uneven edges of the cliffs. Nor were these inordinate numbers of sentries unnoticed by watchers just inside the forest beyond the track.

"Cat brother Chief," Whitetip farspoke Bili of Morguhn, "smelly ones beyond the counting are atop the cliffs, at least one of them to every two-leg length for all of the distance. But they do not seem armed for fighting and no ponies are with them. They simply stare out across the ridges."

"Someone over there has finally dusted off his brains," Bili smilingly mindspoke Pah-Elmuh and Rahksahnah. "Whitetip says that there's at least one Ganik to every couple of yards of the cliffs, and you can safely bet that with a full moon, or almost that, tonight, their orders are to spot our engines."

Rahksahnah sighed. "Then they'll probably attack the engines tomorrow. I wonder how many Maidens will die defending them?"

"None, if I can help it, my dear, and none of the men or the Kleesahks, either. I have other sights than those of operating siege engines planned for the hundreds of eyes on those cliffs tonight," Bili beamed into her mind.

"But I thought . . . thought you *wanted* them to attack, my Bili." There was puzzlement in her return beaming.

He nodded. "Oh, but I do—no war has ever yet been ended finally and completely without a battle. But there are still too many of them for our slender force to take on with any hope of success. I trust that the little entertainment tonight will substantially reduce those numbers, send some hundreds more of them fleeing southward."

At Bili's word, Pah-Elmuh and all seventeen of his Kleesahks left at a ground-eating lope faster than the trot of a horse, weaving easily between the treetrunks and other obstacles of the nighttime woods. They soon were ranged in a single line facing the cliffs, just inside the woods that bounded the other side of the track at the base of those cliffs.

Pah-Elmuh hated bloodshed, thought all of mankind to be

born hurters and killers, incredibly savage toward each other as well as toward beasts. Knowing of old how easily misled and frightened were the common run of Ganiks, it had been his original idea to use the esoteric powers of the Kleesahks to so terrify the cannibals that many if not most of them would flee rather than fight. Bili, seeing in this scheme his duty served with minimum losses from his small squadron, had approved the stratagem, making sure that his men and women cooperated to the fullest possible extent with Pah-Elmuh and the other hybrid semihumans. At the same time, however, the young commander had continued his preparations for the eventual attack by the hard core of the Ganiks. He felt that attack was inevitable, no matter how many cannibals, terrified by Pah-Elmuh and the rest, were sent fleeing as fast as their ponies would bear them down the tracks to the south.

The Kleesahks had carefully rehearsed the events which then unfolded before the gazes—fixed in awe and horror and gut-wrenching terror—of the Ganiks. Even the bullies there found their skins acrawl, while their minds dredged up the shuddery legends that had frightened them as children.

Glowing with an unnatural bluish-green radiance, a pulsing light speedily became a huge and swirling cloud of dense, glowing mist, hovering over the west end of the track. Then, out of that mist, rode a huge armed Kleesahk mounted on a Northorse, glowing as intensely and unnaturally as the cloud that roiled along a few yards behind them. The figures seemed to waver in outline, from time to time, but none of the watchers on the cliffs above failed to recognize both—it was Buhbuh, dead Buhbuh, mounted on the dappled Northorse that had died with him back on the Tongue of Soormehlyuhn.

As the immense hooves of the Northorse paced some foot or more above the ground, the pumpkin-sized head of their dead leader, encased in his tub-sized helmet, was often on the same level—or so it seemed to them, impossible or not—as the unwilling watchers.

Waving his great sword with its very broad, very thick, six-foot-long blade, to emphasize his words as so often he had been seen to do in life, the apparition shouted at them in angry tones, his voice booming hollowly from out the closed and locked helmet.

"Stoopid muthuhfuckuhs!" the revenant roared. "Twicet afore I done give yawl mah warnin'. Them whut heeded me is still livin' and breathin' and they'll awl keep a-doin' it, too. You dumb, bug-tit bastids is plumb *doomed* lessen yawl gits a-headed souf afore of moonup, tomorra. The lucky ones, they'll be kilt owtraht, but yawl pore bastids whut the demons done took them a fancy to, lahk they took a fancy to pore ole Crushuh Hinton . . ."

Slowly, the cliff side of the following mist became less opaque, and through it could be seen a human figure writhing helplessly among crackling tongues of multihued flames. Huge, phantasmal figures seemed to be moving about the wretch, now and then bending over him, and each time they did so, he shrieked in utter agony.

"*Waaaaagh!* Don', *don'* pleez don' do thet to me no mo', *aaaaarrrgh*, PLEEEEZ!" None who had known him could doubt that the screaming, pleading, clearly suffering voice was that of the bunch leader, Crushuh Hinton, and already shuddering, shivering men began to whimper mindlessly in paroxysms of fear.

At a slow walk, the wraith of a Northorse bore his huge, spectral rider along the moonlit track, his progress followed by the boggled gaze of every Ganik along those cliffs. The ghostly rider was followed too by the cloud of luminous mist, within which dark, distorted figures still could be seen to move and from which still came the bloodcurdling shrieks and pleas and screams of Crushuh Hinton, now and then almost drowned out by the fiendish cackling of the demons as they tormented him.

Then the ghost again began to speak. "Thishere be the las' warnin' I'll be a-givin' you mens. I warned the fustes' felluhs thet the demons they meant to kill sum and tek sum away; and the demons they did, they kilt near two hunert and took pore ole Crushuh and them othuh mens.

"I warned the nextes' bunch the rocks they wuz a-gonna fawl agin, lahk they fawled everwher the day I died. And the rocks has done fell two nahts naow, and kilt and mashted up mo' mens. One naht soon, naow, fahr is gonna fawl awn the shelf, demon-fahr, it'll be. And then yawl'll know them ole demons is a-pokin' up the fahrs, a-gittin' 'em ready fer *yawl*. The lucky 'uns, they'll be jes' kilt—lahk I wuz, mah haid laid opun clear to mah eyes wif a big ole axe. Them whut the demons done took a fancy to, they'll be a-jinin' pore ole Crusher, right quick-lahk.

"Yawl ain' gotchew lowng lef' fer to git awn your ponies and do lahk I tol' them mens to start out—ride souf, iffen you wawnts to live. Yawl won' none of you see me aftuh t'naht, no mo'. So yawl awl do whutawl I says, heanh?"

So saying, the phantasm reined about and rode, still not touching the beaten earth of the track with even a single big hoof, into the cloud glowing with wan, blue-green fire. As soon as he and the spectral horse were lost to view in the misty cloud, that cloud began to shrink in upon itself, to grow both denser and dimmer and, finally, to disappear from human sight.

Erica had never seen Merle Bowley so disheartened, so beaten-looking. She quickly crossed the cave to him and laid a hand on his arm. "What is it, Merle? What's happened now?"

He turned a dull-eyed gaze upon her, sighed deeply and said hoarsely, "Don't be lookin' fer your bullies, Lee-Roy and Abner, no more, Ehrkah. Them two wuz part of the bastids whut took awf this mornin', a-ridin' souf. Pore Owl-eyes and some othuhs of the mens trahd to stop 'em, and naow he and them's awl daid, cut down or trompted ovuh."

He pushed past her and sank tiredly into a chair. "Whut with awl the daid 'uns and awl them whut done lit out, naow, the whole bunch is down to way lessen half of whut it wuz whin them Kuhmbuhluhn fuckuhs fust campted up ther in them ridges and commencted a-playin' Kleesahk tricks awn us."

She wondered fleetingly if this was the opportune moment to broach the subject of his coming with her up the airshaft, out of the cave and south, to the Center. Then she decided to wait just a little longer, until she was a bit more certain that his reaction would be one of cooperation rather than opposition to an escape from a place that was rapidly becoming a deathtrap and a situation waxing more and more untenable.

"So what will you do, Merle?" she asked.

"Whut I should awta done fer to staht out, Ehrkah. Hit them fuckin' Kuhmbuhluhners with everthin I still got while I still got it fer to hit 'em with, thet's whut!"

"When?"

"Naow is whin, Ehrkah. Today, soon's Horseface and Counter and the rest as ain' took awf kin git everbody armed and awn they ponies. You kin come iffen you's a mind to, too, but bad as your fahrstick afrahts the ponies, be best you don' brang 'er alawng, this tahm."

Erica Arenstein was not about to ride deliberately into a hack-and-slash contest without a firearm of some sort, so she said, "No, Merle, I'll await you here."

He just nodded, stood up and, with her help, began to don his padded clothing, then the nearly full set of three-quarter plate he wore for serious raids or battles. Just before he set the helmet on his head, he took her body in one steel-sheathed arm and kissed her lips briefly, almost passionlessly. "I'll try fer to mek it back, Ehrkah," were his only words of parting and farewell. Then he settled the helm in its place, buckled the straps securely, stalked clanking out through the high entry, mounted his horse and set it down the terraces toward the lake and the plain beyond.

Everything had seemed to come down at once on Corbett and his hapless command, just as the line of cliffs had come down upon the doomed packtrain, weeks before. One good thing had happened, then nothing but bad.

A hunting party had pursued a wounded deer much farther south than they usually went and Sergeant Cabell had spotted in the near distance a familiar landmark which had told him that they were almost in the territory of one of the reasonably friendly tribes which lived a little to the north and west of Broomtown.

Upon the return of the hunters, Cabell hastened to make a full report to Corbett, and the officer smiled—it was to be his last smile for some time. "Then we've marched farther south than I'd reckoned. That would put us no more than a hundred—a hundred and ten at the outside—kilometers from Broomtown base, itself.

"We'll give Braun a few more days, then we'll hit the track again. It'll be good to get back."

But that evening's examination and rebandaging of Dr. Braun's leg had sent cold prickles racing along Corbett's spine. Seeing the officer suddenly pale, Braun did too.

"What is it, Corbett? Damn you, what is it?"

Jay Corbett sank back onto his haunches and looked his

patient straight in the eye. "It's gangrene, Dr. Braun. I'd hoped earlier that the discolorations would fade as the infections were overcome. Apparently that was just wishful thinking on my part. The only way to save the life of your present body is to amputate this leg, the more of it the better."

"Good God, man!" Braun almost shrieked, his eyes wide and wild. "You don't have the skill to do that kind of a procedure. Or the equipment and supplies, either. If you just tie me down and saw it off, you'll kill me of shock. Then who'll speak for you and your schemes on the Board?"

Corbett just nodded, tiredly, finding that simple act a real effort. He'd been feeling strangely exhausted all day and part of the day before, too, come to think of it.

"No, Braun, don't worry. I'm not going to try to put you through a battlefield amputation. I do have the equipment—there's a full instrument kit with the medical pack—but the drugs are almost all gone. Besides, you're right, it would be premeditated murder, for I don't have the requisite training and skills for such a radical procedure.

"No, in the morning, I'm going to have you tied into the saddle of a mule. Then you and Gumpner and a couple more men will set out at top speed for Broomtown base. I'd not told you this before, but Cabell spotted a landmark he knows, which means we're closer than I'd thought—only some hundred kilometers from the northwestern border of Broomtown. Barring misfortune, you could be there in two or three days. Then you can transfer and let this body finish dying."

But Braun shook his head vehemently, tears welling up in his dark eyes. "Oh, damn you, damn you!" he half-whined. "Haven't you tortured and degraded me enough these last weeks? Do you think I can take the jolting, the pain of riding a damn mule, on just these nauseous little roots? You haven't given me an injection of anything except antibiotics in days, and I know it, too. I can tell the difference between them and drugs, you know."

Corbett sighed. "Doctor, there are only three ampoules of morphine left in the packs, along with a little pentathol. After they are gone, you'll be on toothache roots or nothing. I knew we'd have to move on sooner or later, so I've been hoarding the real drugs against that time."

"*Bullshit!*" Braun snarled. "You just wanted me to suffer,

damn you, wanted to watch me squirm, waiting to hear me beg you for a cessation of the pain, damn you. But I didn't, damn you, I didn't! I'm stronger than you or anybody else gives, has ever given me, credit for."

"Fine," Jay Corbett said soberly. "It's good that you do have a hidden reservoir of strength, Braun, because I think you're going to need it on the ride from here to Broomtown. It's either ride out in the morning, or give me any last requests you have before you go out of your head. Gangrene is not an easy or a pretty death, you know."

But the next morning dawned on disaster. Gumpner and most of the troopers were unable to arise from their blankets, all of them feverish and either writhing and sweating on soggy blankets or in the throes of tooth-chattering chills, their own damp blankets drawn tightly around their shuddering bodies. It was an effort requiring every last ounce of his will for Major Jay Corbett to drag himself out of his own sweat-wet blankets, but his centuries of self-discipline won out, finally . . . for a while.

Sergeant Cabell showed no signs or symptoms of whatever had struck down the rest of the command, nor did Trooper Horner, nor old Johnny Skinhead. So the three became at that juncture the party that would accompany Harry Braun to Broomtown, then send back help to the rest of them.

Under Corbett's supervision, Cabell and Horner put one of the flaring warkaks back on the doctor's big mule, then lifted him into that saddle and tied him in place. The officer gave Cabell the last of the narcotics and a few syringes, warning him to try to make them last.

"Old Johnny will have his bag of toothache roots, of course, and swears that they are common in these mountains. The doctor doesn't like them, but if there's nothing else, he will chew them. Keep going even if he passes out in the saddle, because if he isn't in competent medical hands within two or three days—four, at the outside—he'll be dead, or so far gone that he can't be helped in any way.

"Johnny, you take my horse—he's in better condition than yours is. Cabell, you and Horner take whichever animals you fancy, and spares, too, if you wish. We at least have plenty of mounts."

At that point, the valley began to swim before Corbett's eyes. He stumbled and would have fallen had not Cabell

taken his arm and slowly eased him down into a sitting posture, his back against the trunk of a maple sapling.

"My God, Major, sir, you're hot as a stove! All three of us
can't leave you and the others here. Who'll take care of
you?" Cabell expostulated.

"*Nonono!*" shouted Braun, suddenly. "You heard what he
said, Sergeant. If I don't get back in three days I'll be *dead*!
It's your duty to get me back, to get *me*—Dr. Harry
Braun—back to Broomtown. I'm a highly valuable scientist,
the Center *needs* me, can't you understand that, you cretin?
Major Corbett can be easily replaced if he does die. He's not
valuable to the Center, just another damned soldier."

Jay Corbett had heard little of what Braun shouted, so
loud was the sound of rushing, crashing water in his ears. He
was wondering slowly, vaguely, disjointedly how and when
and why he had arrived on an oceanside beach, when he felt
himself shaken violently. Full consciousness returned as he
looked into the lined, bearded face of old Skinhead Johnny
Kilgore, the Ganik, with the sunlight glinting off his shiny
pate.

"Majuh," he said softly and quickly, "I thank I knows
whut you and the mens has got. Me and my brothuh and my
boy, Lowng Willy, wuz with a bunch sum yars back whut
had done set up camp in a mess of ruins fum way back whin,
and aftuh a coupla weeks, purt neah awl of 'em had done
come down with suthin jes' zackly lahk yawl has, but none of
the three of us got it thet tahm neethuh."

Blinking his eyes rapidly against the salt sweat coursing
down his forehead, Corbett asked, "How many died,
Johnny?"

The older man sighed and averted his eyes. "Bout haf, I
rackons . . . mebbe a maht mo' than haf. But they din't hev
them stick-you thangs, neethuh, of cuss."

Beckoning Cabell, the officer gave his instructions and,
shortly, heedless of Braun's screaming tantrum that they had
not yet left the campsite, the sergeant had gone from man to
suffering man and injected a healthy quantity from the supply
of antibiotics.

After he had given the shot to Corbett, he shook his head
and said, "Major, sir, I still don't think we all ought to just
ride off and leave you like this. Horner and old Johnny, they

ought to be able to get the doctor back. Let me stay here to take care of you and Gumpner and the rest."

With great effort, the officer shook his head. "No, Cabell, thank you, but no. I'll let you help me back to my shelter, but then the three of you take Braun and ride like hell. Old Johnny has led me to believe that this may well be a flare-up of those terrible mutated plagues that killed off millions, hundreds of millions, a millennium ago. The like has happened before. The damned germs lie dormant in old sites for hundreds of years just waiting for a vulnerable human."

Cabell looked around, then stated flatly, "But there're no ruins in this valley, sir."

"No, Sergeant," Corbett agreed, "none that we can see. But how are we to know what may lie under the soil, eh? Or what we may unknowingly have passed through or inadvertently camped upon or among back along the track? No, the best thing that you can do for us all now is to get on the move and send back help from Broomtown.

"When you get there, give your report to the base sergeant major. Old Ted Graham will know what to do from that point on.

"Now, help me back to my lean-to. Oh, and leave the drugs and syringes with me, too."

With the officer tucked into his blankets, Cabell arose, then turned back. "One thing, sir. If we should run into any trouble . . . well, Dr. Braun, he's unarmed . . . ?"

"Oh, hell," Corbett mumbled, feeling a chill beginning. "Give the son of a bitch a pistol. The one he murdered Dr. Arenstein with is in my near-side saddlebag. There's only one other person that I know of he'd like to see dead, now, and that person won't be with you on your ride."

Later, he was to recall those words.

Chapter XIII

Alerted by the powerful farspeak of the watching prairiecat, Whitetip, as soon as the Ganiks began filing down the path from the shelf, Bili had all three hundred and twelve of his male and female warriors standing to arms in their preassigned places when the van of the Ganik mob came onto the crest of the first ridge. Only a few, on the flanks and in the rear center, were mounted. Most of the force were on foot and bearing long-hafted pikes, in addition to their customary sidearms.

Soon the entire ridgetop seemed to be aswarm with shaggy, yelling Ganiks on their weedy little ponies. Anyone could easily see that they still outnumbered Bili's force by at least five to one. But the armored men and women stood fast in the face of the threatening horde, for they knew of things that the screaming mob of pony riders did not . . . yet. Moreover, they nurtured supreme confidence in the sagacity of the very young man who led them—*Thoheeks* Bili of Morguhn, Bili the Axe.

Merle Bowley, in his fine armor, sitting high on his big, well-bred horse, in the midst of a knot of similarly equipped and mounted bullies at the rear of the mob of lesser Ganiks, reflected that whoever was in command of the Kuhmbuhluhners must be either an utter fool or a military tyro to so place his pitiful little bunch. He should have made his stand up on top of the next ridge, so that the Ganik charge would have been slowed, the impetus weakened by the ascent.

But no, the idiot had spread them out in way too thin a line and without even the big horses that gave them an edge over the pony-mounted Ganiks. Now, true, because of the thick growth of brushy woods to either side of that line, it would be damned hard to hit them from all sides—the preferred Ganik tactic. They would all have to hit them in front, but few of them as there were and with the added power of a downhill charge behind them, the Ganiks should be able to tromp right over the two or three hundred, then wheel around on the slope of the next ridge and finish them off, good and proper.

Merle smiled for the first time in twenty-four hours. When he had bid goodbye to Ehrkah, he had been certain that he and the rest were riding out to their deaths. Now he was not so sure. Unless there were a whole helluva lot more of the Kuhmbuhluhners hidden somewheres—and there could not be, not within easy reach, for there was just no place to hide enough to make any difference. The Kleesahks? No, he knew a bit about Teenéhdjook magic, and there were just too many of his Ganiks up here for the Kleesahks to cloud all of their minds.

"A'raht," he yelled at the bullies, "git 'em movin'. Rahd raht ovuh the Kuhmbuhluhn fuckuhs!"

Soon after Merle had left the cave, Erica had saddled her horse, buckled on her equipment belt, slung her rifle and the big binoculars and ridden across the depth of the shelf—now deserted, save for the much-shrunken herd of ponies, and seeming oddly lifeless. She had ridden to the highest point along the cliffs, a spot almost fifteen meters above the track meandering below.

Dismounting at the base of the pile of huge boulders, she tethered her horse to a tough-looking bush and climbed as high as she felt she safely could. Finding a steady seat, she took out the binoculars, removed the protective lens caps, put them to her eyes and began to adjust the focus.

She watched the horde of Ganiks come out of the thickly wooded area between the track and the first ridge and begin to mount that ridge, the knot of bullies—recognizable even at the distance by their bigger horses and steel armor—at the rear of the mob. Bullies, she had learned, did not lead large numbers of Ganiks, they stayed behind, trusting that the ill-armed lesser Ganiks were more afraid of their sadistic cruelties than they were of whatever lay ahead of them.

When all were assembled along the ridgetop, most of the bullies began to ride along the rear of the throng, waving their fine weapons and shouting, their voices thin and tinny with the distance. Then the Ganiks began to wave their clubs and spears and, shortly, move down below the ridgetop and so out of her vision. A small knot of armored men on big horses stayed atop the ridge, observing the charge, but strain and adjust as she might, she could not see clearly enough to tell which one was Merle Bowley.

But then she saw the first of the rocks dropping and a frigid hand seemed suddenly to grip her heart.

Bili waited patiently until the horde of shaggy men had actually started their downhill charge before he mindspoke the signal to the engine crews waiting by their loaded and cocked catapults, for he knew that there would be time for but the one volley before the Ganiks got too close to his own lines to risk a rockfall.

The iron basketloads of one- and two- and three-pound stones came down as a deadly rain upon the mob of shouting, club- and spear-waving cannibals, bashing in heads of man and of mount, smashing through flesh to shatter bones. Including those Ganiks bereft of a pony, Bili estimated that the stones had subtracted perhaps three hundred from the howling throng.

As soon as the survivors had reached the foot of that slope, the archers hidden in the fringes of the flanking woods brought them under fire. As fast as they could pluck up a shaft, nock, draw, and then loose, they did so. They knew there was scant need to aim, for in such a tight-packed mob there was hardly any chance of an arrow not fleshing itself.

Then, when the van was only thirty yards distant, the leading riders became suddenly, terrifyingly aware of just what lay before them, of what they and the bullies had been unable to see, at the onset of the charge, so artfully had it been disguised. The doomed men made shift to rein up, but were borne irresistibly on by the hundreds behind them.

From his place upon the ridgetop, Merle saw it all—first the shower of rocks; then the deadly work of the concealed archers; finally the fiendish cleverness of the ultimate trap. He had thought the Kuhmbuhluhner who set the troops where he did a fool or a novice. Dully, resignedly, he admitted to himself how very wrong he had been in that premature estimate. His rash and overconfident decision had cost the lives of most of what had been left of the main bunch of Ganiks.

Coming down the steep slope of the ridge as they had, the bulk of the mob had simply had no possible way of stopping or even of slowing before they plunged into the deep, wide ditches that lay in front of the Kuhmbuhluhners' small host of warriors. As if the sudden plunge were not enough, the bottom of those ditches had obviously been thickly sown with sharp wooden stakes to impale both man and pony.

Those pitifully few Ganiks who avoided the deathtraps had only done so because the near sides of the long ditch were already clogged to the ground level and above by the kicking, squirming, screaming bodies of those who had not been so fortunate.

Now, while the most of the Kuhmbuhluhners went along the far side of the ditch, the gleaming points of their longhafted pikes rising and falling as they coldly dispatched the trapped or wounded men below them, Merle could see the riders—all armored in fine plate, bearing sword and axe and spear and mace, closing in from both flanks on the bewildered Ganiks between the foot of the ridge and the man trap, and he knew what the end of that grim business must surely be . . . now.

To Horseface, Counter and the two or three other bullies around him, he said, "Ain' nuthun none of us kin do, naow, mens. Twenty-odd bullies won' mean diddlysquat 'ginst awl them Kuhmbuhluhn fuckuhs. Le's us mek tracks back to the camp, git whutawl we maht need and Ehrkah, then head awn souf. It's awl I knows whut to do, aftuh awl thet down ther."

In retrospect, Jay Corbett was certain that none of them would have lived through that savage bout of illness had old Johnny Skinhead Kilgore *not* come back only four days after he, Cabell, Horner and Braun had left. The old Ganik knew nothing of the antibiotics or of how to operate the "stick-you thangs," but his hairless head held a vast storehouse of knowledge concerning medicinal plants and folk medicine. It had been that primitive doctoring that had pulled all save six of the men through, and those six—Allison, Farmer, Cox, Cash, Thurston and Corey—had been dead or nearly so when Johnny had gotten back.

Having been the last to succumb, Corbett was also the last

to recover. When he finally stopped hallucinating, when both his sight and his speech became relatively clear and his mind began to sort some sense out of what his eyes and ears told him, the first sight he saw was the grinning face of Johnny, with the stubbled countenance of a pale-looking Gumpner behind and above the old cannibal.

"J . . . Johnny . . .? Gump . . . ner?"

"Yup, it be usuns, Majuh," Johnny nodded. "Haow you a-feelin'?"

"Like . . . like I've lost track of time . . . a lot of it. Who came back from the base with you?"

The bald head shook slowly to and fro. "I ain' nevuh seed your base, yet awhile, Majuh. I come bek by mahownsef, and a dang good thang I did 'er too. Elst awl yawl woulda been as daid as them six fellers whut is. Too bad too—they wuz awl of them good ole boys, they wuz.

"Naow, you feel lahk you kin eatchew suthin, Majuh? I got sum dang good coon stew, with wil' garlicks and muck weeds in it, too. You gon' hev to start a-eatin' soon, you been down a plumb lowng tahm."

With that, the Ganik produced a spoon and a metal bowl that emitted a fragrant steam. There was so much of importance that Corbett knew it was necessary he obtain from Johnny and Gumpner immediately, but no sooner did he take the last spoonful shoved at him than he found it impossible to hold open his eyelids.

When next he awakened, it was night. But there was a small fire smoldering in a stone-lined pit before his lean-to and old Johnny sat beside that fire, nodding. On the other side of the firepit lay Gumpner, rolled into a blanket and snoring softly. A small kettle sat on a flat rock beside the fire, but it did not just then interest Corbett. He had come awake harboring a raging thirst, and the sole object of his mind was the bulging waterskin hanging from the Y-notched upright above his head. He was straining upward to reach it when old Johnny abruptly awakened from his snoozing.

"Jes' hol' awn ther, Majuh, git back down awn them blankets. You heanh me? *I'll* gitchew sum wawtuh."

Weak as he felt, Corbett did not think he could have reached the skin anyway. And if he had, he knew full well that he could never have lifted it down. Once he had drunk his fill of the icy fluid, he tried hard to recall those questions he needed answered, but before he could remember them, he had again fallen asleep.

It was a morning three days later that he finally got the story from old Johnny.

Sometime after midday the second day out of camp, the mule on which Braun had been riding threw a shoe, so they had perforce halted, lifted the scientist out of his saddle and begun transferring his gear to one of the spare mules. With the spare mule saddled and Braun back in that saddle, one of the other spares had elected to pull loose and head back north, up the track. Cursing, Horner had spurred in pursuit of the runaway, since Cabell was still dismounted and engaged in tying Braun back into the saddle, while old Johnny, too, was dismounted and relieving himself against a trackside tree.

The sergeant had just remarked that they had made very good time and that another day or less should see them quite near to Broomtown when Braun began another of his frequent attempts to persuade or overawe Cabell into giving him an injection.

But the noncom, heeding the instructions of Corbett, just shook his head, doggedly. "No, Dr. Braun, I'm sorry, but Major Corbett said that . . ."

"You've told me more times than I can remember what that strutting jackass said," Braun had shouted, his face purple with his rage at being again denied the soothing narcotic. "Who do you think he is, anyway, you aboriginal ape? What do you think he is? He's nothing but a goddam ignorant professional soldier, with no more medical or scientific credentials than you or that fucking primitive over there have. I've forgotten more than he'll ever know, and I know that if I don't get another shot soon I—this body—will go into shock and die before I can transfer to a new, whole healthy one. He also ordered you to get me back alive, sergeant, *so give me a goddam injection*. Right now, damn you!"

"Dr. Braun," said Cabell in tired exasperation, "there are only two shots left. You've got to get some sleep tonight, so there goes one. You can bet that the pain is going to be worse in the morning than it is now, so I think . . ."

"Think?" shrieked Braun wildly, his voice cracking in his raging tantrum. "You don't know how to think. But I do, and

I think you're trying to kill me with the pain. Corbett gave you secret orders, didn't he? He told you to get me out here where none of the others could see what happened to me and let me die of either pain or infection, didn't he? *Didn't he?*"

Old Johnny had remounted during the "conversation." He did not like the despicable man who was alternately either whining and blubbering like a child or blustering and name-calling and bragging about how important he was and how much learning he had, so he had not really been listening to it. After all, this sort of thing had been going on almost from the moment they had ridden out of the camp.

The sergeant replied as calmly and patiently as he could to the accusing question. "No, Dr. Braun, you your own self heard all of the orders that the Major gave me concerning you, the other morning just before we left."

"Liar!" Braun hissed. "Don't you Broomtown apes know by now that you can't successfully lie to Center scientists? We can see right through your pitiful little fabrications. So admit it, admit that Corbett ordered you to kill me or at least let me die. It will go much easier for you back in Broomtown if you tell me the truth now."

"Doctor," said Cabell brusquely, "for a man as educated as you say you are, you sure have a tough time understanding plain English. Here we go one more time, then we're pushing on. Horner can just catch up best he can.

"All right, now. No, Doctor, Major Corbett gave me no orders to kill you or let you die. And, no, you are not getting any more injections until we stop for the night. Is that plain enough for you, Mr. Valuable Scientist Dr. Braun?"

Braun spluttered, so angry that he could find no words for a moment. Then, "That . . . that's *rank insubordination*! You won't get away . . . damn you, you'll regret having so spoken to a ranking member of the Board of Science."

"No, Doctor, it is not insubordination. You are not my military superior. You are a civilian of whom I am in charge. And, Doctor, you are trying my patience, as well as delaying me in the performance of my assigned mission."

"You and that arrogant West Point bastard, Corbett, must be in this together. I know how you all seem to be in awe of the pig, worship him almost. That's why you're so willing to murder me; because you know that would make him happy. Isn't that right, Cabell?" White patches of foam had formed at the corners of the scientist's mouth and flecks of spittle flew with his excited words.

Toe in stirrup, Cabell swung up on his mount, settled in his saddle, then reined about to face the furious Braun again. There was an edge of anger in his voice as he answered this latest calumny.

"No, again, Dr. Braun. If the major wanted you dead, I am convinced that he is man enough to make you dead with no help from me or any other Broomtown man, trooper or noncom. I have served with the major for most of my life and I have seen him kill many men, but only in combat or in mercy. *He* is not a murderer."

The emphasis was not lost on Braun. "*He* is not? Meaning that *I* am? Is that what you mean? Is that what that damned, lying bastard Corbett told you?"

Cabell shook his head and said, blandly, "No, dear Doctor, that is what *you* told me, told me and everyone else in the column, over and over again. You told us all how and why and when you murdered Dr. Arenstein."

"Well, you won't be able to hold that story over my head, too, damn you!" With the speed of a striking viper, Braun had unsnapped his belt holster, drawn his pistol and palmed back the side. Before Cabell could do more than open his mouth, Braun had leveled the big weapon and fired at point-blank range.

Cabell had been on his left side. Old Johnny was on his right. As the scientist turned toward the Ganik, bringing the smoking pistol back down to the horizontal, wise old Johnny moved every bit as fast as had Braun a second earlier. At the same moment he ducked low in his saddle, he whipped out one of his wickedly barbed darts from the quiver at his pommel and cast it underhanded. Although his aim was spoiled by an unexpected movement of his horse, the sharp-pointed missile struck the berserk scientist high in the thigh of his good leg. It sank deep, grating on bone, and the excruciating agony of it not only caused Braun's next shot to fly wide of his intended victim but caused the heavy recoil of the weapon to tear it from his hand.

Horner, returning with the runaway, heard the shots, let go the lead rope and spurred around the turn of the track to see Sergeant Cabell stretched on the track in a posture possible only to the dead, Braun reeling in his saddle with the thick haft of a Ganik dart wobbling out from his thigh, and old Johnny, the supposedly tamed wild man, in the very act of pulling another of those darts from his quiver.

Drawing a completely logical but completely erroneous conclusion from the testimony of his eyes, Horner jerked his rifle out of the scabbard and had just released the safety catch when Johnny regretfully buried a dart point in the trooper's chest. The shot that Horner's finger squeezed off took the tip off the near ear of Braun's mule, and that beast immediately decided that it would be healthier farther away from this place. He headed south along the track at a full, jarring gallop, with Braun jouncing and screaming in the saddle to which he was securely tied.

That had been the last that old Johnny Skinhead Kilgore had seen of the mad scientist.

When the Ganik had collected the weapons, gear and effects of Cabell and Horner—as he had seen Corbett and Gumpner do—rounded up the mounts and the spares and calmed them somewhat, he had headed back up the track toward the camp.

When Johnny had finished his tale, Corbett shook his head slowly and sadly. "It's my fault, much of it. I should never have told Cabell to rearm that murdering bastard. Hell, if I had just let him die here, instead of two days farther south, Cabell and Horner would still be alive."

"Stop it, sir," said Gumpner. "You did what you thought was right, was the best course. Besides old Johnny here says you were already so sick that morning they set out you couldn't stand up. Like I've heard you say many times before, you can't hold any mistakes against a man or an officer who made those mistakes when he has badly hurt . . . or sick, and you sure were, sir—we all were, that day."

With Johnny hunting and foraging for them until they were well enough to do such things themselves, Corbett kept the unit in the camp for almost a month longer. But when he was certain that all of the men were back in top physical form, he put them back in their saddles and, after crossing back over the ridges to the track, set their faces south, toward Broomtown.

The march was uneventful until they reached the spot

where the murder of Cabell had occurred. Although the scavengers had left no trace of any body, Corbett still had them put up a hand-carved wooden marker for Cabell and Horner. Then he warned them all to keep a sharp eye out for Braun's body or any other trace of him, but such was not found, and they did not discover exactly why until they had at last reached Broomtown base.

"*Jay*? Jay Corbett, is that really you?" Dr. David Sternheimer's voice crackled over the transceiver in the commo center at Broomtown base. "But how can it be? Harry Braun swore you were dead, killed in a landslide or rockfall or something like that, away up north somewhere. What the hell is going on, Jay?"

"Doctor . . . David," said the officer cautiously, not knowing just who else might be in the commo room at the Center, "I think that you should fly up here at once. We need to talk, you and I, privately."

"Jay, I'm very busy just now, and—"

Corbett interrupted the director. "How much of what really went on up north has Braun told you, David? Not much, I'd be willing to bet. Has he told you, for instance, that although we lost the pack train—most of it—we still may be able to reclaim most of the devices and metals and maybe even the books?"

Center Director David Sternheimer arrived by copter some two and a half hours later. But he had to introduce himself to the waiting officer, for he was in a new and quite young body—no more than twenty years old, blond, blue-eyed, tall and rather handsome in a beefy way.

When they two were at last alone in Corbett's Broomtown office, the director said, "Okay, Jay, what happened up there? Harry was brought in here more dead than alive by a bunch of friendlies from up northwest of here. They said they'd found him tied to the saddle of a dying mule, recognized his gear and the mule's brand as being Broomtown, and dragged him in on a travois. He was too bad off when he first arrived to say much of anything—with one leg gangrenous to up well above the knee and the other eaten up with infection its whole length from a peculiar barbed iron spearpoint in his thigh.

"Since he transferred to a new body and returned to the

Center, he's been amazingly close-mouthed and uncommunicative, for a person like him, anyway. You know how garrulous a gascon he has always been. He has given me, however, with much prodding, three different versions of the same story.

"What it all boils down to is this: You botched the setting of the charges so that the eruption, when it came, was days late and far more violent than anyone had expected. As a result of this, the pack train and most of the men were lost beyond any hope of recovery, and you died with them.

"He says that Erica then took charge, since his leg was broken at that time, reorganized the survivors and headed back down here. But he says that she was killed—or captured, depending upon which version he's telling—by a tribe of savages who killed most of the other survivors at that time—or at a later time, or at an earlier time, here again dependent on which of his versions we're using. He says that they are the ones who speared his right thigh and that they pursued him almost to the place where he was found by those friendlies.

"Even before you and your men showed up here, Jay, I did not know whether to believe Harry or not. Now, sitting here with a man who supposedly died months ago, and having just seen and spoken with some of the men who I was told died with him, I'm inclined to disbelieve the entirety of Harry's yarns."

Major Jay Corbett had been fighting a raging battle with himself ever since he and the men had arrived in Broomtown to learn that Dr. Harry Braun had made it to the base alive. On one side of that battle were ranged his basic honesty and his duty to the United States of America, to the service of which he had pledged himself on the plain at West Point more than a thousand years ago, and the Center was the last shred of that once great, once powerful republic now remaining in a much-altered world.

On the other side of the struggle were massed his hopes and plans and dreams for his Broomtowners. These hopes and plans and dreams had so often in the past centuries been thwarted by the Board of Science and the scientists who sat on the Council, who all seemed to look upon Broomtown and its inhabitants as a vaguely interesting experiment which was producing marginally useful human by-products, trainable to a degree but not really sapient.

Corbett had been aware of the criminality of this outlook for years and had fought against it, tried to change it time after time after time, only to see his best efforts derided or lightly dismissed by the members of the Board of Science, then defeated by the Council members who also sat on the Board.

From time to time, David Sternheimer had seemed in some sympathy with him. But although he was the Center Director, his was but a single voice in Board meetings, and he had never, he said, found any real support amongst his peers. Therefore, when Jay Corbett had thought to have found a way to control Harry Braun, who sat on both Board and Council, it had seemed to him that the impossible dream was suddenly become a near reality for him and, through him, for the men and women of Broomtown. But now, after the needless, senseless deaths of Sergeant Cabell and Trooper Horner, he was not so sure that he could or should go through with the extortion of Braun's support.

At last, inevitably, duty, honor, country won out. However, he was resolved to win from the Director as many immediate concessions for his Broomtowners as he could.

"Jay," Sternheimer was saying, his still-unlined, boyish face grave and solemn, "it . . . it's Erica. You know . . . I know you must know how I . . . tell me, is she really dead?"

Regretful of having to do it in this callous way, Corbett said, "In a minute, Dave, but first"—he took a very deep breath—"I want formal commissions for about twenty of my Broomtown men, lieutenancies and captaincies for most of them, and—"

Sternheimer waved a big hand. "Make them all admirals, Jay, I don't care, but about Erica . . . ?"

"Just a moment more, Dave," said Corbett, half hating himself for keeping his friend dangling in suspense in regard to a matter that was so important to him. "I want to start bringing some of the men of the friendly tribes into the army, but I'll need your authorization for that, and . . ."

Sternheimer extracted a pen from his pocket, grabbed a long sheet of blank paper from a box atop Corbett's desk and furiously scribbled his signature at one end of it. "Put anything you want to above that, damn you, Jay, but tell me if Erica's really dead!"

"I will, Dave, I will, but there's just one other thing."

Sternheimer clenched the big fists of his new, youthful body, swelling the muscles of the forearms. "Jay, I've given you a blank check for your damned Broomtowners. What the hell more do you want out of me?"

Corbett mentally crossed his fingers. "A seat on the Board, Dave, that's all."

Sternheimer snorted. "That's impossible, and you knew it before you asked it. To be on the Board you've got to be a scientist. You're not—you're a soldier."

"I hold a Ph.D., Dave. I could claim the title 'Doctor,' did I so wish, did I not prefer a military title."

"Your doctorate was in history, as I recall," retorted Sternheimer with more than a touch of deprecation. "That does not make you a scientist. After all, we have to live, to operate, by rules. Order is necessary to the well-being of man."

"You've bent those same rules before, when there was something or someone you wanted for a purpose, Dave. You've seated psychologists, engineers, even, as I now recall, a M.SW. Are you afraid to have me on the Board, Dave?"

Sternheimer squirmed uncomfortably. "No, Jay, not at all. As a matter of fact, I think a man like you—blunt, honest, outspoken, eminently practical—would be most refreshing among all those prima donnas, those impractical, idealistic dreamers who presently fill many of the seats. And as well as you and I have always gotten on, I might have some real, forceful support for a change with you down the table from me. But, Jay, I'm sorry, it all comes back to the same, indigestible fact. You are not, despite your valid doctorate, a scientist. That's all there is to it."

It had been just what Corbett had been waiting for. He had planned this kill long and carefully. With all of his force, he slammed home the verbal harpoon.

"Oh, but I am, David. I do hold a degree in science. Not a doctorate, true, but a degree nonetheless. My degree is in *military science*, Dave. So when do I take that Board of Science seat?"

Sternheimer opened his mouth to object, to protest, then closed it again. Smiling crookedly, he finally said, "Damn, you're a devious one, Jay. No wonder you've been such a shrewd strategist. You led me and I followed as unsuspectingly as a dumb bullock following a judas goat. I begin to think that you're too inherently dangerous a man to *not* have on the Board.

"Okay, you're at the top of the qualified list, as of now. You get the next vacant seat. Now, Jay, please, about Erica . . . ?"

Corbett sighed. "I didn't see her die or see her dead body, Dave, but still I'm certain that she's dead." Then he went on to tell the director all that Harry Braun had revealed in his fits of delirium, adding that every man in the command had heard the sordid details directly from the mouth of the murderer. He ended with a recountal of Braun's cold-blooded murder of Sergeant Cabell.

Long before he had finished, there was a look in the blue eyes of Dr. David Sternheimer that boded ill for Dr. Harry Braun. Only saying, "Thank you, Jay," the director rose from his chair and strode purposefully toward the door. But then, hand on knob, he turned and spoke.

"By the way, Jay, the Board of Science sits a week from Thursday. There will be a vacant chair—Dr. Braun's. You'll occupy it. The copter will radio when it's leaving for the base, here, to bring you down. Plan to stay overnight, at least. Goodbye for now, Jay."

EPILOGUE

For all that the Kleesahks, who had gone up the cliffs before dawn, and the two cats, who had preceded the column up the single trail by an hour's time, had all telepathically reported no signs of human life on the shelf, Bili still took no chances. So far, there had been no deaths from either his force or that of Count Steev Sandee, and only a few injured or wounded—almost all of those from noncombat causes—and he intended to keep it that way, if possible.

"As long as possible, I should say," he silently corrected himself, as his big black warhorse bore him toward the foot of the trail that led up to the shelf. "Yes, the campaign is concluded. The farmer Ganiks have all been driven south and west, off their lands, and the outlaw Ganiks are now all either dead or on their way out of New Kuhmbuhluhn. All that's left to do now is to regarrison this place and start sending down farmers and stockmen from the north to settle the lands we drove the Ganiks off.

"Yes, the Ahrmehnee and the Confederation nobles are already discussing, planning their return east, all they're going to do when they get home. But I, for one, am not deluding myself. From all that I've heard, all that I know of matters, this Kingdom of New Kuhmbuhluhn is hard pressed in the north by a strong and warlike folk moving down from the Ohyoh country or somewhere beyond. For all his grace and courtesies and sincere-sounding promises regarding this matter and that, Prince Byruhn is as shrewd and devious and slippery a character as ever I've run onto—his personal device should be a fox, not a wolf—and, in his straits up north, I hardly think he's going to just allow a couple of hundred well-armed, well-trained, seasoned and proven veteran warriors to ride out of his little kingdom until he no longer feels so threatened.

"Then there's that weird prophecy—so-called—of Pah-El-muh. His mind is very different from human minds and he does possess talents, powers that I've never heard of, or even imagined in a human mind. It's possible, therefore, that he could have delved deeply enough into my mind without my knowledge that he was so doing to have dredged up all of the needed information concerning my antecedents to flesh out his prophecy—which prophecy is very convenient to Prince Byruhn's goals and objectives, just now.

"But could it be true? Could Blind Hari of Krooguh, the tribal bard who they say was over a hundred and fifty years old when he came east with the Kindred and was fifty or more years older than that—for all that he was not an Undying—when he returned westward with those prairiecats who wanted to get back onto the plains, have really been the so-called 'Eveless Wise One' who made this prophecy among others to Pah-Elmuh's forebears, so long ago?

"And what of this 'Last Battle'? Yesterday was the last battle—if that stinking means of executions and mercy killing could or should be dignified with the name 'battle'—of this Ganik campaign. Yet Pah-Elmuh attested last night that the true 'Last Battle' at which I will be 'Champion' lies in the future, so that is bound to mean we, or at least I, will fight in the north of New Kuhmbuhluhn."

He had not been shielding his mind and his thoughts, and now he received a silent beaming. "If you fight in the north, then so do I, my Bili, my dear love. Remember, I am not one of your soft, eastern women. I, too, am a proven warrior."

"Of course you are, my dear," he mindspoke Rahksahnah, "But fear you not, I doubt me that Prince Byruhn will allow even one of us to freely depart his lands until the king, his father, and he have come to some sort of terms with these invaders from Ohyoh, however long that takes."

The precautions of the young commander proved unnecessary, of course. Aside from the waiting Kleesahks and cats, only the wandering ponies, the fish and frogs in the lake and the clan of stoats in the cave remained of all the living creatures that had for so long occupied the shelf. But the human invaders had been preceded by dark, flapping clouds of carrion birds—ravens, crows, starlings, buzzards, hawks, even a pair of eagles—all now working assiduously at nature's recycling of the scattered corpses of Ganiks and ponies. Bili and his column temporarily interrupted several such grisly feasts on their route up to the cavemouth, much to the loudly voiced displeasure of the avian feasters.

There were two horses left in the cave stable. Both proved capable of mindspeak, and when once Bili had determined from their expressed thoughts that they would be happy with such an arrangement, he took them into his own squadron as remounts. Both geldings were big, clearly well-bred mounts and the previous Kuhmbuhluhn or Ahrmehnee owners were most likely long-dead.

He and his officers helped themselves to the piles of loot, then invited all the others to do the like. Those items that they either did not want or could not carry were left behind for the garrison and, eventually, for farmers who would come soon or late to take over the shelf and caves.

Hornman Gy Ynstyn spotted something gleaming in the light of a torch and stooped to pick up a brace of small brass cylinders, no larger or longer than his smallest finger, each closed at one end by a brass disk in which was centered a smaller disk of red copper with a small depression in its center. Shrugging, he dropped them into his belt-pouch. They might prove useful if he should again need to patch his brass bugle.

They had missed the Witch Goddess of the Ganiks by some hours, but still the future of them all lay ahead . . . waiting.

ABOUT THE AUTHOR

ROBERT ADAMS lives in Seminole County. Like the characters in his books, he is partial to fencing and fancy swordplay, hunting and riding, good food and drink. And when he is not at hard work on his next science fiction novel, Robert may be found slaving over a hot forge to make a new sword or busily reconstructing a historically accurate military costume.